# Dream Makers:

## Book One

## Michael A. Richards

ALL THINGS THAT MATTER PRESS

Dream Makers: Book One

Copyright © 2020 by Michael A. Richards

*Dr. Scott Saxxon and "Nike Jesus" courtesy of Dr. Gary Scott Danford

ISBN 13: 9781734685510
Library of Congress Control Number: 2020941008
Cover Photo: nick-fisher-9QxOmRLDTvs-unsplash.jpg

Cover design © by All Things That Matter Press
Published in 2020 by All Things That Matter Press

This book is dedicated to Dr. Gary Scott Danford. I had the privilege of taking Dr. Danford's course, *Environmental Behavior and Design*, while I was an undergraduate student at the University at Buffalo in the early 1990s. On the first day of class, he walked into the classroom looking quite flustered. He took off his brown leather bomber jacket and put on a white lab coat that he retrieved from his briefcase. He then went on to explain how a meteor had hit the earth near the Sino-Soviet border and contamination from the meteor was killing humans at unprecedented rates. Based on the spread, epidemiologists were predicting the end of all human life within a twenty-five-year period. Preliminary research also indicated that the contaminant could not penetrate two feet of solid salt, ten feet of water, or 500 feet of vacuum. Our project was to design a colony for twelve thousand people in one of these three mediums. To ensure the security of the project, it was decided that it should be hidden in plain sight by conducting it in the open as an academic class exercise.

At the end of the class, not a single student left their seat. Granted, this was 1994, so there were no smart phones, no internet, and no instant way to verify if this was true or not. One student approached Danford and asked him point-blank, "Is this for real?" Danford had already changed back to his brown leather bomber jacket and replied, "Dr. Saxxon is no longer here. I'm Dr. Danford. But Saxxon will be back next week. Just look for the white lab coat." The student's jaw dropped in confusion and he again pleaded with Scott, "Come on, you have to tell us if this is true or not!" Danford simply replied, "It could be!" I remember going home and calling my mom on the public telephone in the hall of my dorm and her telling me she didn't read anything about it or see anything in the news. As the semester went on, I think we all accepted the concept that it could be true, and even if it wasn't, why not be prepared if something like this actually did happen in the near or distant future?

*Environmental Behavior and Design* was by far the most creative and inspiring course I ever took in my tenure as both an undergraduate and graduate student. I was lucky to have Dr. Danford for a few more courses in graduate school and eventually worked with him on a project when I was a research assistant in one of the other research centers in the School of Architecture and Planning at the University at Buffalo. Scott wrote a book entitled, *Nike Jesus* that was an accompanying novel to the course. The book was never published, but it offered much more depth into the end of the world scenario and into the Dr. Scott Saxxon character, who is also featured in *Dream Makers*. When I worked with Scott after graduate school, I promised I would continue his course after he retired. Since I have not been teaching in recent years, I decided writing a book and piggybacking off some of the themes in *Nike Jesus* would be another way to keep this media alive.

Sadly, Scott passed away in 2015, and I did not get this book done in time for him to read it. However, if there is such thing as parallel universes in the afterlife, Scott would be the first one to figure out how to travel between them, and I know he is reading this somewhere, in some time. Indeed, this book would not be possible without him. He was an inspiring educator, a mentor, a colleague, and a friend. *Dream Makers* is for you, Scott.

# 1

I walked through the back patio into the family room of the house I grew up in. Why I was entering the house from the back perplexed me. Perhaps the front door was broken? The décor of the house looked as it did in the 1980s, which was strange because we gutted these rooms after I finished college in 1996. The carpet was burgundy, and the walls were covered with stucco in the family room and wood paneling in the living room. Oddly, there were no window treatments, which was also strange since we always had either shades or blinds that were usually drawn so the furniture and the carpet wouldn't fade. Our house had an interesting, open-plan layout and had many customizations, as the previous owners were a known organized crime family in Rochester, New York throughout much of the 1960s and 1970s and had connections in the construction industry. For example, there was a built-in central vacuum system, an indoor grill, and several secret rooms in the basement. The walls and sub-flooring were also twice as thick as a typical house; the walls were built with two-by-six framing, as opposed to the traditional two-by-four, and were finished with one-inch thick drywall. The floor was constructed with double two-by-fourteen floor joists and had two layers of three-quarter inch subflooring. The windows were triple-paned and could probably stop a bullet.

Perhaps it was this superior mafia construction that explained why our house was the only house still intact in the neighborhood. The family room was surrounded by windows on the north, south, and west facades, which gave me a good view to the outside. Out of the west window, the horizon line of the earth seemed to be skewed. Out of the north window, I could see several balls of fire starting out in the distance and quickly streaming toward the ground. Several of the fireballs were hitting the house, making a loud, explosive sound. As I walked to the front of the house toward the east, the entire structure started to gyrate like a tilt-a-whirl at an amusement park. There was no furniture, so I had to grope the walls to keep my balance. I made it to the window, and what I saw boggled my mind. It was outer space. Pitch black, but with chunks of fire and solid particles hurling everywhere. One of the particles crashed through the presumed bulletproof glass. So much for that theory. I tried to peek my head out the window, but the wind and centripetal force was so great I could barely stand. I forced myself through the window and looked to the south, where it looked like the sun was imploding, melting, forcing the earth to hurl through space and break up into pieces. I fell to the floor and rolled toward the front of the house. I slowly glanced up and could see several large meteors the size of buildings crashing into the ground. One of the meteors hit about a mile away. I could see a wave of ash and smoke slowly approaching along with a delayed tremor in the ground that twisted me back on my feet. I ran back to the family room, where my mom suddenly appeared.

"Larry, what's happening?" She asked.

"This is it, Mom. This is the end of the world."

# 2

I woke myself up with a loud scream, as I often did after having a nightmare. I was used to getting typical night terrors, such as someone standing over me, falling off a cliff, showing up for a test unprepared, getting hit by a truck, or being attacked by dogs, but I'd never had a dream about the end of the world before. It took me several minutes to know where and when I was, but the view from my bedroom window of the University Heights neighborhood in Buffalo, New York was all too familiar. It was about four in the morning, just about last call at the many college bars that lined the strip of the street where my house was near.

This was my sixth year living in the so-called university ghetto neighborhood. I moved here my junior year of college and stayed two years after I graduated to try and make things happen with my band. I applied to graduate school for architecture school merely as a backup plan in the event my music career didn't take off. In 1998, the School of Architecture and Planning called my bluff and admitted me. I was in the first year of a four-year graduate program. I didn't get to sleep until three a.m. since I was in the studio obsessing over a project that was due first thing in the morning. I had to be awake by six for class. I really hated architecture school. I was already prone to obsessive-compulsive disorder before entering the program, but the curriculum just made it worse.

One of the things that did entice me about architecture school was a course I took in undergraduate called Environmental Behavior and Design, taught by Dr. Scott Saxxon. It dealt with the design and implementation of an outer space, under water, or subterranean colony that could safely house ten thousand people for twenty years in response to a cataclysmic meteor impact on the earth. After twenty years, the deadly radiation from the meteor would be inert, thereby allowing humans to repopulate the planet. Since this project had such an impact on me and given the fact that I was now a research assistant for Dr. Saxxon in graduate school, I attributed the dream to rehashing the project in my mind. After all, it wasn't just a project, but in fact a government experiment being conducted in an academic setting as to hide it in plain sight. Just a few days prior, I'd discovered a project file in Scott's archives describing this in detail. The file was from NASA's Near Earth Object Observations Program and identified timelines of various asteroid and meteor collisions with Earth, timetables, and a brief description of Scott's mission to conduct this as an "academic exercise" in the classroom.

Anyway, that's all the dream was, I thought: a by-product of something I read. After all, I told myself, dreams are merely successions and montages of images, fears, desires, ideas, and emotions, right? I tried to go back to sleep, but the fraternity next door was still partying. I looked out of the window and saw that one of the frat members was talking with a young prostitute who lived in the house across the street. The house was full of women, and on warm nights, they'd walk up to the corner and seduce young, drunk college guys. They never solicited me, though, which I though was strange, seeing I used to cut their lawn for them free of charge.

I finally fell asleep and had yet another dream about my studio professor, an eccentric and toxic cougar from the Haight-Ashbury in her mid-fifties named Donna. First, she berated me in front of the class. Then I found myself staring at her trying to figure her out when she suddenly reenacted the scene from the movie *Fatal Attraction* where Sharon Stone intentionally advertises that she wasn't wearing any underwear by slowly crossing her legs. I questioned if this was a desire or fear. In any event, it was better than seeing the world end.

The next morning, I walked to school, which conveniently was only about a five-minute stroll from my dilapidated Buffalo-double house. I was still haunted by the dream but had to get to design studio for yet another pin-up and critique session. Design studio is a bloodbath version of show and tell where students present projects that they've worked on for over for a week straight with little or no sleep and have a bunch of egocentric prigs cut them down in front of their peers. This process is what coined the word "architorture."

As I walked into the building that housed the studios, the smell of dirty hair, cigarette smoke, black mold, and mildew added to my nervousness as always. The stress and tension in this building was palpable, for this was the place where all-nighters and design binges occurred, the place where the thespian culture of architecture school is epitomized. In addition to the raunchy odor, the building had grim lighting, pitiable acoustics, and contemptible ventilation. Built in the mid nineteenth century, it was originally used as a mental hospital. I guess what comes around goes around.

We all placed our projects on the table. The project was to construct a gate and basin based on the connotation of the words and on the concept of typology—at least that's what I derived from the page-long, archi-babble gibberish that described the project. Donna didn't like me. She once told me it was because I was a typical middle-class white male with no culture or eccentricity. She only seemed to like pansexual men and women, non-Americans, or students with a troubled past. She picked up my chipboard model and dropped it on the floor.

"Whose project is this?" she said.

I slowly raised my hand and shakily muttered, "Uh, it's mine."

"Well, what the hell were you thinking, Larry? Did you put any thought into this whatsoever?" She went on, "This project is tongue and cheek, totally white bread. Class, this is what *not* to do. Larry, you should go back to studying earth science."

Yes, earth science was my undergraduate degree. Donna knew this from our first-day introductions and she constantly insisted that I didn't belong in architecture school. I was beginning to think she was right.

I tried to defend myself. "Well, I was trying to emphasize the rel—"

She cut me off. "Stop right there. You are *not* talking your way out of this one."

"Fine," I said, waving my hands in the air like I didn't give a crap.

Donna proceeded to pick up another project. "Whose is this?"

Rachel, a reserved young woman from North Carolina, slowly raised her hand. Donna changed the tone of her voice, so it was softer, but even more patronizing.

"Now, h-how do you think your project c-compares to Larry's project, Rach?" Donna frequently stuttered.

Rachel hated being called Rach but remained silent. She tried to answer, "Um ...well ... I think that ....um ... they are sort of like—"

"Stop right there, sweetie," Donna said in a wicked witch kind of way. "Now, where did you learn to speak? You do know there are more words than um and like, right? And don't tell me things I can already see. You are going to have to learn to be more assertive, honey."

5

The word "honey" dug in deep, as it was meant to be some kind of way of asserting power over Rachel. Rachel's face turned bright red and her eyes began to slightly well up. Donna didn't seem to notice and moved on to the next project. I looked over at Rachel and gave her a nod, welcoming her to the disparaged people club. Rachel looked at me out of the corner of her eye and her frown slowly started to turn into a smile.

I wasn't sure about Rachel's background, but I was used to being insulted. My dad was a Vietnam War veteran who didn't take any crap, not to mention I'd been working every blue-collar job there was for the two years between college and graduate school. As anyone with a college degree who has had to work manual labor knows, people without college degrees don't like people with college degrees. In working construction, I remember hearing things like, "It looks like they didn't teach you how to use a hammer in college there, huh?" I also grew up the youngest in a neighborhood full of older tough guy, mullet-donning bullies in the early 1980s. I was not a fighter, but I was good at breaking up fights, seeing as how my friends would always get into altercations when we went out in public and I had no choice but to play peacemaker.

At the end of the critique, Donna sat on one of the drafting stools to lecture about some esoteric concept that only she understood. She was wearing a long beige skirt. I was sitting to her left and, at one point, was the only one paying attention. She looked me square in the eyes, opened her legs wide, and crossed them back together. She wasn't wearing any underwear.

Later that night, several of us went out for drinks at a college bar, the Blue Goose, on the University Heights strip. I asked if anyone else had seen up Donna's skirt. My classmate Todd burst out into laughter.

"Dude, holy shit! I totally saw her do that! I thought I was the only one who saw it!"

I answered, "Good. I'm glad I have a witness because no one would have ever believed that story." I went on, "You know what the really creepy thing is? I actually dreamt she would do that last night."

My classmates erupted into loud laughter. Rachel looked shocked and somewhat disgusted.

"Eeew," she said. "You had a sex dream about Donna? Really? Donna?"

Another one of my classmates, who was somewhat of a pervert, chimed in. "So, Larry, was she shaved?"

That question didn't surprise me coming from Sam. He used to regularly and openly surf porn late at night in the computer lab.

Before I could answer, Todd shouted, "Are you kidding? She grew up in the sixties in San Francisco. I don't think she even shaves her pits."

Rachel reiterated her original sentiment, "Eeew."

Maryanne was the wet blanket of the group. She was the worst kind of person: the kind who thought they were smart but really wasn't that smart at all. She finally put her two cents in.

"First of all, I don't believe this story one bit. And second, you guys are like children, and, frankly, I think what you are talking about is offensive. I mean, Larry is just pissed because Donna destroyed him today in the crit."

Todd defended me. "Hey, I saw it, too. And Larry has the right to be pissed. Donna has had it out for him from day one. She's like Monica Lewinsky: she has some kind of plan to rid all the men from the architecture program. She did the same thing when she taught at UCLA."

Gary, a quiet guy from Livonia, New York, also piped in. "Yeah, I actually heard from a friend of mine that she had an affair with a student at UCLA. The guy ended up breaking up with her because she was using him like a tool, and she threatened him with a sexual harassment charge to retaliate. Apparently, both she and the student were asked to leave the program."

"Jesus," I said. "That's all I need."

Later that night, I stumbled home to the second floor of the post-World War II Buffalo-double house I lived in. I laid down on the couch and put on reruns of the *Fugitive* on my 1980s RCA tube TV. I quickly dozed off and saw a little girl in a pink hooded one-piece snowsuit walking with her mother on a winter day in Niagara Falls. The little girl ran ahead of her mom to look at the rapids above the falls. She had a big smile on her face and was mesmerized by the water. She looked like a little doll, all bundled up in the snowsuit. And then, in a split second, she slipped on the ice and fell into the rapids. Her mom was hysterical. I ran over and tried to reach over the rail to save her, but I was too late. The little girl went over the falls. I started uncontrollably crying. I then woke up in a cold sweat. My TV was still on but was now airing some public broadcast show.

# 3

Ng Seiko was a Japanese student who didn't speak for the first month of studio. He was diagnosed with schizophrenia and bi-polar disorder but was supposedly fine as long as he took his medication. For most of the year, he was under the illusion that several of us were spies working for the government. He often would stay in the studio late at night, chain smoking cigarettes, ranting his conspiracy theories as he paced nervously around the room, threatening students, or going through our personal belongings. He was always the first one in and the last one out, which led many of us to believe he was actually living in the studio. The night after the gate and basin fiasco, he walked up to me and started mumbling something in broken English.

"You a student, aren't you?"

He had never talked at this point, so, naturally, I tried to be friendly.

"Yeah, that's right Ng, I'm a student. Are you a student?"

He didn't answer at first. "Many people here are not student."

"Really? Who do you think is not a student?" I inquired.

He ran to the door and slammed it with all his might. He closed his eyes and put his hands over his head.

"Shh," he voiced as he put his finger over his lips. Then he pointed to two workstations. One of the stations belonged to Sam and the other belonged to a reclusive student named Gina.

Then Ng went on. "Sam and Gina, they are spy. They have been sent to kill me."

I thought he was messing with me, so I started to laugh. Then I saw his eyes well up.

"I thought you would understand, since you are student like me."

Now, usually, the studio would have been filled with other students. But seeing this was the night after a critique, many of them took the night off. I'd come in to try and figure out what the hell I did wrong with the gate and basin project, and was starting to regret that choice, seeing it was just the two of us. I tried to reverse my carefree demeanor as fast as I could.

"Oh, well … no, Ng, I don't think they are spies. I know both Sam and Gina. Trust me, they are far from being spies. Sam smokes a lot of grass and I think Gina's into the hard stuff, so I don't think either of them would pass the drug screening to become government agents." I chuckled a bit as I said this.

Ng looked at me with a blank stare. I don't think he knew what I was talking about. He lit up a cigarette.

"You smoke with me?"

"Oh, no, thanks," I said. I didn't want to hurt his feelings or spark an episode, so I lied. "I'm trying to quit. But otherwise, I would totally join you."

Ng started to laugh hysterically. He opened the window and sat on the ledge to smoke his cigarette. I went back to work and, after about two hours, noticed he was still sitting in the window.

Ng finally came back into the studio just as I was trying to sneak out. He was crying and speaking to himself in Japanese.

I figured I better say something. "You okay, Ng?"

Ng ran out of the room at full speed and I didn't see him again until our next critique the following week.

\*\*\*

For the next project, we had to observe something as it changed in scale, hierarchy, differentiation, and time, and record its names graphically. The project description was written in some type of quasi-sonnet format that was destined to push someone over the edge. Ng's project of observing consisted of a dollar bill taped to a piece of chipboard. The eye on the pyramid of the bill was highlighted and circled with red ink—or what we think might have been blood. He started his presentation by mumbling some gibberish that was half Japanese-half English. His voice started to get louder as the presentation proceeded. Then, at the top of his lungs, he shouted, "This eye sucks." He pointed his finger and stared at everyone in the class, including the guest critics, who ironically were some of the more laid back, timid professors on the staff. There was an awkward silence; no one knew what to say. Of course, consistent with most of the implausible situations that semester, my project was next in the rotation. I said, "Well, I guess I'll go." I think that was my best review all semester, maybe because I broke the ice and possibly prevented a lunatic from potentially killing everyone in the studio.

I quickly forgot about the Ng situation that night because I was turning twenty-four that weekend. Sam, Rachel, and a friend of mine from my undergraduate college band came over to celebrate. We were drinking Captain Morgan's spiced rum before we ventured out to a local live music dive in the University Heights neighborhood called Moe's. I used to play at this bar in undergraduate and worked the door there to make extra money. The owner, Moe, was a short, scraggly beatnik from the '60s with oversized glasses and a bad, greasy comb-over. Moe saw me walk in and started shouting.

"What the fuck are you doing here? Are you playing tonight?"

"No," I said in a somber voice. "The band has been defunct for two years. I'm back in school now."

Moe was not an advocate for higher education. "Well, why the hell would you do something like that? You guys were doing okay here. I thought you sucked, but I don't give a shit. As long as you could bring in a hundred people on any given weeknight, you could have played here as long as you wanted."

I was feeling somewhat nostalgic that the college band wasn't playing anymore, but putting the band back together was a distant dream at this point. Two of the guys had moved away and I was overwhelmed with work in school.

"Well, if you're not here to play, you can work the door. I need some extra help tonight."

"No, I'm not here to work. Today's is my birthday."

"Well, happy birthday. Karl, get Larry a drink."

That night, one of my favorite local bands, The Walking Carpets, was playing at Moe's. One of the drummers had recently joined a touring band and they still had a vacancy in the drums on stage left. They were using a fill-in on stage right, but he wasn't feeling well, so one of the other guys in the band asked if I knew any other drummers in the area that could fill in for the night. Just around the corner from the bar, I happen to know a group of guys from a band I once filled in with in my undergraduate years. At that point, I was tipsy from the booze but still managed to remember the house. I ran up to the door and barged in. I hadn't seen these guys in over two years, but it was like nothing had changed. It seemed as if they were sitting there – frozen in time, waiting for someone to come and wake them up.

I blurted out, and probably slurred somewhat, "Hey, man, the band needs some drums. Their fill-in drummer isn't feeling well." Cory, the six-foot four guitarist from Korean, started laughing.

"Holy shit, Larry Martin, where the hell have you been?"

I recounted my whole life story in about five seconds.

"I finished college, worked construction for two years, but now I'm back in grad school, tonight's my birthday, and the band needs drums. So grab your rig and let's go!"

Cory continued to laugh. "You can't play drums, you're a keyboard player."

"I know," I said. "But I think I can do it tonight."

As soon as I said that, one of Cory's roommates, a short Latino kid named Roy, put on his hat and grabbed one conga drum for himself and one for me. We bolted out the door. Cory was still laughing. Roy and I ended playing conga drums with the band for the whole second set. I'm not much of a drummer, but after that many drinks, anything sounds good.

At the end of the night, I stumbled down the road and attempted to get back to my apartment. I tripped and fell in the front yard of a church. It was an October night, but it was warm enough for me to want to rest my head on the fresh cut grass. And then I saw an old building on fire. Blood. Knives. Stabbing. A young woman screaming. And the face of Ng. All flashing in and out of sequence.

# 4

I woke up the next morning in a cell in the college police building. A tall, muscular cop came walking over.

"Mr. Larry Martin."

"Yes," I said.

"We found you in the front yard of Saint Michael's church last night about four in the morning. You remember anything about the night?"

"Well, I was at Moe's playing congas—"

The cop interrupted. "Are you in a band?"

"No, I was just filling in."

"Okay, go on."

"All I remember is seeing a guy in my studio, Ng Seiko."

"Where did you see Mr. Seiko?"

"I'm not really sure. It was in a house somewhere in the University Heights neighborhood."

The cop was confused. "But you were outside, Mr. Martin. Did you go somewhere between the time you left the bar and before you passed out on the church lawn?"

"Not that I remember," I said. "I just remember seeing Ng, hearing a young woman screaming, and … stabbing."

"Well, was this some drunken dream, or do you think Mr. Seiko was somehow responsible for you passing out?"

"I'm not sure. It was very vivid, though."

The cop wrote all of it down in a frayed flip-top assignment pad notebook.

"Well, we'll check on Mr. Seiko, but unless he has anything to divulge, you are probably looking at public intoxication and loitering."

"You want anything to drink?"

"Sure. I'll take a Pepsi and some Advil if you have any."

The cop gave me the Pepsi and some aspirin. He told me they didn't have any Advil. Aspirin never worked on me, but I was in so much pain, I guzzled it down. He let me out of the cell to do more paperwork. I started telling him my whole life story, how I couldn't find a job in my field after college, how the love of my life broke up with me because architecture school was consuming all of my time, how my band was defunct, and how I was broke. I told him the story about Donna and the no-underwear leg crossover. He tried not to laugh but started to anyway.

The cop let me stay at his desk while he checked out my Ng story.

"Your boy Seiko hasn't been seen in forty-eight hours," he told me when he returned. "Nobody knows where he is. I'm going to let you off with a warning for this since you don't have any priors ... and you made me laugh. We'll give you a ride back to your apartment."

Between the blackout, the arrest, and the recovery, I missed three days of school, which in architecture school is like missing a month. I was really behind in my work, stressed out, and then began a new cycle of cluster-headaches. Cluster headaches usually consist of intense pain on one-side of the head that comes on daily for a period of one-two months. Each episode lasts one-two hours and are often compared to an "ice-cream" headache or childbirth without anesthesia. Intensity gradually increases so there are multiple episodes a day. Mine usually come on right when I fell asleep ... so my sleep cycle, which was already under strain from the all-nighters in the architecture studio, was now further in jeopardy. I was going to quit the program, but I had just found out my mom wasn't feeling well. To not upset her any further, I decided to stick it out.

When the class gathered around for our weekly critique, I noticed Ng was still missing. I also noticed another female student was missing. Raja was a young, quiet, and studious student from India. Her father was a professor in the engineering department. Raja never missed class ... especially on critique day, seeing each critique was ten percent of the grade.

I presented my project and was once again cut to shreds by Donna. For this particular project, we had to fold a shirt, put it away, and create a design based on the memory of folding the shirt. I honestly had no clue what this project was about. Anyway, Donna claimed my design ripped off the design of an existing building in downtown Buffalo — a building I had never seen before in my life. To humiliate me more, she invited several upperclassmen in to render their opinion.

After the blood bath was over, I decided to go up to see Raja's father, Dr. Raj Patel. I took a course with him in undergraduate and had a good rapport with him. As I walked down the hall, a voice from behind me greeted me.

"Ahh, hey there Larry. What brings you up to the third floor?"

"Oh, I was just wondering if you had seen Raja this week."

"Why no, I have not seen her since last Friday. Was she not in class today?"

"No ... she wasn't ... and that is not like her at all."

Raj dialed out of his office phone and got Raja's voice mail. He left a message half in English and half in Hindi. He didn't seem to be too concerned. I don't think he was that close with his daughter. I think their relationship was more "business-like." He proceeded to ask me how my semester was going. As usual, I went into a lengthy dissertation of how I hated Donna and was unhappy in the architecture program. I guess I'm a bit of a complainer. He didn't have much sympathy.

"Nothing good comes easy, Larry."

"I know, but I'm not sure if there is anything good about it."

On the way back to my apartment, I stopped in at Carbone's—a local Italian take-out restaurant in the heights. I worked there for a brief stint in undergraduate as a delivery person. In addition to great tips, I also had a huge crush on the restaurant owner's daughter who worked there on the same nights as me. I hadn't been back there since I quit, and they still seemed angry with me. During one of my deliveries, one of the customers became enraged because the order was wrong. The next thing I knew, I was surrounded by a gang of thugs hassling me. They threw the pizza at me and refused to pay. Rather than get mugged, I told them I'd give them another order for free that I had in the car. I got in the car, peeled out like a bat out of hell, and went into Carbone's and quit. The next week, my co-worker Mike was shot during a delivery. He survived, but he also quit the following week. Strangely, I remember seeing Mike get shot in a dream several weeks before that. It didn't really freak me out, seeing this was a common occurrence in the heights. The local gangs didn't take kindly to the large influx of students who permeated their neighborhood once the semester started.

Annmarie still worked there, and she still looked great. She was about five years older than me, but we always had good chemistry. I was way too intimated to ever ask her out ... besides, I wasn't her type. I was kind of a skinny hippie. I think she liked more buff, yuppie types.

She was somewhat distant at first. "Hey Larry."

"Hey Annmarie!" I answered. "How are you?"

"Good. What can I get you?"

"Oh, I'm not here for food, I just stopped in to say hi."

"Oh. Are you here visiting?"

"No. I'm back in grad school."

"Really? You don't seem to be the grad school type. What are you studying?"

"Architecture," I said.

"Architecture? Oh my god! Did you hear about the female student?"

"What student?"

"I just saw on the news they found a young woman's body on Lisbon Avenue in a burned down house. I think she was Indian ... Eastern Indian or something."

# 5

My mom called me later that night and had heard the story on the news. She was walking with the cordless phone under her ear and carrying a tray of food out onto her back patio. She tripped on the step and fell face down. A train that ran in my back yard then sounded its horn and woke me up ... I must have been sleeping.

I do remember being on the phone for a long time before that, though, talking to both my mom and several classmates about Raja. Apparently, they were still investigating the cause of death which was difficult because the house was completely burned to the ground, as were her remains. I felt like I was hit by a bus. I was still recovering from the drunken blackout and simultaneously trying to cope with the death of Raja. She was such a sweet person—soft spoken, reserved, and very studious.

Just then I saw the lights of a police cruiser outside my house. I assumed they were coming to break up the frat party at the house next to mine, but then I heard a rapping on my door. It was the muscular cop from the night at the station.

"Mr. Martin, I need to ask you a few questions about the fire on Lisbon last night. Is this a good time?"

"Sure, come on in," I said conformingly.

"Good. Nice car seat. Can I sit in it?"

The officer was pointing to my passenger's side car seat that I removed from my Oldsmobile Cutlas Calais.

"Why the hell is there a car seat in your living room?"

"Oh, that. Yes. Well I removed it so I can fit my piano and amp in my car when I have gigs. I play on an old Fender Rhodes electric piano. It takes up a tremendous amount of space," I explained.

"So, what do you do when you have a passenger?" Officer Stimpson curiously enquired.

"Well, I guess they have to sit in the back."

"What do you do on dates?"

"I don't know. I haven't had a date since I pulled the seat out."

"Why don't you just buy a van?"

"I'm totally broke. This architecture program has bankrupted me."

"Yeah, things are going to well for you lately, are they?"

"No, I guess not," I said disgruntledly.

"Well, I need to ask you some questions about the other night. You said you heard screaming and maybe saw someone getting stabbed—possibly one of your classmates?"

"Yes. I thought I saw Ng Seiko with a knife. Is this about my friend Raja?"

"Yes. She was a friend of yours?"

"Yes, she was. She was a super nice person."

"Did you know her well?"

"Not socially. I've worked on a few class projects with her. She was a very serious student and not into the party scene or anything."

"And you also said you saw fire, correct?"

"Yes, that's right."

"Do you have any witnesses that saw you leave the bar?"

"No. Well maybe Karl the bartender."

"Yeah, we already talked to Karl. He didn't see you leave. Do you think it's possible that you may have wandered around Lisbon Avenue before you passed out in front of the church?"

"No. I don't think so. All I remember is walking up on Main Street, feeling dizzy, and then you waking me up in the cell."

"Do you have a history of blacking out, schizophrenia, or any other manic episodes?"

"No. Just OCD and cluster headaches, but that's about it."

"Well, I'll tell it to you straight, Larry. We don't have any leads on the death of your friend, or the fire, and Seiko is still missing. You either saw something or did something that you don't remember. There was some blood found at the scene. They're going to run it tonight to see if they can get a match, but if not, you may be called in to give a sample."

"Sure, no problem. Anything to help," I said.

"Have a good night. And get that seat fixed."

"Never!" I said half-joking.

The next morning, Stimpson called and told me to go to the hospital and get my blood drawn. He had already submitted the paperwork. I hated getting blood work done. Are they going to wear gloves? Are the needles clean? What if they miss the vein? Ahh, the what-ifs of OCD.

As I was waiting for the phlebotomist, I started thinking about Raja and the images I saw of Ng and the fire. Then I started thinking about all of the other dreams I had that ended up happening: Mike from Carbone's getting shot, Donna berating me and showing me her crotch, and a whole host of smaller premonitions, like dreaming about someone I haven't seen in a while and bumping into them the next day, or a glass falling, or predicting who would be the next student to quit the architecture program. I started to remember dreams I had dating back to grammar school, junior high, and high school. I remembered seeing my friend Rich with a Batman t-shirt on riding his bike past our friend Jack Seafart's house. Rich hit a crack in the road, went face forward over the handlebars, and slid on his stomach across the pavement. When he got to his feet, Seafart was out on his front lawn. The Batman insignia was totally scraped off the shirt and he yelled out, "Did you see that Seafart?" The event then happened about a week later. When Jack told me the story, I thought I was having Deja-vu. I also remembered having a dream about people breaking into Seafart's house.

A day later, Jack called me up and asked if I took the items from his garage, which included a lawnmower, a dolly, a weed eater, and three ten-speed bicycles and put them in his house. I remember cracking up and asking, "Why would they put things *in* your house?" Apparently, the thugs started up the lawnmower and destroyed the carpet in the living room. I also remembered the time when I had a dream that my childhood friend Dan threw a rock at a car and broke the windshield. We used to throw dirt bombs at cars that drove down a road that was cut through the woods in my backyard. I think we were protesting the destruction of the forest, but I didn't realize it at the time. Throwing dirt bombs at cars seemed to sooth our despair. About a week after the dream, Dan picked up a dirt bomb. I thought it looked a little too big and thought it might actually be a rock. We had one rule: no rocks, but I don't think Dan was paying attention. Dan yelled to me, "Larry, look at this one." I saw the rock in the air and a BMW approaching all in slow motion as I turned my head. The rock hit and smashed the windshield. The owner of the car chased us through the woods. Dan and I had to pay for the windshield, and we couldn't hang out with each other for over a year.

Then I also started thinking about all the dreams I had that had not come true yet, like the little girl falling into Niagara Falls, my friend from grammar school hysterically crying, and of course, the dreaded end of the world. My grandmother, who had died several years prior, also came to me in a dream one night and said, "Larry, the lotto numbers, they are Jeanie's numbers." I remember asking my grandmother who Jeanie was, but I ended up waking up before she could tell me. I was starting to think I was some kind of witch.

After my blood draw, I went up to the research center where I worked as a graduate assistant under Dr. Scott Saxxon. He was an interesting guy. He was in his fifties, average height, slim, had side-parted hair that didn't seem to move, and always wore khaki pants with white sneakers and a white button-down shirt with a tweed jacket. He reminded me of Roger Moore, just with a slight Texas accent. He was always studious from a young age. He graduated in the top two percent of his high school class in Texas, then went on to earn a Bachelor of Science, a Master of Arts, and a Doctor of Philosophy in psychology at the University of Houston. To pay his way through graduate school, Scott worked as a contractor at NASA's Johnson Space Center during the Apollo Mission days as an engineering aid, a project coordinator, and as a technical writer. He eventually took a professor position at the University at Buffalo and focused his research on behavioral ecology, the design of complex human-environment systems, and human-space interaction. On the side, he continued to work for NASA in studying space-behavior relationships for humans living in outer space. He drove an old Pontiac Fiero and parked it in the same spot every day, with the front wheels turned at a thirty-degree angle.

It was one of the other professor's birthdays in the research center and Scott and a couple of other graduate students were eating pie.

"Come on in, Larry, and have a piece of pie," Scott said casually in his smooth southern accent.

His office was impeccably organized. He built shelves with cinder blocks and wood and all the books were labeled in the Dewey Decimal system, and he had pictures of his two daughters with their names labeled under the pictures.

In addition to his end-of-the world research, Scott also had a research grant that was measuring personal space in educational settings. The data was consistent with previous research findings suggesting personal space increases with age, is greater for people with mental illness, and is greater for introverts than extroverts. Not surprisingly, physical attraction also had positive correlation, with those that were mutually attracted to one another using smaller distances than those who were not. Saxxon was going to use the findings to change the design of some of the physical spaces on campus.

Every time I spoke with Scott, I felt as though he was breaking me down, or conducting some kind of psychological experiment. I would often wonder if he was monitoring where I sat in the room or if he was recording the direction my head moved or how many times I blinked my eyes.

"You seem a little melancholy today, Larry—more than usual—what's going on?"

"Did you hear about Raja?" I responded.

"Ahh, yes, I did. The student they found in the fire. I didn't know her personally, though. She's never taken any of my classes. Were you two close?"

"Well, we never hung out socially, but she's in most of my classes, and seeing we spend about eighteen hours a day in studio, yeah, I guess we were kind of close."

I went on to explain the black-out and the dream I had of the stabbing and the fire. Scott's interest peaked.

"Hmmm, interesting. Did you see any faces?"

"I saw another student, Ng, who has been missing since the incident."

"And this Ng, has he ever exhibited any signs of violence or unusual behavior?"

"Absolutely. He freaks me out almost daily! He thinks some of the students are spies and are watching him."

"Yes, unfortunately, the school doesn't do a very good job for helping students with mental health problems," Scott explained.

"Tell me about it. My OCD has been out of control lately and there is no one to talk to."

I went on to tell Scott about my recent dreams and how many of the things I dreamt were coming true.

"Is this a new phenomenon, or have you always had dream premonitions?" Scott inquired in typical psychologist fashion.

"Well, I think I've always seen things in dreams that eventually come true."

"What's the earliest one you remember," Scott asked.

"Well, I remember a dream I had in kindergarten where this girl named Krista gave me a valentine and kissed me on the cheek in the coat room."

"And did it happen?"

"Yes."

Scott chuckled. "Do you remember any other dreams that eventually played out in reality?"

"Now that you mention it, several. I remember dreaming about my friend Dick in the second grade."

"Your dick or you really had a friend named Dick?"

"No, his name was Rich, but we called him Dick."

Scott chuckled. "Ahh. What were his parents thinking? That poor, poor boy."

"Well, I think he used it to his advantage. He was always kind of a joker. But anyway, I dreamt he was standing in a corner, crying, and holding a piece of paper up with his nose."

"And did that actually happen?" Scott asked.

"Indeed it did. A few weeks later, Dick wrote 'this is a piece of shit' on this girl Colleen's cut-out fish project we had to do in art class. The teacher made him hold up the fish with his nose and stand in the corner for the rest of the day. I went back to console him, and the teacher warned me not to talk to him or else I would end up in the other corner."

"Jesus. You went to Catholic school, right?"

"Yeah."

"That explains it. They'd probably get arrested for that now. Any other dreams?"

"Well, yes, several more that I'm remembering." I also told him about some of the dreams I remembered while waiting to get my blood drawn. The night before my freshman year in high school, I dreamt that my friends and I were greeting Dick as he was walking down the hall. We all yelled out, "Hey Dick!" He responded in a serious tone. "Guys it's Rich now." That exact thing happened the next day, and ever since then, we called him Rich.

"Write them all down, Larry."

"Why, do you think I might be psychic or something?" I asked.

"I don't know. It could be coincidence, but the only way to know is to analyze this methodically. I would love to work with you myself, but I'm swamped in this behavior-space research. But, a former psychology student of mine now works as a psychic medium and conducts paranormal research in Niagara Falls. She's quite bright. Perhaps you should visit her?"

"You think?"

"Yes. Oh yes. You'll like Dina. Here's her address. And she may be able to help you harness your dreams. This could be a whole new career for you or a whole new research project." Scott started to frantically brainstorm, as he often did. "Or maybe you could use your dreams to change the future or alter the past, thereby changing the present. You might be able to prevent tragedy, fight crime, save lives ... the possibilities are endless. It's like a superpower."

"Well, I should also mention, I had a dream about the meteor collision a couple of weeks ago."

Scott's face turned pale and totally serious. "Like the one in my class?"

"Yes."

Scott looked at his watch. He was late for a class.

"Damn it, Larry. I have to get over to north campus for a class. But we will need to discuss that dream further. And definitely go see Dina."

# 6

The next day, I fired up my Cutlas and headed up to Niagara Falls to see the psychic medium Dina. The front door was locked, so I walked around back. The name on the back door said, "Escape Studio." This must have been another business, or maybe Scott's address was wrong. I walked in and a scantily dressed young woman named Angie welcomed me.

"Hi there. Do you have an appointment, or are you just a walk in?"

"I have an appointment with Dina."

"Oh, okay, she is in the front of the building. You can walk up through the hall."

There were a few other guys sitting in the waiting room. Another woman in a mini skirt and high heels came out of the back and called for a person named Bill. The guy sitting next to me rose, and she took him by the hand into the back hall. Strangely, I recognized him. He was the offensive line coach for the Buffalo Bills.

I walked down a dimly lit hall lined with small massage rooms on either side. A few more women in slutty attire walked past me and smiled. Then I came to a door that read, "Dina Lawrence: Psychic Medium." I rang a bell and heard a woman's voice.

"Who's there?"

"Hi. It's Larry Martin. Scott Saxxon from the university told me you might be able to help me with some dream analysis?"

"Ah, yes, Mr. Martin."

Dina opened the door. She was in her fifties, had long brown/reddish hair, and was dressed in black leggings and a tight black turtle-neck sweater under a poncho. She kind of resembled Susan Sarandon.

"Come on in Larry. Sorry you had to come through the back, but I've had some issues with people from the street coming in the front door. The women in the back help me to sift out the riffraff. And in their business, they are quite good at it. Also, they keep the feds off my back."

I laughed. "Yeah, that's a pretty interesting place."

"Yes, it is. I don't know how they do it. But believe it or not, those women provide much needed therapy to men with some issues that traditional therapy cannot deal with. Most of the guys who come to get massages are usually dealing with some psychological issues. Their wife may have left them, they might be having confidence issues, they might be virgins, they may be lonely, they might have erectile dysfunction, or they just might need someone to talk to. I've actually thought about combining our businesses. I could provide an hour of counseling and then send them back for *physical* therapy," she said and laughed.

She went on. "Then again, sexual therapy is not my forte. I'm more focused on the paranormal and dream analysis. But if our session gets too stressful, I can get you a good deal on a massage."

"That's tempting, but I'm a total germ-a-phobe. I would be paranoid the sheets weren't clean, or the attendant had a cut on her hand, or the massage oil was contaminated, or ...."

Dina chuckled again. "Ah, a little bit of contamination OCD, I see. Have you ever received help for it?"

"Yes. I've been to four different therapists. I've been on five different SSRI drugs and do exposure and response prevention, but none of it seems to work."

"I'm sorry to hear that. Have you always had it, or did something trigger it?"

"Well, looking back on things, I always had something I obsessed over. Whether it be grades, my basketball shorts being too short, stains on my clothing, smells, getting my driver's license, and of course, dating. I've always obsessed. But yes, I did have a trigger."

"Hmm. Interesting. I want to hear about the short-shorts sometime, but what was the trigger?"

"Ahh, you know. I was dating a girl who was way out my league. She got into coke and used to go on binges. Anyway, I found out she was sleeping with several other guys while we were dating and given her inebriated state, she probably didn't always use protection."

"I see," Dina answered sympathetically.

"Yeah, so I went for full panel STD testing every month for a year to be safe. Luckily, everything was okay, but the OCD just kind of snowballed from there."

"That's tough. I take it you don't date much now?" Dina asked.

"Not really. After going through all that testing, I'm not sure it's worth it anymore."

"I hear that. My ex cheated on me as well. But I did eventually get back on the horse. You know there are such things as condoms, right?" Dina said sarcastically.

"Yeah, I know. But I think this monk lifestyle is good for me right now."

I could see her pondering if she wanted to explore this further, but she shrugged it off.

"Well, some of the work I do with dream analysis is interconnected with mental illness, so maybe we can kill two birds with one stone here."

"Yeah, that would be great. Hey, what did you mean about keeping the feds off your back?"

"Oh, a few years back, I was working on a federal grant back at the university that was studying night terrors and suicides in people who took the prescription Zolvid, an anti-depressant. Have you ever been on that one?"

"No," I said.

"Well, I found a definite correlation. The next thing I knew, my accounts were frozen, and stories were circulating about me conducting unethical experiments with under-age students. I didn't have the resources or energy to fight the government or the pharmaceutical industry, so I went underground and opened this *psychic* front in a shady section of town."

"But you're not actually reading people's palms, right?"

"Right. Here, follow me."

Dina pressed a button and the bookshelf on the wall rotated, just like Batman's bat cave door. We walked through another hall and down a set of stairs into another locked room. We then entered a tiered, circular space with green light; there were several pieces of both analog and digital experimental equipment in a control booth on the end and several cameras pointed toward the center of the circle. It reminded me of a room at the university called the "Kiva." Saxxon taught his courses in the Kiva and it was clear to me this space was designed after it. It was perfect for conducting psychological analysis.

Dina then put a white lab coat over her poncho, pulled her long hair into a bun, and put on a pair of glasses. She now looked more like a scientist than a bohemian hippie-chick. This was another one of Saxxon's tricks. He used to put on a white lab coat before lecturing. His lectures were structured like a fictional story and he'd become one of the characters in the story when he donned the lab coat. One time, I asked him a question at the end of class after he took the coat off. He answered me, "Dr. Reardon, the character he was playing, isn't here anymore. I'm Dr. Saxxon."

"You can sit anywhere you want. We won't be using any of the equipment today."

I sat down a couple of rows back as to keep a bit of a shield. Even though Dina had good vibes, I was still a little freaked out.

"Okay. So, tell me about your dreams."

I went on and described several of the dreams that all came to fruition, such as Donna's leg cross incident, several students who I dreamt dropped out of the architecture program and eventually did, and a couple of pregnancies that I not only saw in dreams, but was actually able to predict the sex of the babies as well. I also brought the list I compiled after talking to Saxxon.

She didn't seem phased at all and she had an intrigued grin on her face. She typed all of this on her laptop.

"Interesting. Anymore?"

"Well, yes. I actually had visions of a fire and bloody murder, and the next day, my classmate was found dead in a burnt down house."

"Oh dear, she responded. Yes, I saw that on the news. Now do all of your dreams eventually come true?"

"No. Not always. Usually only the bad stuff comes true."

"Of course it does," she chuckled. "No good things at all ever come true? What about the no-underwear on your professor, wasn't that a good thing?"

"No, it wasn't."

Dina started laughing hysterically. I think she wasn't wearing any underwear under her leggings since they were tight, and I didn't see a line. Just then, the green lights in the room turned to red.

"Oh, don't mind the lights," Dina said. "They're set that way for some light experiments I used to do, and I don't know how to switch the damn thing off."

She recomposed. "Have there been any bad or disturbing things that haven't happened yet?"

"Yes. There are several. I recently dreamt of a girl I knew in high school. I saw her crying and in great pain. I also saw a little girl fall into Niagara Falls and, oh yeah, I saw the end of the world."

"The end of the world, really? So how does it all end? Let me guess. Nuclear holocaust? A super virus? The sun burns out?"

"Actually, a meteor collision."

She wasn't shocked at all. "Oh, well, that's inevitable."

"Yeah, but in our lifetime?"

"Does anyone else in your family exhibit any similar abilities?"

"Well, yeah, my mom actually. Her father died a few days before I was born, and she said he came to her and told her I would be a boy; she also predicted my niece was going to be a girl. She also mentioned she once dreamt the nuns were beating her younger sister in school. The next day, she left her class to check on her sister and arrived just in time. She grabbed her sister and quit the Catholic school."

"Interesting. There could be a genetic component here."

"Would you say you have a fairly vivid imagination in general?"

"Yes, I guess. That's probably why I went to architecture school."

"Could you give me some examples ... maybe when from when you were young?"

I went on to tell Dina about imaginary sports leagues I created when I was a kid. I had a basketball, football, and golf league. I named the basketball league and the football league the MBA and the MFL—Martin's Basketball Association, Martin's Football League, respectively. I had fifty teams for the MBA—one for each state. Each team had roughly ten players, all of which I identified by number. New York was the team I was on and had all my lucky numbers. I would play the games on a small hoop mounted in my bedroom. I kept statistics, held playoffs, had a championship game, and made a trophy for the winners. I recorded all the statistics in a notebook every year. I still have the notebook.

After I explained all of this to Dina, I could see she was amused.

"Interesting," she said with a smile.

"Is any of this related to the dreams?" I asked.

"It could be. I'm just trying to establish the depths of your imagination."

She proceeded with more questions. "What about movies? TV shows? What do you watch?"

"Just about everything," I responded.

"Do you often find that you are living in any of these shows or movies?"

"All the time. My whole life is made up of movie quotes. I prefer fiction to reality."

"What about relationships, Larry? You mentioned you don't date much after the germ incident, right?"

"Right. Even before the incident, I didn't date much. I had a couple of girlfriends in undergraduate, but that's about it. Why?"

"Oh, I'm just curious. Besides the germ risk, why do you think you don't date much?"

"I guess I just don't really connect with anyone."

"Are your fantasy worlds that you create more interesting?"

"Probably," I responded.

"Okay. Let's get back to your dreams. Besides the things you dream that eventually come true, are there any other types of dreams you get?"

"Of course. I also see ghosts."

"Really? How do you know they are ghosts?"

"Well, the house I live in now is actually on the historic register. When I first moved in, I saw three different people at random times standing over me. I usually wake up screaming, punching, or kicking them. Anyway, about a year after I lived there, I had to do a project on a historic building, so I chose my house. I dug up some old photos of the original owners, and I swear to god, the three people I saw in my dreams were all in the photo and dressed exactly the same."

"No way. You're putting me on!" Dina responded. "Are you sure you never saw the pictures before?"

"Positive."

"Wow. That gives me goose bumps. Have you ever tried talking to them?"

"No. They usually scare the hell out of me. I can still see them for a brief moment when I wake up, but I usually swing at them, so maybe I scare them away. One time, I actually used the force and pushed them against the wall."

"Like Darth Vader force?"

"Exactly."

"I assume you are a huge *Star Wars* nerd?"

"Yes, I am."

"Any other dreams?"

"Well, just your typical things. Like getting chased and not being able to run, drowning, getting buried alive, falling off a tower, getting captured and not being able to scream, and showing up to school and being unprepared for a test. Oh, I also am frequently visited by dead relatives … and I can fly. That's right, I can fly in my dreams."

"Wow! You think these are typical? Do you talk to your dead relatives?"

"All the time. My grandmother actually tried to give me the lotto numbers once."

"Really? What happened?"

"She told me that the numbers were Jeanie's numbers. The next day, I called my mom and asked if we knew anyone named Jeanie. She said we had an aunt named Jeanie. We called her up, gathered all her vital numbers, age, address, birth date, social security number, phone number, you name it. We played every combination of numbers, but we didn't win."

"Interesting," Dina responded. "What percentage of your dreams actually come to fruition?"

"I'm not sure. Maybe sixty or seventy percent? It's usually just the bad stuff."

"The good things don't ever come true?"

"No! If they did, I'd be having sex with super models daily."

Dina chuckled. She took her glasses off and closed her laptop.

"Well, the timeline of these dreams is something we're going to have to pin down. I suggest you start keeping a journal so we can ascertain if you are seeing things that already happened, are happening now, or are going to happen. Once we figure out when these events take place on the timeline, the next step will be to teach you how to better control what you see."

I was a bit in disbelief.

"Wait, so you actually think this is real and not just a coincidence?"

"I'm not sure yet. You seem to be honest, but I don't know you well enough to know if you're bullshitting me. That's why we'll run some tests."

"What kind of tests?" I asked nervously.

"Well, much of this is experimental, but there is equipment that can lock on to your brain waves in your REM sleep and map your images onto a monitor."

I laughed. "You're kidding, right?"

"Oh no, not at all. The technology was actually developed in Switzerland."

"Has it ever been done?"

"Mostly on animals. The FDA hasn't cleared it for human trials. However, some human subjects volunteered, but the results weren't very conclusive."

"Jesus. Are there any side effects?"

"Well, so far, it has been relatively safe in animals. But with any trans-cranial stimulation, there is risk of seizure and hallucination. I think this happened in one of the six humans who volunteered."

"That's almost twenty percent! You're not selling me on this."

"Oh, come on Larry, have some backbone. It can't be any worse than any of the drugs they gave you for your OCD or your cluster headaches, right?"

I started laughing, but I hadn't told her about the headaches.

"How did you know about the headaches?"

"Oh, don't forget, I am technically a psychic," she said with confidence.

"Come on. Really, how did you know? Did you hack my medical records or something?"

"No, nothing like that," she quickly answered.

She then took off her glasses and let down her hair.

"Larry, my gut tells me you have a strange connection to the universe; the scientist in me remembers a few case studies that associated cluster headaches with vivid dreams that could alter reality. Plus, I'll be honest with you, I've been scanning your brain with the lights since you walked in here."

"What, wait a minute!"

She started laughing. "I'm just playing with you Larry." But was she?

"So what do you say, do you want to try the dream analysis software?"

"I'll have to think about it. I assume I would have to sleep here?"

"Oh no, not at all. I'll inject the chip into your head, and I can connect to it wirelessly."

"Whoa. Wait a minute, it gets injected into my head?"

"Yup."

"There's no way I'm getting anything injected into me."

"Why not. It's totally painless. And I can take it out just as easy as I put it in."

I started frantically listing all the things I was afraid of.

"Well, what if it screws my brain up? What if it makes me brain dead? What if it gets infected? What if other digital waves interfere with it? What if someone else hacks into it? What if—"

"Ah, the what-ifs. I see your OCD is taking over."

"This has nothing to do with that, this is a legitimate concern," I emphatically explained.

She chuckled. "No, it's on a secure network. Besides, it's only your dreams. It doesn't read your mind or anything."

"Well, right now, I'm going to have to say no. Is there any more research on it?"

"I can send you links to some articles on it, but there isn't a whole lot of research on it yet. But I'll let you think about it. Anyway, I have another client coming in. Here, I'll walk you out."

She gently took my arm and walked me back upstairs to the psychic lobby. She smelled like vanilla and she seemed to have healing hands. My anxiety subsided when she touched me.

"What do you say, do you want me to set you up with a massage?"

"No, not today," I said and chuckled.

"Okay sweetie, you know where I am. But seriously think about the chip. It sounds like this gift you have could be something."

"Gift, it's more like a curse," I responded.

"Ah, the dilemma of all superheroes."

Dina gave me a hug in hippie fashion. I then walked out the back of the massage parlor and the Buffalo Bills coach was just finishing his massage. And then I remembered seeing him on a massage table in a dream a few years prior, trying to get his mind off the huge heartbreak when Scott Norwood missed the kick in *Superbowl 19*. Strange.

# 7

I arrived back in Buffalo at about midnight. Since the bars were open to 4:00 a.m., the activity was just getting going. The fraternity in the house next to me was being filmed on MTV's new show, "Fraternity Life." I dozed off on the couch and once again dreamt of my friend Cindy from high school. She was sobbing, her mascara was running down her face, and she was wearing a ripped prom dress. I woke up to sirens on my street. Apparently, a local gang tried to get onto the set of MTV's show. When the producers refused, the gang became violent, vandalized the house, and injured several people at the party. I fell back asleep and had an erotic dream about Dina, but my damn alarm woke me up right when it was about to get good. The strange thing was that the alarm wouldn't turn off. I tried every switch and even unplugged it, but the voices on the NPR channel that I woke up to wouldn't stop. Then, I really woke up, apparently. I was still dreaming that I was shutting off the alarm—a dream within a dream.

The semester was coming to an end. Our final critique was a couple of weeks away and Donna had trashed my project at the previous critique and essentially made me start from scratch. Between the eerie dreams, the stress of school, and the cluster headaches, I was noticeably stressed out. I had a full-grown beard and my hair was getting long. I had been wearing the same flannel jacket and cargo pants for about a week, and my diet consisted of cola, candy bars, and cheese filled pretzels out the vending machines.

For the next few weeks, I worked until four in the morning. I rode an old three-speed bike that I garbage picked to and from studio. The bike was old enough that it wouldn't get stolen and also lessened my chances of getting mugged in the university heights ghetto. I rode past all the drunk undergraduate students coming out of the bars and past the long line of stoned kids waiting for late night slices at Carbone's. I put on the TV and fell asleep to reruns of *Family Ties* and had a disturbing dream that my mom was in great pain. I was so busy and pre-occupied, that I hadn't had time to call home.

The day of our final critique had finally arrived. Final critiques in architecture are like the Super Bowl of architecture school. They are catered events, any guests are welcome to attend, and outside critics are brought in to bring their angle of archi-babble to the circle.

I looked at the roster. Donna put me dead last at four-thirty, so I had to sweat it out the entire day. I kept seeing the stress drop from the faces of each of my classmates after they presented. I don't think my stomach could make it to the end. This was no accident. She gave all her favorites morning slots when everyone was in a good mood. To get me through the day, I brought a flask of black-berry brandy. This was an old family remedy to settle your stomach. I nipped on it all day, and have to say, I was pretty much hung-over by the time I had to present.

Maryanne was one of the first to present, which was no surprise as she was one of Donna's favorites. All semester, she had been stealing other people's ideas, including mine, and passing them off as her own. In architecture school, this is a huge taboo. However, Donna was blind to this. In one of the previous critiques, she accused me of copying Maryanne.

After I presented, Donna cut me down as usual, but at that point, nobody seemed to care. The guest critics liked my project. Donna didn't like this and argued with one of the guests. This just reaffirmed my notion that Donna had it out for me from day one. However, even with the praise from the guest critics, I realized I really wasn't a talented designer. I had no intention of returning to the program the next semester—that was until my sister called later that night.

Apparently, my mom had been sick for the past month or so, but they didn't want to tell me because I was so stressed out from school. Two of her close friends died of cancer in the preceding year and she came down with the same symptoms. The doctors ordered a full panel of tests over the course of the December and January. I saw the whole thing weeks before in a dream, and I did nothing. Not even a phone call because I was too absorbed in some absurd goddamn fictional project. It was then and there I decided I would make the appointment with Dina to put the chip in after the holiday break. Also, as to not upset my mom any further, I decided to stick it out in the blasted architecture program.

The school had a sixty-year tradition of having a happy hour called "x-bar" every Friday in the building that housed the design studios. Every week, one of the studios would host the event and were responsible for the food and for sneaking the alcohol in. And it became a fierce competition; each studio would try to up the event from the previous week. During one of our weeks hosting x-bar, Sam decided to enhance the flyers a bit with pictures of booze and people smoking grass. In the past, the flyers were subtle as to not draw attention…a simple "x" with a bar line under it and the studio room number. Sam's flyers seemed to work, though. The turnout was so big we had to move the party into one of the lecture halls down the hall and had to go purchase more beer. I went with Sam to pick up the beer. When we came back, Sam dropped me off and I hoisted the cases over my shoulder. When I walked into the lounge, there were two university police officers standing at the door.

"Stop right there. What's your name?"

"Larry."

"Are you a student here?"

"Yeah. A graduate student."

"Are you the one that has been supplying the alcohol to this party all night?"

"No. I'm just helping someone unload it."

"You didn't actually purchase it?"

"No. I'm just unloading it."

"Who purchased it then?"

"I'd rather not say. In the neighborhood I grew up in, we don't rat people out."

"Okay. That's fine. Then we'll just charge you."

"Charge me with what?"

"It's illegal to have or serve alcohol on campus."

"Really? But I'm 24 years old."

"It doesn't matter. Besides, there are people in this room that are under 21, right?"

"Well, we did have someone proofing people at the door."

"Where's that person?"

"I don't see him."

"Ahh. You don't want to rat him out either, huh?"

"No."

"Fine. We'll have to book you."

As I looked up, several of the students and the professors were sneaking out of the room. After all, the faculty promoted this event. If they were connected to it, they could lose their jobs.

"Okay. I'll take responsibility."

Just then, this bad-ass woman named Lana came charging for the cop.

"Hey fuck head. Don't try this divide and conquer crap on us. You can't arrest one person for this. We all contribute to this. We all payed for the beer. He's just kind enough to carry it in."

"What did you call me, young lady?" The cop snared.

"Fuck head."

The officer grabbed Lana by the arm.

"You're coming in as well."

"Fine, arrest me."

The police officers cuffed Lana and I and put us in the back of the cruiser. When we arrived at the station, they booked us and put us into separate cells. Ironically, a strange calm came over me. I remembered dreaming about this exact incident several years prior after a night when my college roommate was arrested for smoking a joint at a Springfest concert. I couldn't remember the outcome of the dream, but I had a feeling it would end all right.

The officer came into my cell.

"Sorry about all of this, Larry. We were just going to let you go in the parking lot, but since that girl yelled us, we had to act. She's got some brass, eh?"

"Yeah. She's a tough one. I wouldn't mess with her."

"And trust me. I actually respect you for taking the heat and not ratting out your friends."

"Oh, well, like I said, that's how my neighborhood was growing up. And I understand you are only doing your job. But I have to say, I honestly didn't know the event was against school policy."

"Yeah. You can officially host an event, but it has to be done through the university event services department. They have people who are licensed to serve alcohol and will hire one of us to monitor the event."

"Ahh. I'll keep that in mind."

"Well, you can have the beer back."

"Really?"

"Yeah, we don't want it."

"Are you sure? Come on, take a six-pack home for later tonight."

"Well, I can't know about it so maybe you will just 'forget' to bring a few home," the officer said as he winked at me.

"Ahh. Right," I said.

Sam picked me up at the station. Apparently, the entire party went out to the Blue Goose after the x-bar was broken up. When we pulled up to the bar, the bad-ass Lana was also pulling up.

"Hey crime buddy. Did they let you go, too?"

"Yeah."

"The cop told me the only reason he let me go is because you were cool. So, thank you, Larry."

Lana then gave me a kiss on the cheek.

When we walked into the bar, the place erupted in cheers and applause. Lana and I were the heroes of the night, and for a brief moment, I think people thought I was bad ass. I don't remember paying for a drink that night. While we certainly spared others from getting in trouble, we killed the tradition of x-bar. From that point on, the Blue Goose became our Friday night go to.

The night started getting out of hand. People were drunk, several people went home together, including some of the professors and students. I considered working off the momentum of the night and flirting with Lana, but by the time I got up my nerve, she was already tongue-deep with a professor from the program.

At about three a.m., I walked back to my dismal apartment. My five minutes of fame were over, and I already was 'awake' hung-over. That night, I had two strange dreams. The first was one of Maryanne. The dream was hazy because I had several drinks, but I woke up and saw her for what she was: pure evil. I fell back asleep and had another dream of a group of students having an orgy and one of Donna and Sam having an affair.

# 8

Things started out just as stressful the second semester. About half of the class dropped out of the program, and many were surprised I made it back. Believe it or not, Donna passed me. News quickly surfaced that Ng, who was still missing at our final critique, had killed himself in New York City. The police were able to match his DNA to the house fire and murder of Raja.

The good news was that our new studio professor seemed to like me quite a bit. We had her for a few guest critiques the previous semester and I always had a good rapport with her. And, she was no fan of Donna or Maryanne. Margaret was an English woman in her early thirties with short black hair and a soft voice. She kind of looked like Lois Lane. She was one of the professors who encouraged me not to quit when I threatened to in the fall semester.

Margaret was very fair in the critiques, but some of Donna's "starchitects" from the previous semester were no longer getting preferential treatment. After several lackluster reviews of her work, Maryanne decided to make sexual harassment claims against several of the male students. She had a huge crush on Sam. She used to follow him home and pester him for dates. After he rejected her, she moved onto Phil, a tall good-looking guy who was an intense student. Phil called her out for stealing other people's ideas. Margaret actually agreed and spoke to Maryanne about it. She obviously wasn't happy.

Several of us were called down to the dean's office to testify before the school's ethics committee. The assistant to the dean called me into the room. I sat down in front of a panel of twelve people—some students, some faculty, and some administrators. I was glad to see Saxxon was on the panel. He was probably chosen for his background in psychology. The head of the committee then proceeded to introduce everyone at the table.

"Mr. Martin, it has come to our attention that a hostile work environment has been fostered in your studio. There are accounts of lude language, vulgarity, and unwanted advances. Have you witnessed any of the like?"

"Well, what constitutes lude language? Swearing?"

"Yes, any cursing or inappropriate comments, jokes, or innuendos."

"Well sure. I think everyone swears. I mean, these projects are frustrating."

"Has it ever gone beyond basic swearing, into more of hate language against women or minorities?"

"Well, I think most of us may have called Donna a bitch a few times, but can you blame us?"

The room was silent. Saxxon looked up from his notebook and I could see he was trying to hold back laughter.

One of the female students on the panel quickly responded. "What about a cunt. Did anyone ever call her a cunt?"

"No, not that I witnessed. Just bitch."

The young woman proceeded. "What about stories of professors not wearing any underwear?"

I chuckled a bit. "Oh, that. Well, that actually happened."

"So it was discussed?"

"Yes, but I don't consider the topic vulgar. I think most of us were just shocked and it seemed like she did it on purpose."

The chair of the committee then chimed in. "But would you agree that that might be considered offensive to some of your classmates?"

"No. I didn't hear anyone object when we were discussing it. Everyone was either laughing or recounting what they saw. That goes for both the male and female students."

"Okay, let's move on. What about some of your male classmates making passes at the female students. Have you ever witnessed this or have acted this way yourself?"

"No, I never have. But Ng, the student who was found dead, often made threats against students. And one of the students who dropped out used to always ask one of the students to take her top off."

"And who was that student?"

"Ahh, his first name was Steve, but I actually don't know his last name."

The person to the right of the committee chair responded, "That's Steve Maston. But as Larry said, he's no longer enrolled."

"Well, as awful as that is, we are only investigating this semester since the complaints were just recently filed. And we are well aware of the Ng Seiko issue."

"Well, the only harassment I've seen came from one of the female students."

"And who is that?"

"Maryanne Daniels. She was in love with Sam Bowen and used to follow him home and pester him for dates. She then started hitting on Phil Malone, but then they got into a fight over a project."

The chair continued. "Well, it is Ms. Daniels that has filed the complaint." I was somewhat shocked he outed her, but then again, the department had a stern policy of being transparent in these types of cases.

I freaked out. "No way, man, no way. She's just mad because Sam rejected her, and she was called out for plagiarism. She's fabricating this claim to get even with Sam and Phil, and me ... and all the other people she doesn't like, I guess."

"Thank you, Mr. Martin. Is there anything else you would like to say?"

"No. I really hate this program, but I guess that's a discussion for another time."

"Yes, it is. Thank you for cooperating, Mr. Martin. We are interviewing everyone from the class, but if you would, please keep our discussion confidential."

"Of course."

As I was walking back to studio, Todd passed me on the bridge that connected the two buildings.

"Hey, did you meet with the committee?"

"Yeah," I responded.

"Can you believe that Maryanne? I told you, she's like Monica Lewinsky!"

"I know. You remember I had that dream about her last semester, right?"

"Yes! Dude, you totally predicted this!"

"I know. I think I might be a witch—or a warlock or something."

I went back to my dismal apartment. I was so angry with Maryanne I couldn't even eat dinner. That night, I dreamt of my grandfather, who died in 1981 from a heart-attack. I told him about Maryanne and how she was pure evil. I cursed her. I cursed her straight to hell. I also had a dream that one of our other professor's was fired for sexual harassment.

\*\*\*

Coincidentally, the site for our final project was in the Niagara Gorge and was only about a half-mile to Dina's psychic studio. After learning about my mom at the end of the first semester, I called Dina as soon as I returned after the winter break to tell her to get the software ready. After our first site visit for the project, I broke off from my classmates and went to see Dina to get the dream monitoring device inserted in my head.

I walked through the dimly lit massage parlor. It was quiet that day with only one woman working.

Dina welcomed me at the door. "Larry! I'm so glad you decided to try this. I think we are on the verge of a big breakthrough here."

"Well, I hope so, because I've been freaking out lately. I think I'm a witch."

"Any new dreams?"

"Yes, several—"

"Don't tell me yet. After I insert the OC17 chip, we'll have to calibrate the software. I'm not sure, but it may be possible to get a backlog of your dreams, or at the very least, get you to go back into a previous dream."

Dina then put on some latex gloves and pulled out a gun-looking device.

"Is all this sterile?" I nervously asked.

"Of course. Nothing to worry about. Look, right out of the autoclave."

She then came behind me. I could smell her vanilla perfume. I thought about that when she counted to three to inject the device into me.

"Owww," I screamed.

"Oh, quit being a baby. I didn't even put it in yet."

"Ready? One, two, three."

The device went in. I barely even felt it.

"I didn't even feel it!"

"I know, I told you."

She then turned on one of the monitors.

"Okay, you may feel a little tingling while I calibrate the device."

"Oh, yeah, I feel it."

Dina laughed. "Again, I haven't turned it on yet, silly. Ready? I'll count to three. One, two, thr—"

"Ahh, there it is, now I really feel the tingle."

"Good, that means it's working."

Up on the monitor, a series of three-dimensional waves forming a complex tetrahedron were circulating. There were also windows with images of my brain. It was like a real-time MRI.

"So those are your brainwaves. As you can see, you have an abundance of activity in your basal ganglia which probably explains your OCD."

"Great, can you turn it off?"

"Unfortunately, no. Okay, I am getting a few images, but since you are not currently in REM sleep, they are just memories and are somewhat spotty. Here's the first image. Do you recognize it?"

The image was a group of students in a circle—they were all naked. This was the orgy dream I had at the end of the previous semester.

"Larry, you old devil you!"

"No, there's no sex involved. In the dream, I just walked in on the circle because I was at the party earlier in the night and I left a bottle of booze there."

"Sure, Larry."

"No really, I don't even like any of those people."

"Well, this is the only image I can retrieve. The other thing I want to try is to see if we can program you to go back into a dream. Is there any one in particular you want to see again?"

"Well yes, all of them."

"Well, let's start with one. Maybe a simple one."

"There's the one of my friend Cindy from high school. I see her crying and in great pain."

"Perfect," Dina answered. "Do you have any images of Cindy?"

"Yes, in my old yearbook, but I'll have to have my mom scan it in and send it to me. My yearbooks are still at my parents' house."

"Sounds good. In theory, I should be able to upload an image and it should trigger your memory when you are in REM sleep. Also, I'll give you some phrases to repeat throughout the day that may spark your memory when you fall asleep."

"Wow!"

"I know, this is cool stuff. But don't get your hopes up. Like I said before, it didn't work for everyone in the human trials."

"Yeah, and let's hope I don't get a seizure or start freaking out."

"Right. Ahh, I almost forgot. There's one more critical piece to this technology. I'll have to inject a receiver chip in my head and one in Saxxon's as well."

"A receiver chip?" I asked.

"Exactly. The receiver chip will connect Saxxon and I both to your dreams, thus putting us in the timeline relative to you. Does that make sense?"

"No, not really," I responded.

"Well, since Scott and I don't seem to have this dream altering ability like you do, we need a way to be synced to your dreams if there is a change in the timeline. We can view your dreams on the monitors, but if you were to go into a past dream and change events, it could create a ripple effect in the timeline that could displace all of us in space and time. With the receiver chip, our time will be relative to your dream. This way, if something is changed, only you, Saxxon, and I will remember the multiple timelines."

"Ahh, I get it. So let's say I have a dream and I go back in time and marry my high school sweetheart. This might lead me to never live in Buffalo, never go to architecture school, never meet Saxxon, and thus never be here talking to you."

"Exactly. But you'd remember both timelines since you are the one altering it. The receiver chips will keep Scott and I connected to you, so we will both remember both timelines as well. And we would come and hunt you down if we didn't like what you did."

"Wow. Very interesting."

"Yes, well, in theory, this is how it works, but like I said, it's never been fully tested."

"It's like a checks and balances for altering time?'

"Exactly. If Saxxon sent you to me, I trust you. But in the wrong hands, this technology could have devastating effects on humanity. That is, if it works." Dina chuckled.

\*\*\*

When I arrived home, I called my mom and had her go into my drawer and get out my old yearbooks. I had to walk her step by step on how to scan in the image, save it to the computer, and attach it to the email. It took about two hours.

The image finally came through on my email and I forwarded it to Dina. It was midnight, but luckily, she was still awake. Dina sent me back a message saying the image is uploaded into the software and will transmit into my OC17 chip when I go to sleep.

I had a difficult time falling asleep that night because I was anxious for the device to work. It was a Monday night and the WCW and WWF wrestling shows were on. I flipped between the two and eventually fell asleep on the couch.

And there she was, Cindy Swain, as clear as day. Once again, she was sobbing. Her mascara was running down her face and she was wearing a long, light blue, satiny dress. Her hair was French braided, but it was pulled out of the braids. The shoulder of the dress was torn, and she wasn't wearing any shoes. I had to go to the bathroom really bad, but I was trying to stay in the dream. However, the urine pressure became too great and I woke up. It was about two a.m. I sent an email to Dina.

"Did you get it?"

She responded right away. The software alerted her of the dream. "Got it. Can you come by tomorrow night so we can go over the images?"

"I'll be there," I responded.

# 9

When I arrived at Dina's lab, she had the entire video spliced together of the dream. There were more parts and much more detail than I remembered.

"It's working. I'll have the entire movie spliced together in a minute. Hey, you dream in color!"

"Hmm. Interesting, because I'm actually color-blind in real life."

We sat back and watched the dream unfold. We were like two kids in the theater seeing *Star Wars* for the first time. Cindy was the same age as she was the last time I saw her, which was about seven years prior. She was walking away from a house, crying, and her dress was ripped.

"Wait a minute. I know that house. Can we zoom in and sharpen in a bit?"

Dina worked her magic on the computer. We were able to zoom into a number—89.

"That's it. It's 89 Chestnut Drive and I know the guy who lived in that house. His name was Erik and he was a dick."

"Do you know where Cindy lives now, Larry?"

"No. Let's look her up."

On another monitor, Dina did a search and found she lived near Albany, New York.

We zoomed in further and saw a couple of cars: a Pontiac 6000 and a Dodge Aries K-Car, both classics from the mid-eighties/early nineties.

"So, this is obviously the past," Dina explained. "She looks the same as you remember – although that might just be your memory of her. There are old cars in the distance, and she's wearing a prom dress."

"This must have been her prom night, 1991."

"Were you at the prom, Larry?"

"No. I didn't go to prom."

"Ah. Big surprise," Dina said sarcastically.

I started to postulate. "Something must have happened. Maybe she broke up with her boyfriend, or maybe she got into a fight, or, oh god, maybe she was attacked."

Dina did more searching. "I found an address and a phone number, but there is no other digital footprint of her. You may have to call her."

"I know, but what do I say? I can't just blurt it out."

I dialed Cindy's number and got the answering machine.

*Hey Cindy! This is Larry Martin from high school. I bumped into Jeff the other day and he mentioned you were living in Albany. I'm going to be in Albany this weekend. Let me know if you want to grab a drink. My number is 716-555-2727. Talk to you soon.*

Dina was a bit skeptical. "Do you think that will freak her out? And who's Jeff?"

"Jeff was a guy she dated in high school. I was also friends with him, and he actually goes to UB, so I can tie it together."

That night, it was snowing heavily out, so I decided to crash on the couch in Dina's lab. It was very comfortable. It was a U-shaped sectional couch with a lot of pillows. I then dreamt I was in a warm lake on a hot summer night with a beautiful blonde woman. She was riding on my back as we swam out to an island. When we arrived at the island, she started kissing me, but then I woke up. I never saw her face.

In the morning, Dina brought up all my dreams on the monitor. There were actually a few more that I didn't remember: a car stuck in the snow, and my studio teacher Margaret crying in the hall of the architecture building. Dina played them all back, but of course I was most intrigued about the swimming dream.

"Oh, Larry, who's the lucky gal in the dream?"

She zoomed around and tried to patch more of the waves, but all she could make out was that it was Lake Champlain. Her family used to vacation there, and she recognized the Adirondack back drop.

"Have you ever been to Lake Champlain, Larry?"

"No."

"Ahh, this could be a promising future!"

"Yeah, but remember, only the bad stuff comes true."

"Right," Dina confirmed.

I made it back to campus just in time to take a shower, eat a bowl of cereal, and go to studio. I was about five minutes late, but when I walked in, you could cut the tension with a knife. Apparently, Phil had decided to lambaste Margaret, attacking her teaching style, her knowledge of architecture, and her general intelligence.

"This studio is a total joke. I came in with high expectations because you're a Harvard grad, but this project is completely useless and is a waste of our time."

Being soft-spoken and methodical, Margaret tried to reason with Phil.

"Well, does anyone else feel this way?"

Maryanne spoke up. "Yes, compared to last semester where I was totally energized, I have completely lost my motivation in this studio."

Then I spoke up.

"Don't even bring up last semester, Maryanne. Donna loved you and kissed your ass, but she shit on the rest of us!"

The class, including Margaret, chuckled a bit.

Phil went on. "No. This isn't funny. We're paying big money to be here. We are here to learn and better ourselves and Margaret is totally incompetent. I'm going to bring this up with Dean Williams. And fuck the rest of you. You all complain about her behind her back, but when I confronted her, no one spoke up."

Maryanne chimed in. "Well, I said something, Phil."

"Fuck you, Maryanne. How's your fake sexual assault lawsuit coming? I don't want to hear anything from you."

The whole studio was chaos. Everyone started chiming in about their gripes, whether it was school related or not. Margaret quietly slipped out in the hall. It looked like studio was over for the day.

After the dust settled, I decided to go over to the computer lab to check my email. On my way over, I saw Margaret in an alcove in the basement and she was crying.

She saw me coming and wiped away her tears.

"Hi Larry. Interesting class today, huh? I have to say, I didn't expect that, but thanks for sticking up for me."

"Oh, no problem."

"Do you think my studio is a failure? Am I incompetent? You can be honest."

"No, not at all. I'm enjoying your studio. It was Donna's studio that I hated."

She laughed a bit. "Yeah, Donna is a piece of work."

"You know, I wouldn't listen to Phil or Maryanne. Phil is just stressed out because of some personal stuff he is going through, and Maryanne is a complete psycho!"

"Yes, I gathered that," she replied. "But I've never had anyone hate me like this. I'm not sure what to do. I may resign."

"Hey, you were the one that convinced me not to quit, remember? These studios are like movies—some people like them, some don't. And each semester is a different cast."

"That's a good point, Larry. You remind me of my brother."

It looked like she wanted to hug me, but I refrained.

"Are you going to the computer lab?"

"Yes," I said.

"Okay. I'll walk over with you."

I think she would have gone anywhere with me at that point—it's like she needed protection.

I walked Margaret back to her office and then went into the computer lab. Much to my surprise, there was a voicemail from Cindy on my *Motorola* flip phone.

*Hey Larry. I got your message. It's good to hear from you. I work as a waitress at a restaurant called Aiko's in Saratoga Springs. I have to work this weekend, but feel free to stop in and say hi. Talk to you soon.*

I was planning to take a field trip to Albany anyway. Even though it was a few years away, I was considering doing a large-scale transportation plan for my thesis; there was a proposal for a light rail system between Albany, Schenectady, and Saratoga Springs and I thought this would be a good case study.

The next morning, I looked outside and there was six feet of snow—no joke. This is quite common in Buffalo with the lake effect snow off Lake Erie. My slumlord owner of the house I lived in didn't plow the driveway, so I had to back the Cutlass out of the garage through six feet of snow. The car ended up spinning. I hit the post of the garage and the entire roof collapsed onto the car. Oddly, the only damage was to the passenger side mirror and a small dent on the hood. I somehow managed to get the car out from the garage and to the end of the driveway, but I got it stuck on the curb where the plow went by—which was probably seven feet of solid ice and snow. About ten miles out of Buffalo, the roads were completely clear and there was only a couple of inches of snow. You have to love the Great Lakes.

Albany is about four hours from Buffalo and the Thru-Way is quite bland. Aiko's was kind of a rough place. I was surprised Cindy worked there since she was always such an introvert in high school.

I sat down at the bar and ordered a drink. I looked around the bar and finally saw Cindy. I tried to get her eye, but she was busy. After a few sips off my Jack and Coke, she finally saw me and motioned she would be over in a minute. She looked tired and very ragged, almost like she was ten years older than me. In high school, she was a nerdy librarian type. Her hair was always perfectly groomed, and she wore sweater vests and long pleated skirts. She now looked kind of haggard and a bit slutty. She had a short tight skirt on, a lot of eye shadow, and a low-cut shirt. Her hair was frizzy.

She finally came over and seemed happy to see me. She smelled like cigarette smoke.

"Larry, oh my god, you actually came. I didn't think you would."

"Oh yeah, well, Jeff told me to check in on you."

"Oh really? And how is Jeff?"

"Ah, he's okay. He's in medical school now. The medical school is near the architecture school, so I sometimes see him at lunch."

"Medical school? Oh my god, I wouldn't trust him to do anything on me."

"No, me neither."

Cindy laughed. "Well, I have about another hour before my shift is over. I'll join you for a drink when I'm done."

For the next hour, Cindy kept getting me free refills. By the time she sat down with me, I was three drinks deep. We talked for about an hour about old friends, junior high, high school, college, and family. Cindy drank three vodka-tonics and chained smoked four cigarettes in about fifteen minutes.

Since we were both fairly buzzed, I decided to just blurt it out.

"I'm going to be honest with you. The real reason I looked you up is because I had a disturbing dream about you. You seemed to be in great distress. Is everything all right?"

She laughed. "I don't know. I guess so. A disturbing dream? What did you see?"

"You were leaving Erik's house in tears. Your dress was ripped, and you weren't wearing any shoes. You walked back to your house in the rain. A car drove by you and the water from the road splashed your light blue prom dress."

Cindy tried to make it like it was no big deal. "Oh my god, that sounds like my prom night. Who told you about that? Did Jeff tell you something?"

"No. I'm not really friends with Jeff. Like I said, I just see him in the cafeteria sometimes."

"Then Jason must have told you something."

"No, I haven't talked to him since freshmen year."

"Really? You guys were always pretty tight, right?"

"Well, we were, but he kind of turned into a dick after freshmen year."

Cindy was happy to change the subject. "Why, what did he do?"

"Oh, it was over some girl."

"Of course it was." She laughed. "Who was it?"

"It was Michelle."

"Oh, I remember her. What did Jason do, steal her from you?'

"Yeah, basically. He made up some crazy stories about me."

"What stories?"

"I don't want to talk about it."

"Come on, you drove all the way here, you might as well tell me."

"All right. He told her that I had weird sex fetishes."

"Well, did you?"

"No, of course not. He was describing himself to her—that's the whole ironic part. Anyway, she totally lost interest in me after that. I couldn't convince her he was lying."

I tried to veer the conversation back to prom night.

"So was my dream accurate?"

Cindy's smile vanished. "Kind of. What are you, some kind of psychic?"

"You may say that. So, what happened?"

"It was a long time ago. I don't really want to go into it."

"Aw, come on, I shared the sex story with you."

"You're right. It was nothing. We all had too much to drink and ended up at Erik's house. I went to the prom with Jeff, but he disappeared at the party and I ended up hooking up with Jason."

I could see Cindy was trying to shake it off. But her defense mechanism was failing. She started to get angry at first.

"Ugh. I can't believe I did that. Jason. I fucking hated that guy. He was such an asshole. I didn't even want to do it. I kept telling him no, but he kept insisting. It was awful."

"So it wasn't consensual?" I asked.

"I don't know. I mean, I had a lot to drink. All I wanted to do was kiss a little. I mean, he was a jerk, but he was kind of cute. But then, he just …"

Cindy gasped in anger, then put her hand up to her forehead and started crying.

"I can't believe I'm reliving this again. How did you know? Who told you, Larry? Is this dream bullshit for real?"

The bartender interrupted us.

"Is everything okay here?"

Cindy recomposed herself. "Oh yes, one of our good friends recently passed away and we were just talking about him."

I nodded my head to the bartender. I then grabbed Cindy's hands. She continued.

"Not a day goes by that I don't think about that night. It ruined my life."

"Well, did you ever confront Jason?"

"Yeah, of course. He thought nothing of it. He told me I never said no."

"Did you call the cops? Or go to the hospital?"

"No. It would have been a he said/she said. Besides, I didn't want anyone knowing about it. But then Jason blabbed it all over the school, anyway. I'm sure you heard it from someone."

"No, honestly. I knew nothing about it. I kind of became a recluse after freshmen year."

"So you just had this random dream, huh?"

"Yeah."

"I still don't believe you."

I persisted. "Do you have any pictures from that night? Especially anything inside of Erik's house?"

"Why? Are you going to re-open the investigation? Jason is some big-time attorney now."

"What if I told you I might be able to change what happened?"

"Like travel back in time?'

"Yeah, something like that."

"I would say you're crazy or high or something. Are you high?"

"No. Not at the moment," I joked. "Just send me any pictures you might have. I might be able to prove what he did."

I could see from her expression that she thought I was totally crazy. But something inside of her conceded.

"Look, I don't know what you're up to, but if you can burn Jason while keeping my name out of it, then by all means, do it. I'll see what pictures I can find. I have them in a shoebox in my closet."

Her face looked as distraught as it was in my dream. She took out a bottle of Ativan and popped two pills. "This is how I deal with that night."

She finally calmed down after about twenty minutes.

"Well, I guess I should get going."

"Yeah, me, too. I have to get back to Buffalo."

"You're going to drive all the way back? You can crash at my place if you want."

"Well, I'll come by and get the pictures, but I don't think I can stay."

Much to my surprise, there was a dude in her apartment when we arrived. The guy was a total douche, too. There was a bong and an eight-ball of coke on the table. Cindy tried to introduce us.

"This is my boyfriend, Chris; this is Larry, he's an old high school friend and needs to crash here tonight."

I put my hand out to shake Chris's hand. He walked by me and barely acknowledged me. He and Cindy started to fight violently.

"What the fuck, Cindy? Now you're just bringing random guys home? What if I brought girls back here? You would flip out."

"I'm not the one who cheated, Chris."

"Oh no, what about that bartender?"

"He kissed me."

"But you led him on. You're a whore. I don't care what you do with this guy. But don't call me when you need more blow."

This went on for about twenty minutes. It was very awkward. I didn't know if I should intervene. I finally interjected.

"You know, I really just came for some old photos. I actually have to get back to Buffalo."

Chris put his arms in the air. "I don't give a fuck what you do, dude. I'm out of here."

Cindy was upset. "Don't leave because of him. If you need to stay, just stay."

"No, really, I have to go. But do you have the photos?"

"Oh, right, they are right in the closet."

Cindy pulled out an old shoe box. There were pictures of her and Jeff getting into the limo, pictures at the prom itself, and one picture of the party at Erik's house of a bunch of guys doing keg stands. Jason was in the background funneling a beer through a beer bong.

Cindy gave me a hug. "Thanks for coming to see me. Sorry about Chris. Hey, so what exactly are you going to do with the pictures?"

"I'll let you know." I said.

I was saddened on the four-hour drive home back to Buffalo. Cindy had so much potential, and her life looked awful.

The next day, I called Dina and explained the meeting with Cindy. I then scanned in the pictures and forwarded her the images so she could upload them into the chip in my head. I also wrote down the description of the night that Cindy gave me and memorized several key phrases to repeat to myself throughout the day.

Oddly, it didn't work this time. No dreams of Cindy that night. Instead, I had a repeat dream of the little girl who slipped into the rapids above Niagara Falls. This time, there was a bit more detail. The little girl and her mother were on one of the observation platforms on the American side of the falls. I recognized it because of the multiple trips I took to the site for our studio project. A man was also on the observation platform reading a newspaper.

The next morning, I bumped into Todd on the way to studio.

"Hey dude, hear this. Maryanne's husband was just arrested for illegal stock trading. And she may be tied to it. Dude, Maryanne is going to jail!"

This was a new scenario. I cursed Maryanne in a dream and wondered if that could have caused this arrest to come to fruition? Now I was really freaked out.

# 10

The semester was starting to wind down. Like the previous semester, I was completely stressed out again. Several weeks had passed, and I still couldn't get back into the dream about Cindy. Dina tried to enhance and reboot the images into my chip several times, but it didn't seem to work. She was also interested in my "damnation" of Maryanne dream, seeing she and her husband were being indicted for illegal trading, and the dream of the little girl falling into the Niagara River. Dina tried to isolate the date from the newspaper the man was reading but couldn't enhance the image. She was able to read the time off the mother's watch, though — eleven-forty-five a.m.

I was working about twenty hours a day trying to finish my final project. This project was difficult because we had to construct the site at a scale of one foot equals one inch, which meant the site model took up an entire classroom. From there, we had to build our model into the site along with drawings and a written dialog. Several of the other students didn't take the project seriously and started placing all kinds of props on the site model. There were bras, underwear, jock straps, and a penis enlargement pump that people anonymously placed. Margaret did not find this funny.

Our final presentation was being held in a pavilion right near the actual site in Niagara Falls. Seeing Margaret liked me, I was given a morning slot this time to present — eleven a.m. This presentation was a complete one eighty from my final presentation first semester. The criticism was constructive and, for the most part, positive. I finished up at about eleven-forty and went over to the buffet table to get some food. I was talking to a few of my classmates and gazing out the window of the pavilion and there they were — the mother and the little girl in the pink one-piece snowsuit on the observation platform.

I ran out of the pavilion. I was awake, but I felt like I was in a dream. I seemed to be moving in slow motion. It was May but was still winter in that part of region. Snow still coated the ground and large chunks of ice were floating in the river and accumulating at the base of the falls. The mother took out a camera to take a picture. The little girl let go of her hand and was running to edge of the platform. The old man was reading his newspaper but barely noticed me as I frantically ran by.

The mother screamed out the little girl's name. "Maggie. Get away from the edge."

I slipped on the ice and fell headfirst and was sliding toward Maggie. She slipped through the railing and into the icy river. I slammed into the railing and lunged my arm into the river. I was able to just grab the hood of the pink one-piece snow suit. Maggie was screaming. Her mother ran to the edge, saw I was slipping, and grabbed my legs. My bicep was starting to give due to the current of the river. Since the mother was holding my legs, I was able to get my other arm into the water. With all my strength, I hoisted Maggie out of the current back onto the platform.

By the time I regained my composure, there were several people gathered around. Many of my classmates also ran out of the pavilion to see what had happened. The old man reading the newspaper called an ambulance, and a brigade of sirens and news reporters were soon on the scene. Maggie's mother hugged and kissed me about one hundred times.

# 11

After my five minutes of fame was over, I had to figure out what to do for the summer. I was completely broke and accruing more student loan debt every day. I ended up going back to Carbone's to work as a pizza delivery driver. That summer, I had several dreams that presented me with personal gain opportunities. However, as we expected, it seemed I couldn't personally benefit from any of the dreams. Dina and I noted a negative reaction if I tried to benefit from a premonition. In 1991, I dreamt the Buffalo Bills defeated the New York Giants in Super Bowl XXV and took my entire paycheck to my bookie. As the game played out, Scott Norwood missed the forty-seven-yard field goal wide right in the fourth quarter and the Buffalo Bills lost. The same thing happened this past year when I dreamt of the outcome of the 1999 Stanley Cup finals between the Buffalo Sabres and the Dallas Stars. The game ended with a contentious goal by Dallas where Brett Hull's foot was in the crease. In my dream, the goal was called off, the game went into overtime, and the Sabres won the cup. I once again went down to a local bookie and put $1000 on the Sabres to win. When the game was played, the referees never reviewed Brett Hull's foot in the crease and the goal was counted. The Stars won the cup and I lost $1000 dollars.

As I pondered more, I remembered more negative ripple effects from me trying to benefit from a premonition dream. In chaos theory, this is known as the "butterfly effect" where "a small change in one state of a deterministic nonlinear system can result in large differences in a later state." In my case, the differences were indeed always negative. The first case I could remember was a dream I had in kindergarten where I saw the girl who kissed me in the coat room, Krista, place her bookbag that was sitting on the bus floor on her white band pants. The bag was covered in mud and her pants were ruined. Seeing we went to strict Catholic school, the nuns wouldn't let Krista participate in the music recital because her uniform was ruined. She was heartbroken. So, I devised a plan where I would come to her rescue with a new pair of white pants. The night before the recital, I stole a pair of pants from my sister who was about the same size as Krista. After she ruined her pants and was getting berated by the nuns, I came to her rescue with the new white pants. Krista gave me a kiss on the cheek, and I became her kindergarten boyfriend. Two days later, I was given an after-school detention for being in the bathroom when two of my classmates climbed out of the window. I never thought anything about that incident until now. Was I being punished for using the dream to get Krista to like me? Did altering the dreams have to truly be altruistic for nothing bad to happen? I continued to ponder.

In fifth grade, I played youth basketball. One night before a game, I had a dream that told me which shots I would make and which ones I would miss. The next day at the game, I pumped the ball up in every place that was a basket and passed it off in the miss spots. I ended up the high scorer in that game. A few days later, my neighbor broke my clavicle in a game of "kill the man with ball." I couldn't play basketball for the rest of the year. Coincidence? I thought not.

Around the same time, one of my classmates, Diane, started flirting with me. Because of immaturity, I was intentionally mean to her. One day when we were on a ski trip with the school's ski club, Diane tried to follow me on some of the runs. I intentionally went down a difficult trail and left her by herself. In school, our teacher used to periodically check the binders on our textbooks to see how worn they were. If they were in bad shape, we'd get a "bad" check mark on our report cards. I swear the teacher used to favor Diane and not wiggle her binder as much. I called out the teacher on it and rabble-roused the whole class into a rebellion. This resulted in one of my classmates damaging some of Diane's books so she would get a check mark.

Diane and I became friends again later in high school and I started to like her. But this time, it was she that broke my heart, citing the time I stranded her on the ski trail. A few nights later, I went back into the dream when we were skiing in the fifth grade. This time, I stayed with her and skied with her the entire night. We ended up kissing on the ski bus on the way home. When I woke up in the present time, I thought I had fixed things with Diane, but instead, I made things worse. In the past, I ended up being her boyfriend and taught her to be an expert skier. Diane became a prodigy and was an Olympic hopeful in slalom. She ended up breaking up with me for some stud on the racing circuit and I never heard from her again. Once again, I was punished. I went back into the dream a third time and didn't leave her by herself, but I also didn't become her boyfriend. She still ended up hating me later in high school.

In college, I utilized a dream I had where I saw the answers to an exam I was about to take. I aced the exam of course, but the next night, my mom fell off the step on the porch and broke her hip. I also noted that merely mentioning a premonition dream out loud would prevent it from happening. For example, I'd dream that certain people would not be in class the next day and to try and impress my classmates, I would announce it. "Yeah, I guarantee Mark doesn't show up today." But when I announced it, the opposite would happen. I started explaining this to Dina, but she wasn't at all surprised. However, neither she nor I had any scientific explanation for it. We weren't exactly sure if my dreaming ability was flawed, or if the "spirits" were just warning me not to try and personally benefit from the power. Over the years, I learned I couldn't benefit from the dreams no matter how I spun things.

Early in the summer, I had another dream of an armed man on the Buffalo Metro line. He pulled out a handgun and shot several of the people on the train, including me. I immediately called Dina to see if we could figure out when this was going to happen, but there were not any clues in the images. My plan was to just not ride the Metro ever again, but then I realized there were several other people either injured or killed on the train. I called the Metro authority and asked them about their security. They assured me they had measures in place, but from what I could see when I rode the metro, there was nothing—no metal detectors, no cameras, no armed guards in any of the cars. Since the Metro authority ignored my concerns, I ended up writing an editorial in the newspaper on how the Metro was an accident waiting to happen. I figured this might make passengers and workers more cautious. I decided to just let the natural course of action play out. After all, not all my dreams came true, and at that point in my life, I wasn't afraid of getting shot. One of my family members was a cop, so I did have her loan me a bullet-proof vest.

About a month went by, and my downstairs neighbor asked me to go to a concert with her at Lafayette Square. I offered to drive, but she insisted it was much easier to take the Metro. I figured this was it. There were about three more stops to go until we reached the square, and nothing had happened yet. My neighbor, Theresa, could see I was nervous about something. And then the guy I saw in the dream with the gun boarded the train. As in the dream, it was clear he was high on something, probably crack or cocaine. He pulled out the gun and started his rant. I reached up and pulled the emergency stop cord. The train came to a halt and the thug fell on the floor, dropping his gun. The doors opened and I yelled for everyone to get off the train. I then grabbed the little girl and the mother who was shot in the original dream and bolted for the door. The drugged man reached for his gun and shot me dead square in the vest. I fell right on top of the woman I saved. The thug ran off and was never caught. Strangely, there was no media coverage and no police response to the event. The conductor came out to make sure everyone was okay and then restarted the train. I was glad there was no coverage. After saving the little girl at Niagara Falls, I think people would have started to become suspicious of me, like I was planning these events to be a hero or something. Theresa and I went for a drink after that. She asked why I was wearing a bullet proof vest. I think she was suspicious. I decided to tell her about my dreams. Theresa was studying for her PhD in psychology and started to psychoanalyze me. She disbelieved that I could predict outcomes in my dreams; she thought I was delusional, and I just happened to get lucky. We started to argue, and I eventually told her she was way out of her league. She didn't appreciate that much.

A few weeks after the event, she knocked on my door and asked if I would help her with a project. She had to design a Meyers-Briggs type test and test it out on subjects. She told me to make up answers to the questions to test her methodology, so I did so. At the end of the quiz, she diagnosed me a manic depressive and suffering from delusions of grandeur. I laughed.

"Yes, that is exactly what I was going for with my answers."

"What do you mean?" Theresa responded.

"Well, I made those answers up, like you said to do."

"Well, that's something we just say so you'll actually answer honestly or so you won't manipulate the test."

"What? What the hell are you talking about? So you ask me to lie so I will tell the truth?"

61

"Precisely."

"Well, I didn't tell the truth. Let's do it again and I will answer truthfully as me this time."

"No. I have what I need. You know, Larry, there are some medications that might help. I also know several colleagues who specialize in this sort of thing."

"You want the truth. I think there is something seriously wrong with you, Theresa."

"Of course. Deflection is very typical of your condition."

"All right, let's reverse rolls. I'll ask you the questions. Oh, and make up the answers."

Theresa wasn't amused. "No. You are not qualified to conduct this test."

"This isn't a real test. This is an exercise."

"Okay, fine." Theresa agreed.

After she answered the questions, I used her chart to examine her outcome.

"It says here that you are schizophrenic."

"No it doesn't. Let me see that."

I handed her the chart. She looked surprised.

"Well, you were making up the answers, right? It's not really true?"

"Right," she said shakily. She slowly walked out of my apartment. "Thanks for helping me with this."

Oddly, Theresa stopped talking to me after this.

At the end of the summer, I noticed my wardrobe was in shambles and the one thousand bucks I lost on the Sabres game wasn't helping. I had been wearing the same clothes since undergraduate and was really starting to look shabby. I went into Walgreens and ended up buying five tourist t-shirts that had "Tonawanda, New York" logos on them and five pairs of sear-sucker shorts for twenty bucks. This would be my uniform at the start of the fall semester.

Our new studio professor for the semester was a really laid-back guy named Fred Knight. Fred didn't fit the typical profile of an architecture academic. Instead of all black suits typically donned by architecture professors, Fred wore jeans and flannel shirts. He was a Vietnam veteran who worked in construction and eventually went back to school later in life after a knee injury on the construction site. Even though Margaret liked me, her studio was still intense. I could see Fred's studio was going to be much more chill and down to earth.

That night, I ended up falling asleep on the couch and much to my surprise, I was back into the night of Cindy's prom. I walked with her a bit this time and talked to her. She ended up hugging me in the dream, but then the pain of the cluster headache returned, and I woke out of a dead sleep. Damn it.

I emailed Dina about how the dream was cut short and she told me she figured out a way to communicate with me while I was asleep. In essence, she could talk me through the scene so I could better control the dream. I was all for it.

That semester, our project was to design an environmental education center on a wooded site. It was part of a national competition among architecture schools, so the program was stringent. I decided the best environmental education would be to build nothing at all, but rather put a foot path with interpretation signage through the woods. When I presented the project, I was ridiculed by several of the guest "starchitect" critiques.

One of the critiques was from Harvard. He was dressed, no surprise, in a tight black turtleneck sweater and tight skinny black pants. He also donned a scarf and designer glasses.

"Well, that's really noble, Larry, but you didn't meet the program requirements. If you were in practice, the client would fire you."

"But this isn't practice, this is school. It's fake," I responded.

Another one of the internal critiques cut into me as well.

"Larry, I think you hate this program so much, that you'll do anything just to go against the grain. If we told you not to design a building, you probably would clear cut all the trees and do the opposite. Either that, or this is just a cop-out. You realized you can't design buildings, so you decided to just take the easy way out and build a path. Maybe you don't belong in this program?"

I started to lose my shit again. "Are you talking about me, or are you talking about the project? Because it sounds like you are talking about me."

"Whatever. You, the project. It doesn't matter. There is nothing to discuss because you didn't do any work."

I actually did do quite a bit of work. I had several drawings and did various studies of the topography, vegetation, and species on the site.

"Why don't you talk about the ecology of the site; how it's a Class 2 wetlands; how there are twenty-six species of birds residing there and thirteen different species of trees, many of them old growth."

Another critic responded. "Because that's not architecture. If you don't want to design buildings, then switch degrees and go into forestry or something. I mean really, we have nothing to talk about here. What do you want us to talk about?"

"I want you to talk about the project," I responded.

"There is no project to talk about."

The young cocky professor from Harvard was on his feet and in my face. He pointed his finger at me. "Maybe you need to take a step back and reconsider your career options."

I responded. "No. You need to take a step back. I don't think you understand anything else but designing some signature statement."

I then grabbed his shoulder. "And you better get that finger out my face, or I'll break it off!"

Just then, Fred intervened.

"Whoa, whoa guys, this has gotten way out of hand. Everyone needs to step away and take a deep breath. And I take responsibility for this. I encouraged Larry to find a way to minimally disrupt this forest. Granted, he still needs to meet the spatial program requirements, but I think his environmental analysis is a solid start."

The Harvard critic then turned away and started laughing. "I can clearly see there is no reasoning with you."

I walked to the back of the room and Sam was laughing. "Nice, Larry. Way to stand up to that Harvard prig."

"I'm all right, I'm all right," I said with a chuckle. It was all an act and most of my classmates knew it.

***

64

There were several more confrontations during that critique. Another student also almost came to blows with another professor and they had to call campus police to intervene. A few other students left in tears. It was a blood bath.

After the critique, several of us went out to the Blue Goose for drinks to drown our miseries. The stress of the program was starting to take its toll. Rachel was super drunk that night and couldn't drive home. Seeing I lived just around the corner from the bar, I let her crash on the couch. I think she wanted to hook up, but quite honestly, I was too drunk, tired, and miserable to do anything about it. Besides, she had a crush on some pretty boy from one of the other classes and didn't stop talking about him. I think I was a back-up.

I made us a couple of grilled-cheese sandwiches and she started to tell me how one of our communications professors was hitting on her. I told her to report it, but she said she really wasn't sure, maybe he was just being nice. Just then, Rachel's car alarm went off. It seems some street thugs broke into her car and stole her laptop off her seat. By the time the cops arrived and all the reports were filed, she was sober enough to drive home.

It was about two a.m. and I finally was able to fall asleep. The alcohol had triggered several episodes of cluster headaches throughout the night while we were out at the bar, but it seemed to be at bay for the moment. I had several vivid dreams that night. The first was similar to the end of the world dream I had a couple of years prior. This one, however, was more like the scenario in Saxxon's class—a large meteor hit the earth and the radiation from it would wipe out life. Then I saw the evacuation of 10,000 people into space shuttles headed for a large space colony orbiting earth. As the shuttles took off, there was a large explosion. I woke up screaming and in a cold sweat. I went to the bathroom and drank a glass of water and quickly fell back asleep. I then had a quick flash that Fred was in great pain, but suddenly, I was back into Cindy's prom night, and this time, it was before she left the party.

I was wandering around through Erik's house when I suddenly tripped and fell through the floor. I was just about to hit the basement floor, but I woke up in my parent's house all alone and a burglar was trying to get in. Just then, I heard Dina's voice.

"Larry, you're dreaming from a dream. You need to wake up and go back one level to Erik's house. Yes, you tripped, but you did not fall through the floor."

Dina's voice was soothing. She was right. I just tripped, but I was still in Erik's house. I managed to pull out of the second dream back into the first dream. As common in many dreams, the images of Erik's house that I was pulling from my memory were distorted. Rooms were out of scale and the lighting was either extremely dark or extremely bright. Familiar faces from high school were all over the house. I zoomed into some and faded out others; some of their voices were loud, some were faint. My mind started wandering, but Dina's voice once again was in the background.

"Larry, look around. Do you see Jason?"

I looked around the house and was able to focus on the faces a little better.

"No, he's not here."

"What about Cindy?"

"No, I don't see her, either."

"Okay, go up the stairs and check the bedrooms."

As I walked up the stairs, the steps turned into a broken escalator. As I pushed down on one of the treads, it would sink but I wasn't able to ascend. Dina's voice came through again.

"Straddle the steps and put your feet along the side. Use the railings to hoist yourself up."

Strangely, I was able to do it. It was like one of those rope ladder climb rides at an amusement park.

Upstairs, there was a lot of smoke. I also heard the sounds of people having sex. I gravitated toward one of the rooms and became mesmerized by the sounds of the woman.

Dina interrupted. "Larry, you're too focused on the woman moaning, you pervert. Look in the room. Is it Cindy?"

I opened the door. It wasn't Cindy. Shit. We were running out of time. The images were starting to fade, and I was leaving the dream and entering another dream where I was in a car with my father and my sister.

"Larry, stay in the house. Your notes say there is a finished basement. That's the only other place she could be. You are going to have to jump through the floor and go into the basement."

"Can I do that?"

"Sure, you can do anything. It's your dream."

Just then I remembered I can usually fly in my dreams. It's kind of like swimming, but in the air. I also often avoid getting mugged in dreams by flapping my arms and hovering in the sky.

I decided I could also jump through the floor. I jumped up off the edge of the stairs and broke through the floor into the basement. Oddly, I sustained no injuries nor did the subflooring cut me on the way through. I think I was starting to understand how to control the dreams.

I opened my eyes, and much to my surprise, I had no injuries.

I then proceeded down a dark hall. I heard heavy breathing, but it was all from a guy. And then, in the finished part of the basement, I saw Jason on top of Cindy. They still had their clothes on. She was clearly resisting but seemed too drunk to fight him off.

Just then, I woke up.

"Damn it," I yelled out.

I was only half awake and I could just make out Dina's voice.

"Larry, you are in control. You can go back to sleep and get back into the basement."

"Yeah, you're right. I can go back in."

I put my head back on the pillow and re-entered Erik's basement. This time, I felt much more at ease. The images were clearer and less distorted. I walked up to Jason, grabbed him by the hood of his sweatshirt, and threw him through the wall. Surprisingly, I had great strength in this dream. I picked up Cindy and covered her in my coat. I carried her outside and she was able to get on her feet.

"Are you okay?" I asked.

"Yes, I'm fine, thank you so much." She hugged and kissed me, and then the image faded.

# 12

I woke up after the dream with one of the most intense cluster headaches in my life. The pain level was a ten on the cluster headache pain scale—also known as the "kip" scale. At the time, I was getting about four to five episodes a day. Each episode only lasted about one to two hours, but it's one to two hours of intense pain. It feels like an ice-cream headache that won't go away. The entire cycle usually lasted four to six weeks. The pain drained me. However, this episode was different. I read about oxygen therapy as a remedy, but my doctor wanted to start with the more traditional prescriptions.

I stumbled out of the house and somehow managed to drive to the 24-hour pharmacy to pick up a prescription of Imitrex nasal spray and it seemed the doctor wrote down the wrong strength. The pharmacist wouldn't fill the prescription.

I started to freak out. "Just fill the damn prescription. It's a freaking typo. It only comes in one dose, for Christ's sake!"

The pharmacist responded in a condescending tone. "Sir, I'm going to have to contact the doctor on Monday."

"Do you know the amount of pain I'm in? You're not a doctor. You're nothing but a fucking chemist at best. You're really just a glorified cashier." I couldn't keep myself from shouting.

"Sir, I'm calling security."

"Go ahead and call them," I yelled back. "I'm leaving."

As I walked out, I knocked over the sunglasses display and threw a bunch of items off the shelf. It was a real scene, but that's how bad the pain was.

I peeled out of the pharmacy. I pulled over to the side of the road and dialed Dina's number, but before I knew it, everything went black.

I woke up the next day in Dina's lab. Luckily, she was able to triangulate my cell phone signal and get to me before the police and paramedics showed up. They would have most likely found the chip in my head, and seeing the technology was not FDA approved, Dina and I would have faced some repercussion.

"Welcome back, Larry," Dina said softly.

"What happened?"

"Well, there's good news and bad news. The good news is that you were able to alter history through your dream. You saved Cindy!"

"Yes, I remember throwing Jason through a wall."

"Indeed, you did. You were amazing. This is amazing. We altered history, Larry!"

"It worked? Where is she now?"

Dina pulled up the timeline grid on one of the monitors. It was a really interesting graphic. There were two lines with infinite branches and sub-branches. The software highlighted the differences between the two timelines, similar to a "count if" or "Vlookup" function in Microsoft Excel.

"Yes, it worked. Look what I found." Dina found it hard to contain her excitement.

Dina zoomed into a current node on the timeline that read: *Cindy Swain: District Judge.*

"She's a judge, Larry. She made a name for herself as a prosecution attorney—mostly going after sexual predators and sexual assault assailants. She worked her way up to judge."

"Holy shit! Do you think she remembers me coming in the room?"

"I'm not sure. Maybe you should call her?"

"I will. So, what's the bad news?"

"Well, it seems this amount of energy—the energy it took to go back into a dream and alter history caused intense pressure in your brain and sparked a seizure. I think I made it to you just in time."

"Does this mean I can't jump back into dreams? Because I have a lot of things I want to fix. I mean, I could go back in time and beat up the bullies that beat me up in sixth grade. I could ask out girls that I was too afraid to ask out. I could prevent my cat from getting sick!"

Dina was shaking her head. "Well, besides killing you, I don't think this power works that way. You said it yourself that none of the good things you dream about ever come true, just the bad things. Remember your bets on the Bills and Sabres? And didn't you also say your dead grandmother gave you the lotto numbers once?"

"Oh, yeah, she did. She said they were "Aunt Jeanie's numbers.""

"And did you ever play those numbers?"

69

"Yes. Every combination. Her birthday, her social security number, her house address, her phone number, you name it."

"And did you ever win?"

"No."

"Precisely. Like I said, I don't think you were given this power for personal benefit."

"Well, I'm still going to try, damn it."

"And risk killing yourself?"

"Why not. My life stinks anyway."

"You just saved a friend from getting date raped on her prom; you also saved that little girl from falling into Niagara Falls. You're a hero, Larry."

"Yeah, I guess. That reminds me, I want to call Cindy to make sure that event was really erased."

"Good idea. We also need to examine the timeline further to see if there were any other ripple effects. And, we need to go over some of the other dreams you had. But call Cindy first."

Cindy's number was disconnected, which was a good sign. This number was from her "previous" timeline. We looked her information up at the courthouse and found an email address. I quickly composed something generic and sent it to her:

*Hi Cindy! This is Larry Martin from high school. I recently read an article about a case in your area and I saw your name. I am really proud of you that you became a district judge and at a young age! How are things?*

I left my email open to see if she would respond. In the meantime, Dina checked the timeline.

"So here's what else changed. Since Cindy never gets raped, she never goes into a downward spiral. In the original timeline, her depression drove a wedge in her family. Her parents divorced and her mom became an alcoholic, eventually getting cirrhosis. In the new timeline, none of this happened and her parents stay together and are still living in Florida."

"So that's good, right?"

"Yes. But there's more. It looks like Jason stormed out of the party and gets pulled over for DWI. Hmmm."

"What?" I asked in a concerned tone.

70

"Well, this alters his life quite a bit for the worse. Instead of going to law school and becoming a partner in his father's firm, he ends up working as a mechanic."

"Well what's wrong with that? Mechanics make good money and hell, maybe he's happier?"

"I guess. But I'm not sure about this, Larry. I don't know if we should be messing with things. Every change has consequence. In this scenario, it doesn't seem too bad, but I can imagine much worse." Dina said in a concerning manner.

"Well, if we screw things up really bad, can't we just go back in and reset them?"

"I'm not sure it's that easy, but we'll just have to see, I guess. Let's look at some other dreams."

Dina brought up the dream I had of Fred. The flashes in my dream were vague, but I saw him in a great deal of pain. Dina spliced the images together and refocused them. We were able to see that Fred was in a hospital bed. A doctor was in the edge of the frame and we could just make out the name tag: "Carlson."

Dina did a search on doctors named Carlson in the area and our worst-case scenario came true. Joel Carlson was an oncologist at Roswell Park Cancer Institute. Fred was going to get diagnosed with stage IV colon cancer.

I was horrified. "Do we know when this is? Are there any clues?"

"None yet. Does he seem sick?'

"No, he seems fine right now in class."

"This has to be sometime in the future, then."

"Yes, I agree, and I think it is the near future. He does not look much older than he is now. I have to go warn him."

"Wait, Larry, what are you going to say?"

I put my coat on and ran out of the lab. "I don't know, I'll think of something."

"Wait, Larry, you're not well enough to leave yet. And we still need to go over this space colony dream."

I yelled back. "I'll come back tomorrow."

"Well, be cautious, and please, don't alter past dreams until I figure out what almost killed you."

"Yeah, yeah, I won't."

# 13

Dina was right. I was not well enough to leave, nonetheless drive. Besides, the car was in really bad shape after I crashed it. Surprisingly, it started up. It was about ten p.m. I'm not sure why I was rushing back to studio since Fred wouldn't be there right now anyway. But then again, he was the type of guy who used to check on students late at night in studio. Unlike other professors, he'd tell us to go home and that we were working too hard. Fred was a nice guy. Nobody deserves cancer, but especially not Fred.

I quickly swept the halls. It was a Sunday night and it was quiet. The only people around were two students from India and a guy surfing internet porn in the computer lab. After the trip to Albany and the blackout, I was behind in my work.

I was going to check my email in the computer lab, but the guy surfing internet porn was creeping me out. I went back to my apartment. My downstairs neighbor, the uptight psychology major, heard me in the vestibule.

"Oh my God. You scared me! With that black hat, and that black coat, you are scary looking. Scary, Larry."

She then slammed the door. That was the end of that exchange.

I opened my laptop and much to my surprise, Cindy wrote me back:

*Larry, so good to hear from you! It's been a long time. Yes! I became a judge about a year ago. I really like Albany. It is in the middle of New York City and the Adirondack Mountains. How are you? Are you back in school? Do you talk to anyone from high school?*

Based on her response, it occurred to me that Cindy had no recollection of our meeting at Aiko's a few nights prior. But it was still unclear if my prom night interference was successful. I didn't beat around the bush.

*Yes, it has been a long time. I think the last time I saw you was at Erik's party the night of prom. Yes, I'm back in grad school for architecture. I hate it! No, I don't talk to anyone from high school. I sometimes see Jeff in the cafeteria. He is a medical student and is in the building next to mine. Are you married? Any kids?*

I made a grill cheese sandwich. Before it was done, Cindy responded.

*You were at Erik's party? I don't remember seeing you, but then again, I was pretty plowed! Yes, I'm married. But no kids yet. How about you?*

I realized Cindy may have had no memory of seeing me.

*Married? Wow! No wife or kids for me yet. Hey, you didn't end up marrying Jason, did you?*

Cindy responded.

*Jason? Eww, no! I hate that guy. Do you know he tried to have sex with me that night when I was passed out? Luckily, something woke me up. I kicked him in the balls, and he fell backwards right through the dry wall! Actually, it was because of that night I decided to become a prosecution attorney and put date rapists like Jason away. You don't still talk to him, do you?*

I was somewhat disappointed she didn't remember me saving her, but like Dina said, I wasn't given this power for fortune or glory. Cindy and I traded emails for a couple of hours. We agreed to meet sometime if either of us were ever in each other's vicinity.

Feeling a bit let down, I decided to ignore Dina's advice and test out the "personal gain" theory again. Jason ruined things for me with Michelle in high school. I was going to see if I could change that. I honestly wasn't afraid of dying. I hated school, I had no love in my life, and I was otherwise miserable. It was worth the risk. I busted out my old photos and yearbook and compiled everything I had on Michelle. Without Dina's help of uploading the images into my chip, I had to enter these scenes manually. I reminisced about one of the dates I had with Michelle before Jason made up the sex lies about me. I recited the stories to myself and examined the images carefully before I went to sleep. But it didn't seem to work. The only dream I had that night was of Fred, and it was at his funeral.

I tried to reach Dina in the morning, but there was no answer. That day in studio, Fred was going around the room doing individual desk critiques to see how we were progressing on the project. I figured this might be a good time for me to warn him, but I had no idea how to broach the subject.

"Mr. Larry. How's it going? Are you still sticking with the save the trees theme?"

"Yes, I sure am, but I think I found a compromise."

"Good! Good man," Fred responded happily. "So, what's your plan?"

"Well, I'm going to build the spaces around the trees, kind of like the Ewok Village in *The Return of the Jedi*."

"Ahh, you're a *Star Wars* guy, huh?"

"Yes. I'm a big fan."

Sam yelled out from across the room. Yeah, he's a total *Star Wars* nerd."

Fred looked over my drawings.

"Why is everything designed so square? The forest isn't a perfect orthogonal grid, so why should your design be? That is unless you have a reason."

"No, that's a good point. It should be more organic."

"Yes, definitely more organic. Let it flow with the trees. Use the force, Larry."

"Well, I have the visions, but I just can't get them out on the paper."

"That's the challenge that makes it interesting. But don't let your graphic skills limit you. It's better to fail at the impossible than to succeed at the easy."

Fred was always good for one-liners.

"So, how's everything else going? You kind of look like shit, Larry."

"Yeah, I've had a rough couple of days."

Right then, I thought I had an opportunity to inquire about Fred's health. Using my dry sense of humor, I just blurted out, "Yeah, I haven't been feeling, well, with my luck, it's probably cancer or something."

Fred chuckled at my wry joke. "Well, make sure you take care of your health. These projects aren't worth it. Life is too short."

Fred moved onto to the next student. I couldn't ascertain if he knew he had cancer. But I thought at the very least that my mere mention of it might get him thinking about it. Maybe he'd go get screened and catch it in time. I'd have to try again when the situation was more apt.

Later that night, as usual, I fell asleep on the couch watching re-runs of old eighties sitcoms on *Nick-at Night*. I dreamt of my birthday when I played congas with the Walking Carpets at Moe's. At first, I was excited to be back in this dream. After all, it was a fun night. Then I suddenly remembered that was the night I passed out on the church lawn and had the bloody nightmare about Ng and Raja. Raja's house—the place that was burned and where her body was found—was a couple of blocks from Moe's. I was torn. Part of me was listening to Dina's warning of not altering past dreams. So, should I just stay and enjoy the feeling of playing with the Walking Carpets? But part of me wanted to walk up the block and see if I could save Raja.

Although Dina had not yet figured out what exactly was causing me to flat-line when I altered the past, I thought I could control the amount of time I was in the dream enough to prevent any adverse consequences. I remembered my head started hurting about midway through the dream where I saved Cindy. So as soon as I felt any pain, I was going to wake myself up.

I walked up Lisbon Avenue past the rows of student-ghetto Buffalo-double style houses. There was a gang of thugs approaching me. One of the thugs picked up a crowbar. His buddy yelled out, "Yeah, throw that shit at him."

I turned around and the crowbar was coming directly for my head. I somehow managed to dodge out of the way at the last second. The gang then charged me. I started running, but my feet didn't seem to be moving. The gang was just about to tackle me, and I remembered that I could fly in my dreams. I flapped my arms just like I did when swimming the breaststroke in water and suddenly I was about twenty feet in the air above the gang. I then could see the roof of Raja's house. She lived on the second floor, so I landed on the balcony. I walked into the apartment. It was pitch black. And then suddenly, Ng Seiko was behind me and hit me over the head with a crowbar. Again, with a crowbar? I thought as I fell to the ground.

Ng left me on the ground unconscious, but I could see him go into a room in the back and I could just make out Raja. Ng had her duct-taped to the bed. I heard screaming and struggling, but I couldn't move. I was paralyzed. It was a nightmare, for sure.

Then I heard Dina's voice.

"Larry, I thought I told you not to alter past dreams."

I really couldn't respond, as the pain from the crowbar still seemed to have me in a daze.

"Well, I'm not going to preach to you, Larry. You need to get up. It's your dream. You can control it. You're not really hurt."

As a kid, I was a huge pro-wrestling fan. Hulk Hogan's signature move was to "Hulk-up" after he had been beaten, overcome the pain, and go on to kick his opponent's ass. Suddenly, I could hear Hulk's theme music playing. I pushed myself up off the ground and started shaking off the pain. Dina was cheering me on. I charged back to the room. Ng came at me with the crowbar again. He swung it, but I put my arm up and blocked it. I felt no pain as the bar hit my arm. I then kicked Ng in the face, and he fell to the ground. I grabbed his arm and took his knife away from him. Ng reached for his lighter and lit the bed, which was soaked with gasoline. I was trying to cut the duct tape, but the knife wouldn't cut it.

Dina then chimed in. "Use the scissors in the drawer."

I needed that assist. The scissors worked. I grabbed Raja and ran toward the porch. Ng grabbed my ankle and we fell to the ground. I was stuck again and was starting to wake up.

Dina once again chimed in.

"Larry, start your swimming motion and fly off the porch."

I started moving my arms and suddenly built up some momentum. Ng lost his grip, and Raja and I flew out of the window. The house went up in flames.

Just then, my head started pounding and I remembered I had to wake up. I told myself to wake up, but I couldn't. Instead, I ended up back at Moe's playing congas. I eventually left the bar and once again passed out on the church lawn.

I then let out a scream and woke up on the couch in my apartment. My head hurt, but I was alive. I didn't flat-line this time.

Both my landline answering machine and my cell phone had several messages from Dina. I called her back.

"Are you okay?" Dina asked nervously.

"I think so. My head hurts, but I woke up in time, I think. Am I really awake?"

"Yes. You're awake. Phew! It seems as if you just pulled out in a nick of time."

"So that's the trick then, I just have to wake up when my head starts to hurt."

"We don't know that yet, Larry. You didn't wake up. You went backwards in the dream."

"So, did it work? Did I save Raja? Is she alive?"

"Unfortunately, no. I just checked the timeline, and she still ends up deceased."

"What?! I don't get it."

"Well, your brain made a choice. In going backwards in the dream back to the point where you were playing congas, the alternative reality of saving Raja never happened."

"Son of a bitch!"

"Yes, but Larry, that may have saved your life. Until we figure this out more, you have to promise me not to try and alter any dreams."

"Well, I'll try, but sometimes, that is just where the dream goes."

"I know. It gravitates towards your fears and desires, but you need to control the outcomes. If you get an urge to alter something, just observe it from afar. I'll also be watching and will divert your thought process."

"You're becoming a dream Nazi, Dina."

"I know, but it is so you don't die, dummy."

# 14

The fall semester had come to an end. Since our final project was a national competition, we had a slightly different critique format. All the students pinned their work up in one of the large lecture halls, and a panel of judges from the competition went around the room critiquing and scoring the projects. We then broke off into smaller rooms where we had to present the projects. My Ewok village design did not go over that well. The critics cited a disconnection between my concept and what was displayed in my drawings. Surprisingly, Fred didn't have much to say. I could see he was not feeling well.

"I still like the concept, Larry, but I think there were better ways to do it."

I was kind of bummed Fred didn't help me out, but he was right. In the hall, a Canadian student named Otis saw me hanging my head.

"Hey Larry. How did it go?"

"Ahh, my design work sucks, Otis."

In his thick Canadian accent Otis responded, "There's nothing you can do aboot it! Just push through—getting out is the goal."

"I guess. How is your thesis going?" I inquired.

"It's like a joogling oct. I can't even breathe this semester. I would go as far to say that this program is unethical."

"It is unethical. I actually think I'm going to quit."

"Really?"

"Yeah. I'm going to talk to the chair tomorrow."

"Ah. Let me know what he says."

Ted Simmonds was the chair of the program. He was a Stanford graduate and hated that he was working at a second-tier state university. One of the first things he did as chair was remove the ability for students to get course credit for constructing homes through Habitat for Humanity. This sucked because I had participated in the program the previous summer. The last time I met with him was an argument over the volunteering credits. I remember him saying, "There's nothing educational about swinging a hammer." Ironically, I learned more about construction technology building those houses than in any of my academic courses.

"Mr. Martin, come on in."

Ted had removed all the furniture in the office and replaced it with sawhorses and doors.

"Have a seat. What brings you in today?"

"Well, I'm realizing this program is not for me. I'm a lousy designer, I'm running out of money, and my mental and physical health are in jeopardy."

"Who have you had for studio so far?"

"Donna, Margaret, and Fred."

"How did those studios go?"

"Well, Donna's was a nightmare, Margaret's was fairer but extremely difficult, and I actually liked Fred a lot, but my work is just plain lousy."

"Well, you'll be able to choose your upper level studios, so you can hone your interests more. What are your interests?"

"That's the thing, Ted. I have no interest in becoming an architect. As a matter of fact, I tried to not design anything last semester. I tried to save the trees instead."

"Well that's fine. You don't have to become a practicing architect. You can go into landscape design, or planning, or set design. You could write screen plays or work in animation, be a graphic designer or a videographer. The architecture degree is so much more than building design. And besides, it's going to be a doctorate soon, so you will be able to teach across disciplines."

"A doctorate? Really?"

"Yes. Plans are underway to convert all graduate programs to professional doctorates. It should happen in a year or so. Yours would be granted retroactively."

"Interesting, but I don't think I can stomach another two years of this. What if I just converted my graduate credits to undergraduate credits and came out with a second bachelor's degree?"

"That's the most ridiculous thing I've ever heard. That can't be done, and why would you want another bachelor's degree? I'm telling you, the degree will be converted to a doctorate and you're so close."

"So, you're saying I can't quit?"

"Well, I can't stop you from quitting, but I will not convert your credits. If you quit, it is a loss of two years of work and money. I'm suggesting you might as well stay."

Ted was right. I really didn't have a choice at that point. And with the prospect of a doctorate, I was a little more enthused to stay. After all, four years for a master's degree was far too long.

Later that night, I went out to the Blue Goose with some classmates. I explained how Ted wouldn't let me quit and they found it amusing. I also told them about the doctorate. Todd seemed to know about it already.

As I stumbled home to my miserable apartment, I bumped into one of my roommates from the dorms from undergraduate at an ATM machine. He was pulling out five-hundred dollars and it was four in the morning.

"Hey Pauly."

"Hey, what's up Larry?"

"Not much. What the hell are you pulling out that much at four a.m. for? I'm guessing it's drugs, gambling, or prostitution?"

Paul giggled. "Dude, there's a brothel on Northrup Place."

"Yeah I know, those are my neighbors."

"Do you ever go over there?"

"Well, I cut their lawn sometimes because they don't have a mower, but no, I've never been inside the house."

"Dude, you've got to go. They'll do anything. Some of the girls are really freaky."

As tempting as it was, my contamination OCD wouldn't allow me to do it. Besides, I was too drunk, depressed, and tired to get it up anyway.

"No. That's not my thing. But be careful. Make sure you wear a rubber."

"All right dude, your loss."

I made myself a grilled cheese and looked out the window and watched Paul go into the brothel. It didn't surprise me he was still into prostitution. When I lived with him in the dorms, I frequently came home to a prostitute in the room either in the act with Paul or waiting to get paid. Paul also used to work on one of the Indian reservations and used to bring back ditch weed and sell it out of the room. And in addition to the prostitution and the drug dealing, Paul also was big into gambling.

One time, two no-necks dressed in zoot suits showed up at the dorm looking to get their cut that Paul owed them, which I believe was the second of four Super Bowl losses by the Buffalo Bills. Paul bet his entire second semester student loan money on the game and lost.

I dozed off on the couch and soon fell into a dream. The dreams seemed to bounce all around, probably from the alcohol. I briefly saw images of Fred fading in and out, Raja, Pauly in the brothel, finally settling on the meteor dream from Saxxon's class. This time, I was able to see more of what was happening. I saw a clear image of a large group of people at a resort being evacuated to a colony in outer space. I had a decent look at many of the faces of the people, but my mind wandered into a dream about Michelle. It was about time, I thought. After all, I had been trying to get back into a dream with her ever since I saved Cindy. I remembered Dina's warning, but after the amount of drinks I had, I said to hell with it, I'm going in!

We were back in high school in my mom's Buick Regal at a drive-in movie outside of Rochester, New York. I decided to lay it all on the line.

"So, did you know that Jason has a thing for you?"

"Yeah, I kind of knew."

"Well, he doesn't really like you. He's just trying to get in your pants. And he's jealous that we've been going out, so he's been talking trash about me."

"I believe it. He's a total asshole. He treats women like shit."

"Oh good. I thought you were into him, and that would have sucked because I really like you."

"I know, Larry. I really like you too."

Michelle and I started kissing and then suddenly, I heard a young lady scream outside the window.

"Get the hell out of here. You are a sick guy! What the fuck is wrong with you?"

Then I saw Paul running out of the house with his pants down. Waking up to this may have inadvertently saved my life. I was starting to alter the past again in that dream and seeing I was kissing Michelle, I wasn't about to stop.

Just then, my phone rang. It was Dina.

"I can't believe you would throw everything away for some chick back in high school. What is wrong with you?"

"It wasn't my fault. I was drunk. But did it work?"

"Did what work? You patching up a doomed romance? Oh Jesus. No, it didn't work. Your magic kiss didn't do anything. Michelle still ends up breaking your heart. So, like we postulated, you can't personally benefit from altering your dreams."

"Damn."

"That's right. And you know what else? Instead of Jason date-raping Cindy, in your new timeline, he date-rapes Michelle."

"Oh no! I have to go back in."

"What? Are you crazy? No. Absolutely not! I might not be able to save you this time."

"It will be quick. I just won't tell Michelle anything in the dream."

"No. Wait until tomorrow and you can sleep here under a controlled environment. This way, I can wake you up when your pain level hits a certain point. I was able to isolate the exact moment when you lost consciousness."

"No. It has to be right now while it's still fresh. I may not get back in for another month, or six months … or ever! I can't live with this. I made this mess and I have to clean it up."

I hung the phone up and went to the cabinet and downed two Benadryl to get back to sleep. I could still hear Dina screaming, but suddenly, I was back into the dream. This time, I didn't tell Michelle about Jason. I never told her how I felt, and we never kissed —just like it happened the first time.

I woke up on the floor of my living room apartment the next day. There was a large needle sticking out of my chest and Dina was sitting on my couch.

"You're lucky I got here in time. I told you to wait."

"What the hell is this needle?"

"It's epinephrine. I used it to revive you. I had to look up in my books on how to do it. You're lucky it worked."

"Did I fix things with Michelle?"

Dina opened the timeline on her laptop. There was an image of Michelle's wedding and she was married to Jason.

I was livid. "How did that happen? How did she end up with him?"

"I don't know," Dina said somberly. We talked about this. There are always multiple ripple effects—even from the tiniest change. You must have done something to alter the space-time continuum. Either that, or you're being punished for trying to use this power to help yourself."

"Really? Have we really proved that yet?"

"I'm not religious, but at this point, anything is possible," Dina said rather casually.

"You mean you're finally accepting the fact you can't and shouldn't try to benefit from altering a dream?" Dina yelled.

"Well, I thought maybe that only applied to seeing things in the future, but I guess I can't benefit from altering the past, either."

"Duh. That might have been good to know before you tried to fix things with Michelle," Dina responded in an agitated fashion.

"I know. But I wonder why? How is this power able to differentiate what is truly altruistic versus what may be personal gain?"

"I have no idea. Karma? Spirits? The gods? Who knows? But we need to get back to work. And forget about Michelle. She seems like a bitch, anyway. We need to focus on the evacuation dream. We have some great images."

I was still bummed out about the Michelle situation and a little shocked from having a needle sticking out of my chest.

"Well, can you first pull this thing out of me?"

"Oh yeah, that."

Dina pulled the needle out and brought up the images of the evacuation dream. She put the images on a slide show.

"Larry, what is the one thing consistent about all these pictures?"

I perused through them but was still kind of dazed. Then it hit me.

"Holy shit!"

Dina responded, "I know, right? We have to go see Saxxon."

# 15

Coincidentally, Saxxon was my studio professor for spring semester of the second year of the four-year graduate program. Scott also still taught his undergraduate course about the end of the world and hired me as a teaching assistant. Every Thursday, Scott, Dina, and I would sit down and go over more of my dreams related to the end of the world and the evacuation. Scott had been conducting this research for NASA's Center for Near Earth Objects program since the 1970s. As an environmental psychologist, his research centered on sustaining the human race in response to a meteor collision that would destroy all life on earth. His primary objective was to program the space for a colony that would house 10,000 people. These citizens would eventually repopulate the earth when the radiation levels from the meteor had subsided to safe levels. In addition to space programming, Scott was also charged with the selection and evacuation of the inhabitants. Scott framed the course as an academic exercise, but in reality, he was gathering data from students on how to design and populate the colony, and after twenty-five years, he had quite a bit of data to work with. He often changed the location of the colony. For example, other data showed that a hundred feet of water could potentially shield humans from the radiation; so some semesters, the notion of an under-water colony was added as an option. One semester, he added a subterranean option as well.

Scott told us about all the different scenarios his students came up with over the years. Some were really creative, some were inconceivable, and some were just plain scary.

"Larry's dreams are consistent with some of the more disturbing scenarios," Scott said with a calm smile.

Dina chimed in. "Well, this isn't what you recommended to NASA, is it Scott?"

"Hell no! I may be from the south, but I'm a progressive. This *superior race* colony is something a villain out of a James Bond movie would conceive."

I was a big Bond fan. "Right, it was in *Moonraker*."

"That's right," Scott replied. "According to your dreams, someone is planning an all-white colony made up of physical marvels."

Scott's recommendation to the government used a more democratic solution. He took all the responses of his students and tallied them. This was essentially a "blind" study. Since the students didn't think it was real, their solutions were candid. Although there were some extreme proposals—such as the single-race, gender, or religion colony—most of the students tried to maintain the diversity on Earth. Some students went as far as to enact a lottery to ensure a random sample of the population.

However, in my dreams, it seemed that those in charge went against Scott's diversity recommendation and decided to create some kind of ultra-beautiful, non-flawed, white-supremacist colony. The biggest question was when this would happen. NASA's Near-Earth Objects Observations website did not seem to show any major meteor collisions in the immediate future. Saxxon still had a few contacts at NASA that he was going to consult and he suspected the government hid some of the information.

Over the course of semester, Dina, Scott, and I worked on getting more details from my dreams. Dina worked tirelessly on giving me scripts to recite and uploading images into my chip to get me back into the dream. Between the dream research and my school workload, I was starting to have a difficult time understanding the difference between fiction and reality and this wreaks havoc on OCD. I was using so much digital drafting and 3D animation software, I ended up writing a song about it:

*paper space and model space*
*it's alright with me*
*your life has finally bottomed out*
*it's your destiny*

*pull down tabs and key commands*
*the screen will melt your face*
*real life won't let you undo*
*copy trim or paste*

*a line from earth to outer space*

*a travel back in time*
*can't distinguish what is real*
*finally lost my mind*

*3d trees and figure skates*
*your spline is quite askew*
*cut a portal through the page*
*freeze and thaw your view*

*two dimensions is for the birds*
*these trees will knock your socks*
*mirror a vast array of words*
*you can always insert blocks*

*extrude your world from x to z*
*design won't get you fame*
*set your limits so you can see*
*this grid will kill your brain*

*slice a union to its shell*
*carve a bar of soap*
*overrated show and tell*
*smoke and mirrors will help you cope*

*meshed my thoughts right on the page*
*don't tell me you forgot*
*a reference to another world*
*just wait until you plot.......*

*wait for you .... I'll wait for you to plot .... wait for you .... I'll wait for you*
*to plot*

I continued the dream research over the summer. I also landed a job teaching AutoCAD at the community college. Dina and Scott felt I was burned out, so they decided to stop feeding me information about the end of the world dream. For the rest of the summer, most of my dreams were about relationships and romance. For example, I dreamt Sam and Donna hooked up again. I dreamt about an upperclassman named Jenna that contracted several STDs, a Vietnamese student who was desperate to get married, and me kissing a woman on a navy ship. I also re-visited the orgy dream and saw all the grades that everyone was going to get in the new fall studio. None of these were tantalizing and most of them were just vague images. I also saw an image of Saxxon and Dina kissing, but that was obviously an odd ball. Saxxon was pretty straight edge and happily married. I decided to let that one go. Dina would probably see it on the monitor, anyway, so I really couldn't hide it.

That summer, I also noticed I was developing the ability to jump into a dream via falling asleep in front of the television or listening to the radio. I used to watch re-runs of the *Fugitive* late at night on the couch. One night, I was trying to help Richard Kimball escape from the U.S. Marshalls. On another occasion, I woke up to my clock radio and there was a story about the Iditarod Trail Sled Dog Race on NPR. They were interviewing one of the racers and suddenly, I was in the sled with the cold wind blowing on my face. Both of these were interesting scenarios. I wondered what would happen if I changed the outcome of the television show in the dream. Would the show take a different course? Would that affect any of the actors in the "real" world? For the news story, I wondered if I could alter the outcome as well. What if my sled crashed into the sled that was supposed to win the race, thus changing the results? This was something that Dina needed to research more. Quite frankly, the power of that scared me somewhat. I'd never do something nefarious, but what if someone else with bad intentions had the same ability as me? Luckily, I still couldn't control the dreams I entered without the data uploaded into the OC17 chip and even that wasn't quite one hundred percent yet.

Before the start of the fall semester, we had quite a bit of detail on my end of the world dream. In several of my original end of the world dreams, I saw the sun imploding and the earth spinning out of its orbit into space. But a closer look at the images confirmed that there were multiple meteors hitting Earth. Some were solid and some were large fire balls. Large sections of land were detached from the earth and the force was so great, the land masses blasted through Earth's gravitational field and drifted into space. We also were able to home in on the bunker of beautiful people exiting Earth to a space colony via shuttles. There were no images of the space colony itself and Saxxon was having a fit. After all, he submitted designs of the colony and was curious if those in charge of the exodus used any of his ideas.

That fall, I took a studio in urban design. It was a little more practical than some of the previous studios that were more theory-based. We spent a lot of time in the city of Buffalo designing urban renewal strategies. Early in the studio, I had a dream that Rachel's brother was paralyzed from the neck down. Before our first critique, I was shocked when I overheard Rachel telling some of the other students that her brother was going skydiving.

"Wait, did I just hear your brother is going skydiving?"

"Yes, and I'm so nervous about it," Rachel responded shakily.

"Do you know when he is going?"

"This weekend."

"Rachel, you have to tell him not to go."

"I know. I tried. He won't listen. He is bent on doing it."

I didn't know how to tell Rachel that I saw her brother paralyzed in a dream and there is a good chance it would come true. Besides, Dina calculated that my "future" dreams were only about seventy-five percent accurate. However, the twenty-five percent that didn't come true were mostly personal desires. The horrifying dreams I saw were more around the ninety percent range. I had to convince Rachel somehow. I called Dina and had her email me the images from the dream. Luckily, on Friday, our studio went out to the bar for drinks. Rachel was drunk and needed a place to crash, so I offered my couch. Living in the heights had its benefits, I guess.

"Rachel, I have to show you something, but try not to freak out."

"Oh boy, what are you up to, Larry?"

"Well, for the past couple of years, I've been dreaming things that eventually come true."

"What? Come on. Like what?"

"Well, like when Donna crossed her legs and showed the class she wasn't wearing any underwear, or Maryanne getting arrested, or when Phil attacked Margaret in class. I saw all of those before they happened."

"Okay," Rachel said and giggled. "But it's probably just coincidence. Nobody can predict the future."

Clearly, Rachel thought I was joking. She kept laughing about Donna.

"No, I'm serious. I also saw Ng kill Raja."

"Now you're freaking me out. Come on, stop, Larry."

"Rachel, I saw your brother in a wheelchair. Look, I have the images."

"Larry! How could you say that! Stop. Is this a joke? Did you Photoshop that image?"

"No. It's hard to explain, but I'm able to record my dreams."

Rachel started inconsolably crying.

"Larry, I always thought you were one of the nicer people in the program, but I was wrong. This is just plain cruel. Why are you trying to freak me out?"

"I know it's scary, but you have to believe me. You have to stop your brother from going skydiving."

"I'm leaving. You're mean. And you're a freak."

"At least take the images and show them to your brother."

Rachel grabbed the images and crumpled them up and threw them back at me. She ran out of the door. I chased after her, but she just screamed and told me to get away from her. One of the frat boys came out and grabbed me.

"Hey man, leave the girl alone, bro. Don't you know no means no?"

Rachel ran back up Main Street and peeled out in her car.

The next morning, I emailed Rachel the images and wrote a long letter trying to plea my case, but she didn't respond. I then called the skydiving outfit and told them to cancel the jump. They hung the phone up and threatened to call the cops. My last chance was to go in person and knock Rachel's brother out before he got on that plane. I jumped in the car and sped to the skydiving site. They were just boarding the plane. I ran out on the runway and waved my arms.

"Stop! Don't get on that plane!"

Then I saw a security truck speed towards me. They fired a large net over me, and I fell to the ground. A large man was then standing over me and knocked me out with a night stick.

I woke up in the back of a police cruiser. The cop was breaking my balls.

"Don't you know you can't run out on a runway like that? What the hell were you thinking?"

Just then, a call came over his radio. There was an accident back at the skydiving site.

I didn't see Rachel for a couple of weeks after the accident. Honestly, I didn't think she would come back to school, and if she did, I didn't think she'd talk to me. And for the first week or so, she didn't. Then one night there was knock on my door. It was Rachel. She hugged me and started crying.

"You were right, Larry. You were right."

# 16

The year is 2020. President Ned Beaumont was lying in bed with a prostitute in the penthouse suite of one of his hotels, reflecting on the biggest scam in American history. Beaumont inherited a hundred million dollars at the age of eighteen from his father, Perry Beaumont, who owned a large oil refinery. Ned was a playboy who eventually opened a chain of casinos in Nevada and Atlantic City. He also owned a TV network where he hosted a game show, starred in a reality series about his luxurious lifestyle, and created a news outlet. He also produced a show where people would compete against each other in a series of mental and physical challenges. Over time, Ned's lifestyle started to get boring, so he decided to run for president to fill the void. In 2016, he won the election, beating out the progressive incumbent. The win was a shock and analysts were still working on theories of how he won. Beaumont ran on the platform of shrinking and privatizing many portions of the government and exporting citizens of non-Anglo heritage back to their native countries. The public never took his white nationalism agenda seriously and were instead mesmerized by his charisma and charm. But now he was in power.

The young prostitute climbed out of the bed and turned the television on. Breaking news was on every channel and the scrolling headlines ran across the screen:

*Meteor shower to hit Earth on 07/04/2020. Destruction will be widespread. Beaumont yet to comment.*

Beaumont jumped to his feet and grabbed his cell phone. The young prostitute seemed excited. Beaumont pressed a button and security came in and forcibly took her away. Beaumont dialed his Chief of Staff, Bryce Patrick. As he dialed, he could see the mayhem on the streets outside of his penthouse window as it was simultaneously displayed on the news.

"Mr. Patrick, what the hell is going on? How did this get out?"

"We're not sure yet, Mr. President, but we have a few theories."

"Do they know about the evacuation plan?"

"That's unclear. The press seems to be releasing several stories at the moment."

"That goddamn fucking press. I should have repealed the first amendment when I had the chance! So, what are we going to do?"

"Well, sir, we already have a plan to counter the story on one of your networks."

"Good. Tell them it's a hoax and make it believable. Tell me some of your theories on how this got out."

"Well, our lead scientist on the OC17 project has found an anomaly in the code."

"What the hell is the OC17 project, Mr. Patrick?"

Bryce ducked out into a hall at the White House and lowered his voice. "It's the dream analysis program, sir. You know, the program we used to fix the election."

"I know nothing about that, Mr. Patrick, remember?"

"Of course, Mr. President."

"What the hell is this anomaly in the code?"

"Well, it seems someone else beyond our four subjects has been using the software."

Beaumont stood up and was irate.

"Do we know who it is?"

"Almost, sir."

"What the hell do you mean, almost?"

"Well, we are having a difficult time triangulating the signal. They must be extremely far away or it could have been used in the past."

"Jesus Christ, Bryce! They assured me this program was secure. We need to find out everything there is on this and bury it. If this gets out, we'll all go down."

"Of course, Mr. President."

"Well don't just stand here, go get to work."

"Of course, Mr. President."

Bryce Patrick boarded a helicopter and flew to a secluded building on one of President Beaumont's private clubs outside of Washington D.C. Patrick went down an elevator into a secluded bunker and proceeded down a hall through several check points that required ocular scans. He finally reached an octagonal room surrounded by monitors. In the

93

middle of the room, four human subjects were asleep on recliners. A team of scientists were on computers stitching the imagery from the subjects together. The lead scientist, Harold Mitchell, was at the main workstation.

"Mr. Mitchell, how are we doing? Were you able to isolate the signal?"

"Yes, but there is an issue."

"I don't want to hear any excuses. The president is losing his patience!"

"Well, we were able to pinpoint the signal. It's coming from Niagara Falls, New York."

"Okay, good, so let's go get the bastard."

"Well sir, the problem is the signal is coming from the past."

"You've lost me, Mitchell. How is that even possible?"

Another scientist in the background popped his head up.

"Oh, it's quite plausible, sir. The software was developed in 1998. Someone could have obtained a pirated copy and hooked it up to someone with dream sensitivity."

"I thought we identified all the people with dream sensitivity. Didn't we kill the ones who wouldn't participate?"

Mitchell responded. "Indeed. The four in this room are all that are left in 2020. But we never identified anyone before year 2000 because the program didn't exist."

"So, do you think it is this person who leaked the story to the press?"

"That could be. If this person has dream sensitivity and manipulation abilities, they could have dreamt of the meteor collision and our plans to evacuate sometime in the past."

"Is there a way to stop this person?"

"Well, there are a few problems with that. First, we don't know who it is; we just have a location. Second, we don't know when it happened yet, and lastly, we don't know what they know and who they have told."

"So basically, you don't know shit, is that right Mr. Mitchell?"

Just then, another one of the techs popped his head up.

"Actually, we do know when it started. The code has a history that we were able to extract. It originates from the year 1998."

"Jesus Christ. That's 22 years. And we never saw it?"

"Well, we weren't looking, sir."

"This is unacceptable," Bryce said irritably. "What are our options?"

"We may be able to send one of our dream makers back to the year 1998 and stop this person, which may ultimately stop the meteor story from being released."

"Is that even possible?"

"Of course it is. Our subjects can go into past dreams just like they went into future dreams when we rigged the election."

"They can change the present by changing the outcome of a past dream?"

"Indeed. And it's even better than that. One of our dreamers lived in the Buffalo-Niagara region in 1998. Since the location and time is already in her subconscious, all we have to do is recreate scenes from 1998 in Niagara Falls and then upload these scenes into her OC17 chip."

"Okay, get to work and keep me posted in real time."

"Sure thing, Mr. Patrick. If we can rig an election, we can stop one measly person from changing the present in the past."

"I hope you're right, Mr. Mitchell, for your sake. Your place in the evacuation can be easily replaced. Remember that."

Mitchell's goofy smile suddenly disappeared.

"Of course, sir."

# 17

Our final presentation for the fall semester was a blood bath. Our studio professor pulled a one-eighty and just decided to belittle many of us in front of his colleagues. He argued with me because he claimed my work looked too computer generated.

Against Dina's wishes, I did try and go back into the dream of the skydiving accident, but without her help, I couldn't conjure the images. Besides, she and Saxxon were too busy working on the meteor collision dream. I also dreamt of a classmate from my first year named Gina. I saw her lying motionless on a rooftop with a hypodermic needle in her arm. This was something I needed to review with Dina. Unfortunately, I hadn't seen Gina in a while. She dropped out of the program after the first year and no one had heard from her.

After our final presentation, we all went to the Blue Goose for drinks. Todd heard about a party at Jenna's house in the Elmwood neighborhood of Buffalo. We piled into Todd's car and went to check it out. I ended up bringing my portable suitcase bar, which was a big hit at the party. When we arrived, you could tell they didn't want us there. It was mostly students from the class ahead of us and several professors. Sam and I decided to split and go check out a band at one of the nearby bars.

The band playing was a compilation of musicians from the sixties Haight-Ashbury scene. The room held about one thousand people and was packed wall to wall. I never liked crowds, so we decided to hug the perimeter but get as close to the stage as possible. We were on the right side of the room and had a good view of the stage and the backstage area. And then Sam noticed Donna was backstage.

"Hey, isn't that Donna back there?"

"Holy shit, it is. It looks like she's partying."

Donna always liked Sam, so it was no surprise her eyes lit up when she saw us.

Donna was wired—most likely coked up on the white lady. She hugged and kissed both of us and invited us backstage.

"Ssssaaammm! And Lararary!" Donna stuttered. "I knew you guys would show up. Aren't these guys great? And they're just the opening band. The headliners are in the back."

She grabbed both of our hands. "Come on, I'll introduce you to the band."

It was evident that Donna was either tagging or trying to tag one of the guitar players. There were several joints being passed around and ample amounts of coke in the back room of the green room. Sam joined in but being the germ-a-phobe I was, I was weary to put my mouth on something that twenty other strangers put their mouth on. I ended up talking to the keyboard player about playing tips and gear. I drank a few seven and sevens and realized Sam and Donna had disappeared into the back room to blow some coke. They were both lit up when they came out. I decided to be blunt with Donna.

"So why did you hate me so much in studio?"

"Hate you? No! Where did you get that idea? Are you kidding? I loved all you guys!"

"Really? But what about throwing my project on the floor? Telling me to quit? Berating me every day?"

"Oh, Larry, I was just trying to get you to realize your potential. I'm mean, I was hard on everyone. Isn't that right, Sam?'

Sam was two sheets to the wind. "Yeah man, it was the best studio I've had so far."

I started laughing. Just then, the guitar player grabbed Donna for a photo. Sam had a huge grin on his face.

"Dude, I think Donna wants to go home with me."

"What? Really? Are you considering it?"

"I don't see why not. What do you think?"

"Don't ask me, man, I hate that woman."

"Oh come on. She's not that bad. And look at that skirt."

"Yeah, probably no underwear on, either."

"Even better," Sam exclaimed. "You're going to have to leave me here later. I'll pretend I'm stranded and get a ride with Donna."

"Jesus. All right. Who am I to stop you?"

After all, I did see this happen in a dream a few weeks prior. I just never thought it would come to fruition.

After I left Sam and Donna, I walked back to the party to see if I could get a ride from Todd. When I got back to the party, the house was completely dark. I knocked on the door a few times, but there was no answer. I didn't see Sam's car, but I remembered I left my portable suitcase bar in the kitchen. The door was open, so I walked in. Just then, Jenna came out of nowhere half naked.

"What the fuck, Larry? What are you doing here, I thought you left?"

"No, I just came back for my bar."

I looked past her into the living room. It smelled like sweat, smoke, perfume, and incents. And there it was. A circle of twelve people or so all naked. It was mostly students, but there was a husband and wife from the architecture faculty and another female visiting professor in the midst of the orgy. I had to ask.

"What the hell is going on in there?"

"Nothing. Just take your bar and go home, Larry."

"Is Todd in there? I need a ride."

"No. Todd left a while ago. Now go, Larry."

Jenna physically pushed me out the door.

I ended up walking from the Elmwood neighborhood back to the University Heights neighborhood. It was about ten miles or so and I had to walk through several rough neighborhoods. I made it about halfway or so and suddenly a car pulled up next to me and beeped the horn. It was Todd.

"Dude, where are you going? Get in."

I jumped in Todd's Volkswagen Golf. There was strangely a lot of headroom in the car.

"You are not going to believe what just happened," Todd said excitedly.

"Let me guess. Orgy."

"Holy shit dude, how did you know?"

"Because after I left Sam and Donna—who were both all coked up and are most likely hooking up as we speak—I went back to the party to get my bar and walked in on it."

"Wait, Sam and Donna are hooking up?"

"Yup."

"Holy fuck!"

"So why didn't you stay for the orgy?" I asked Todd.

"Honestly, it got weird in there, dude. Then, three faculty showed up, no one was wearing rubbers, and that Jenna … she is something else. Stay away from her, she's bad news."

"Yeah, she practically beat the shit out of me when I showed up for my bar. And mark my words, she's going to get some kind of STD."

"She already has herpes," Todd responded.

"Really?"

"Yeah. She caught it from that guy Andy last year."

It occurred to me that I dreamt about Sam and Donna, the orgy, and Jenna's STD all in the same night. Two of the incidents happened that night. I wonder if Jenna's was a past or future event? I thought about contacting Dina when I got home to investigate more, but I honestly was too tired and Jenna kind of pissed me off that night, so I decided not to pursue it.

Todd dropped me off at my apartment. That night, I had several vague nightmares: getting chased and not being able to scream or run, people standing over me, getting shot, and falling off a building and waking up right before I hit the ground. Hopefully, none of these were going to happen. Then, all the nightmares subsided, and I was in a field with a Queen Ann style barn in the background and a lake along the side. The most beautiful woman was approaching me. It was the same woman I dreamt about swimming with several months prior. She was tall with long blonde hair and sort of looked like an older version of Diane from grammar school and junior high. She smiled at me and I woke up.

# 18

Over the winter break, we received an email communication from the school.

*It is with great sadness that we share that our colleague Fred Knight has passed away after a long battle with cancer. Prior to joining the faculty, Fred served in the U.S. Army during the Vietnam War; after the war, he worked for the Army Core of Engineers repairing infrastructure from war ravaged communities. Fred then went back to school to get his master's degree in architecture and went on to teach at seven different colleges. He has been with the University at Buffalo for 17 years. Fred was an inspiring professor that was adored by the students. His presence will certainly be missed.*

I was devastated, to say the least. The spring semester of my third year started out somber. Fred was one of the only nice people on the faculty and it just seemed grim without him having our backs at the critiques. Evidently, Fred had battled colon cancer for about a year before I started the program. He was in a brief remission, but it came back right around the time I tried to confront him about it in his studio. I wasn't sure if my warning forced him to get checked or if it was already too late. And then I thought, maybe if I didn't say anything, he might still be alive? After all, many people end up dying when they are told they are going to die. I was distraught. I called Dina as soon as I read the obituary to see if she made any progress on my ability to alter past dreams without the near-death experience. She mentioned that she had a few ideas, but she still had some tests to run before we were ready to try it.

For spring semester, I chose a landscape design studio, which really was more on par with my interests. The professor was a female in her early sixties named Christina who had longer hair. She was a hippy from the sixties, and I got along with her quite well. As a matter of fact, if she wasn't my professor, I would have considered dating her.

I wasn't getting that many dreams that semester, and the ones I was seeing had no relevance. I did keep getting the recurring dream about the beautiful blonde on the dock. And this image wasn't just confined to my dreams. I also seemed to be seeing her when I was awake. I would be sitting in class and suddenly she'd appear. At first, I thought I was dozing off in class, but this wasn't the case. I was wide awake, and the image was right in front of me like a hologram.

I also had a dream about my grammar school crush, Diane, who somewhat resembled the blonde I kept seeing in my dreams. Diane went to college with me as well, but neither of us had the courage to start the friendship back up. I always regretted this, since I really thought she was my soulmate. Diane was big into her sorority in college and one of the rules was that members could not date guys that were not in a fraternity, which is a totally elitist and ridiculous policy. However, my band was doing quite well and circulating the basement and college-bar scene in the University Heights neighborhood. One particular show, we were lucky enough to get hired to play one of Diane's sorority mixers. All night, I saw Diane watching me out of the corner of her eye; she even grinned at me a few times. At the set break, I went up to her and started turning on the charm and everything felt right. Then I suddenly felt a grip on my shoulder.

"Hey, what's up Ray Manzarek?" The voice said sarcastically. "I didn't know you knew the guys in the band, Diane?"

The guy was about my height but about twice my width and all muscle. Apparently, he was on the UB football team and a member of the fraternity that was at the mixer. He put his arm around Diane.

"Oh, this is Larry. I know him from grammar school. Larry, this is Jordan, my boyfriend."

Jordan gripped my hand so hard I had to loosen it up before I went back on in the second set. And that was it. That was the last time I ever spoke to Diane.

Even before my premonition dreams, I dreamt about Diane on a frequent basis. In the current dream, we were back at the night of that sorority party. At the end of the night, I proclaimed my love to Diane and convinced her to come home with me. We ended up at the mansion of one of my former music teachers named Jim. He played in several local bands but made millions when he played guitar with the *Grateful Dead* for a tour shortly after Jerry Garcia died. Jim recently became ultra-religious and was quite perturbed that I brought a woman back to his house. To test if we were really in love and worthy to stay in his house, Jim put Diane and I though a daunting test. We were seated in the car of a roller coaster that weaved throughout the mansion. The car would stop at stations where the "love" questions were posed. If our answer showed we were truly in love, we would advance slowly to the next station. If our answers showed we weren't in love, the car would go on a daunting ride with twists, turns, dark tunnels, and loops. At the end of the dream, Diane and I ultimately passed Jim's test and could stay in the house together. When I woke up, I really hoped this dream changed the present, but after a quick internet search, and the fact that Diane was not by my side, I learned Diane was happily married with two kids. So once again, this proved that the fortunate dreams never came true for me.

I was still working for Saxxon as a graduate assistant. I went down to his office and told him about the "daydreams." We called Dina on the conference phone.

"I have the images of the blonde from when you were asleep, but I'm not seeing anything when you're awake. You better come by the lab so we can run some tests. Oh, and who is this Diane? I have to say, I'm a bit jealous, Larry." Dina went on. "Also, I may have found a safe way for you to change outcomes in dreams."

"Really?"

"Yes, but it involves psilocybin."

"You mean mushrooms?"

"Yup. And it may also help with you cluster headaches and your OCD."

Saxxon chimed in. "Yes, I've read a few of these studies. It seems the psychedelic compound can release control of the DMN."

"What the hell is the DMN, Scott?"

"That is the default mode network. It's the part of the brain that controls the sense of self. The shrooms also enhance serotonin signaling in the brain."

Dina chimed in. "Yes. And it seems when you are attempting to alter a dream, a severe cluster headache episode is triggered. The sheer pain of the attack is causing a mini-stroke and causing seizures and heart failure. If you were awake, we could use pure oxygen or triptans to treat the episode. But since the attack is happening in a deep state of dreaming, you are not waking up. You are essentially dying in the dream. The tryptamines constrict blood vessels and attach to serotonin receptors."

"So, what do I do, trip out on mushrooms every day? This may not be practical."

Saxxon laughed. "Well, your design work may become really interesting."

Dina chimed back in. "I'm working on a clinical dose that won't cause hallucinations. We'll have to just try this empirically and see what happens."

"Jesus. Okay, I might as well try it. I'll come by later this week and pick up the shrooms."

"Great. And I also have the images compiled of your friend Gina on the rooftop."

"Oh good. Can you pinpoint a time-frame?"

"I think so. Since it is on a rooftop, there's a clear image of the night sky I think we can tell when it is by the alignment of the stars."

"Hmm. Won't that just give us a season?"

"Yes, but that's better than nothing. If the expanding universe theory is true, we could run the images by an astronomer to see if they can calculate a distance, but I don't know any astronomers, do you?"

"No."

"Me, neither," Dina responded. But it's probably not a good idea to bring in too many other outsiders on this."

"Right. I'll come by on Friday to test the shrooms. That way, if I freak out, I have a couple of days to recover."

"Yes, good thinking, Larry."

# 19

Back to year 2020. Harold Mitchell calls Bryce Patrick on a video conference.

"Mr. Mitchell, I hope you have some good news for me."

"Indeed. We were able to send one of our dream makers back into a dream from 1998 and find the perpetrator."

"Really?"

"Indeed. Our very first recruit is Mr. Martin's age and is from the Buffalo area. As it turns out, she lived there right before Matt Brennan brought her to us and fortunately, it was just before the time when Martin started using the OC17 software. We were able to re-create her memories when living there, so sending her back was relatively easy."

Just then, Dream Maker Number One, Melanie Merriman woke up. Her images from her dream were compiling on the screen. In year 2020, the OC17 technology was much more sophisticated. Harold could send his subjects into any of their dreams at any time that he had in his archive. He could also digitally model things that would project into the dreams. Dina and Larry were trying to do this in year 1998 but hadn't quite perfected it yet. He sent Melanie back into a dream she had about six months after she was recruited for the end of the world project. Melanie's dream in year 1998 was a memory she had of a party she was at where she hooked up with a guy. Before she went home with him, her friend was cautioning her to not go through with the one-night stand. Harold was able to model an alternate where Melanie's friend warns her about someone using the OC17 dream chip instead of the one-night stand. Melanie was able to give her 1998 self the information about the future through the dream.

"Excellent. What do we know about this person?"

Harold's software quickly started splicing Melanie's images. Before the splicing was finished, Melanie chimed in.

"His name is Larry Martin. He's getting help from a rogue psychologist named Dina Lawrence."

"So how do we stop him? Can we just kill him in 1998?"

"I'm afraid killing him will not solve the problem, Mr. Patrick." Melanie answered emphatically.

"We will need to hack into his chip and reprogram his dreams."

"Ahh, so he'll never see our evacuation project?"

Mitchell responded. "No, he's already seen everything, and we can't undo that. And Melanie is correct about not killing him. We don't know how many other people are tethered to his timeline or where or when they hid information about the space colony in the past, present, or future. So merely killing him may not necessarily prevent the plan from getting out. But until we figure this out, we can alter what he sees. For example, we could give him a false date of when the earth will be destroyed … maybe in year 2024. Then when it actually happens later this year, any plans he and his collaborators put in place to warn the planet will be too late.

Bryce seemed frustrated. "It sounds too complicated. I still say we just kill him and anyone he has told about the project."

Melanie responded, "That contingency plan is in place, but like Harold said, we need to know who else is tethered to his timeline. Besides, he may be a useful asset to us. This ability is rare and so far, I have been the most productive dreamer out of the four of us. Martin's abilities may be on my level."

Bryce was still frustrated. "Well, what about just going back in time in a dream and killing his parents and prevent him from ever being born?"

"That is also not possible," Harold responded. "We currently cannot alter the present in a past dream unless one of our dreamers actually lived or dreamt that exact event."

"Well, do what you have to do," Bryce responded. "But time is wasting. There is pandemonium in the streets. Soon, the press will release the plans for our colony, and everything will be ruined."

Harold Mitchell brought up the news on another monitor. "They already have, sir."

A news reporter reported the story:

*Sources tell us that Beaumont and a private team have known about the meteor collision for the past two years. While the meteor collision will damage Earth and kill countless people, Beaumont's team is planning on hitting the meteor with a nuclear arsenal, which has the potential to wipe out all life on*

*Earth if not executed properly. As far as Beaumont and his team, sources tell us he has an evacuation plan in outer space for 10,000 people that he hand-picked. And from the list, it looks like he is creating a colony of super-beings.*

# 20

It took me longer than usual to get to Dina's lab in Niagara Falls. The traffic was backed up on the Grand Island Bridge. Apparently, a boat's engine failed and was headed fast up the river toward the falls. Everyone who lives in the Buffalo/Niagara region has some story of almost going over the falls. My mom swam across the river when she was young and claimed she drifted two miles; my uncle claimed his boat came within a half mile of the falls due to engine failure, and then, just before they entered the rapids, the engine miraculously started back up; one of the students in the architecture program actually claimed he went over the falls and survived when testing a floatation device for one of his upper level studios. I never believed any of the stories until I saw how fast the boat was drifting. By the time I crossed over, it looked like the Coast Guard had captured the boat.

Dina had the psilocybin ready to go. I was expecting actual mushroom caps like I saw in my band days as an undergraduate, but she had extracted the compound into a tincture so she could measure the exact amount.

"So, am I going to freak out? I remember seeing many kids in college have bad trips."

"No. You shouldn't. There are only five mg in each vile. I think a recreational dose is about twenty mg."

"You think?"

"Well, I watched a video on how to do the extraction. I think I did it right."

"Oh Christ! I don't know about this."

"Settle down, Larry. If anything, it's weaker than five mg, so you have nothing to worry about."

Dina continued. "But before I give you a dose, I want to show you the images of your friend Gina."

Dina brought up the images on the screen. We were at an art opening in downtown Buffalo. The opening was a public sex booth that an architecture student designed for his final thesis. I was able to see the student.

"Yes, I know that guy. He is a year ahead of me. He'll be presenting his thesis this spring."

"Excellent," Dina said. Because things don't turn out very well for your friend Gina. It looks like she overdoses on the rooftop."

The presentation was in an alley of a building in Allentown. Sometime during the presentation, Gina climbs up a ladder onto the roof of an adjacent building and scores heroin from some shady looking guy.

"Well, I guess I'll be at that presentation."

"Indeed. You better show up early."

Dina proceeded. "Okay, so the psilocybin, in theory, should allow you to go into a past dream and prevent you from developing a cluster headache, thereby preventing the stroke, and ultimately, well, prevent you from dying."

"Well that's good. You know they always like it when I don't die."

"Funny, Larry. Isn't that a Jerry Garcia line?"

"It sure is."

"So which dream should we start with?"

"It's up to you. Which one do you think is easiest to manipulate? That might be a good one to start with."

"Hmmm," I said. "Which one do we have the most footage on?"

"That's easy. The Ng/Raja dream. And you already went back into this one once."

"I know. I almost died."

"The dreams of Rachel's brother in the skydiving accident and Fred dying of cancer were both future dreams at the time. We'd have to recreate scenes before their deaths to get you to go into the dream. This may take some time."

"Then Ng/Raja it is."

"Right. The only other past dream we have is your friend Cindy, and I don't want to mess with that again."

"Yes, I agree. I don't want to screw up that timeline."

"I'll load the images into your chip."

"Is this stuff going to make me sick?"

"It shouldn't at that small of a dose, but you never know," Dina answered. "Besides, it's mixed with a small sedative that should put you to sleep and relax you. The sedative has an anti-nauseate in it."

Quoting *Indiana Jones and The Last Crusade*, I proclaimed. "Well, there's only one way to find out." And then I downed the clear liquid in the vile.

For the first half hour, I was wide awake, and nothing was happening. Then suddenly, I was laying on the carpet of Dina's lounge. The fibers of the carpet started growing to the size of trees. I then started to weave my way through the fibers but couldn't find my way out of the maze. Just then, I heard the water ticking in the base-board hot water; it was the same sound the heat in my bedroom made in the house I grew up in. I then found myself in my room, very sad, reflecting on my life, my OCD, my lack of love, my hate for the architecture program. I then started weeping. I walked through my house, but it was completely empty. I looked out the windows and didn't recognize any of the neighbors. I then heard Dina's voice.

"Try another path."

Suddenly, I was back into the carpet climbing through the fibers. Then I heard music at the other edge of the carpet.

"Go toward the music, Larry."

The song playing was one of the songs I played at the bar the night of my twenty-fourth birthday—the night I passed out on the church lawn and dreamt about Raja. I then smelled beer and cigarette smoke. Dina mentioned she was going to be playing music and emitting aromas to trigger my memory. And then I climbed out of the carpet toward the stage lighting. I was on the stage at Moe's playing the congas with the Walking Carpets. I was in the dream.

The mushrooms made everything distorted—more than the usual distortion that often happens in dreams. The stage was about ten feet higher, the audience looked like a fishbowl, and the lights were intense. At the set break, I walked up Lisbon Ave. to Raja's house. I remembered from the last time I went into this dream that there was a group of thugs that harassed me on the street. I didn't see them this time. Perhaps I was a bit earlier than the previous time. I jumped up to Raja's second-floor porch. This time, she was in the kitchen making a sandwich and there was no sight of Ng.

So I wouldn't frighten her, I jumped back to the ground and knocked on her door. Just then, I felt a large jolt on the back of my head. It was Ng

109

and he once again knocked me out with a crowbar. I could see him going up Raja's stairs but could not move. Suddenly, I saw the blonde that I had been seeing at a farm barn. She was walking up to me in slow motion. She grabbed the back of my head and started kissing me. I thought if this was death, it wasn't that bad.

I heard the song *Eye of the Tiger* playing in the distance. I could hear Dina's voice yelling at me. "Get up, Larry! Get up. You're not really hurt. Listen to the music."

The music worked just like in *Rocky 3*. I pushed myself up and went up the stairs. Ng had a towel dipped in chlorophyll and had it over Raja's face. I grabbed Ng by the back of the hair and gave him a DDT, a wrestling move where you put your opponent in a side headlock and slam them to the ground, through the kitchen table. I grabbed Raja, who was half-unconscious, and ran to the balcony. I went to jump so we could fly off the porch, but Ng grabbed my leg. I tripped and fell off the balcony with Raja in my arms. I woke up right before I hit the ground, but I wasn't at Dina's lab. I was at my apartment a couple of blocks away. I realized I wasn't really awake, but in another dream. Suddenly, Dina's voice was in the background.

"You're in another dream, but you can just go back to the first dream. It's only two blocks away."

She was right. Who's to say I couldn't slide back into the other dream? These are my dreams, after all. I climbed out onto my porch and climbed high up a tree. I could see myself laying on the ground two blocks away on Lisbon Ave and Raja trying to wake me up. Ng was coming down the stairs.

"Run, Raja, Run," I yelled from the tree. "Run to Cory's house on Minnesota Avenue."

Raja had no idea who Cory was. He was the guy who I borrowed the congas from to play with the Walking Carpets that night. But in the dream, she knew Cory, or at least that was how I was programming the dream. She ran into Cory's house and closed the door. Ng was in the street yelling. He had lost her trail. Just then I woke from both dreams, and I was back in Dina's lab.

I was still somewhat hazy, as the mushrooms were not completely out of my system.

"How are you feeling, Larry?" Dina asked.

"Okay."

"Any pain?"

"No, just a little groggy."

"Fantastic. It looks like the psilocybin worked. You're not in shock and you're not dead."

"Is Raja alive?"

Dina went over to the other monitor and searched on Raja. Unfortunately, she was still deceased.

"What, how can that be? I saved her. You saw it."

"Altering a past scenario is one thing but bringing people back from the dead is a stretch, Larry." Dina empathetically explained. "I mean, you're not god, for Christ's sake."

Dina went on. "But let's check the timeline for Ng." And then she zoomed in on a node and found a headline. She read, "Suspected serial killer at large. In the original timeline, Ng killed Raja, burned down her house, and ended up killing himself in New York City. In the new altered timeline, Ng didn't kill Raja in the house on Lisbon Avenue, but instead killed her walking home from studio a few weeks later and then went on a killing rampage that took the lives of twelve young women. He was still alive. It seems we made things worse."

"I have to go back in and wipe this guy out."

"You're not a murderer, Larry. But you could try and get him arrested. In any event, you'll have to wait at least twenty-four hours before taking another dose. Otherwise, you might go insane."

I agreed to try again the next day. That night I went to sleep and dreamt of the mysterious blonde on the dock again.

# 21

Dina and I tried several times to go back into the dream and capture Ng, but we seemed to fail every time. I either ended up getting killed in the dream and waking up or getting knocked out and transferred to another dream. One time, I found a police officer and told him about the event, and he ended up arresting me instead. It was very frustrating. I was distraught that twelve innocent people were dead because I tried to save my friend and frustrated that we could not control the dream better. It seemed like the harder we tried, the more the dream floundered, and the more ripples were embedded into the timeline.

Dina was also concerned I was taking too much of the mushroom extract, and I think she was right. I looked in the mirror and I looked like shit. My hair was all frizzy, I had deep black circles under my eyes, and I lost about fifteen pounds. We shifted gears for a while and tried to recreate images from Fred's life before he was diagnosed with cancer. However, since I didn't know Fred before he was diagnosed, recreating the imagery proved to be difficult.

To add to the stress, the semester was winding down and my final project was due. Dina and I decided to take a break from the past dreams until the end of the semester.

As I walked down Crosby Hall, I saw that Malcom Green's final thesis presentation was being held at a building downtown called the Arts Riot. Apparently, his public sex booth project was deemed too controversial to be held on campus, which is ironic seeing architecture is one of the most liberal degree programs in higher education. I now had a date, time, and place to prevent Gina from overdosing. Even though I couldn't undo Ng's murders or save Fred, I decided to focus on this event.

I met up with Sam, Todd, and Rachel to go to Malcom's presentation. I hadn't really talked to Rachel since her brother's skydiving accident, but I could see she was not doing well. I was so focused on fixing the Raja/Ng event for the past month, I totally forgot about Rachel. I made a mental note to work on recreating the skydiving scenes with Dina.

Just as in my dream, Malcom's presentation was being held in an alley between two buildings in the Allentown neighborhood. There were about five-hundred people in the audience. His public sex booth was a fairly minimal structure. It basically looked like a large phone booth covered in an opaque latex. He had a live band that played techno music and he hired a male, female, and trans-gender erotic dancer to dance behind the opaque screening while he presented his thesis. You could see the dancers' silhouettes as they acted out sex acts behind the screen. His thesis was that people would use this public exhibition booth at the party, but no one other than the dancers seemed to use it.

Between the light show, the live music, and the crowd of people, it was difficult for me to locate Gina. Then, I noticed a fire escape ladder on one of the buildings like the one I saw in the dream with Gina.

As the night went on, people started getting intoxicated. Malcom and a few of his friends decided to strip behind the sex booth. Just then, I saw Gina. She didn't seem to even be there for the presentation. She was talking to a sketchy guy and the two started climbing the ladder to the roof. Todd saw me looking at the ladder.

"Hey, isn't that Gina?"

"Yeah, it is."

"What's she doing? Who's that guy she is with?"

"I don't know, but I'm going to check it out."

Todd didn't approve. "Dude, are you crazy? That situation looks totally sketch."

"I have to. I have a bad feeling."

Just then, Rachel looked in my direction. Since I told her about my dreams, she knew I knew something.

I climbed up the ladder and peaked over the edge. I could see Gina was buying heroin. I tried to play dumb.

"Hey Gina! So, this is a cool spot, huh?"

"Larry? What are you doing here?"

Just then, another thug appeared at the top of the ladder and kicked me in the face. I fell off the ladder and landed right on the public sex booth. The rubber screening that Malcom used on the top and sides turned out to be pretty strong. It broke my fall, and I landed in the booth between three naked people. The audience thought this was part of the show and started applauding. I looked up on the roof. Gina and the thugs were nowhere to be seen. The good news was Gina didn't end up overdosing that night. However, she was found dead two days later in her apartment. I guess fate is inevitable.

I was happy the spring semester was wrapping up. My project was decent—I removed the roads along the Niagara River and designed a linear park. My review went well, but it was bittersweet. I thought about Gina, Fred, Rachel's brother, and the twelve women Ng murdered. The failure to help them overshadowed the positive reviews of my project.

I fell asleep as soon as the critique was over and dreamt my mom fell and was hospitalized. I had this same dream about a year prior. I woke up and called home, but I was too late. The event seemed to happen at the same exact time I had the dream. What good is that, I thought? She wasn't seriously injured, but she had some cosmetic damage to her face. I thought if it bothered her enough, I could try and get back into the dream and prevent the fall. However, my dreams seemed to be spotty that spring. It was like something was blocking them.

I did randomly dream about a family Christmas party I was at when I was a kid. Events seemed to be occurring in the dream that never actually happened at the party. I started to worry that these "historically inaccurate" dreams might affect the present if I interacted or altered them in any way. The site of the Christmas party and all the people in attendance were both accurate, but in the dream, I ended up getting angry about something and threw one of the gifts on the floor. The gift was a box of glass cups that all inevitably broke. My tantrum caused a huge fight that escalated and caused our extended family to be on non-speaking terms. I woke up completely distraught that I was some kind of villain.

As I said, I was unsure if this dream impacted reality. However, I was too tired to try and figure it out, so I decided to just go back to sleep to see if I could fix the event. Much to my luck, I was able to go back into the dream. This time, I contained my anger and didn't throw the box of glasses. However, one of my cousins still remembered me breaking the glasses in the original dream. For a moment, I thought he had dreaming ability and was jumping into one of my dreams trying to make me the bad guy. But then, I was able to go back into the dream a third time and somehow prevented my cousin from being able to see both outcomes. It worked, but this time, I ended up getting attacked by a dog. The dog ended up biting my fingers off, so I had to go back into the dream a fourth time and both prevent my cousin from seeing all the outcomes and prevent the dog from biting me. It seems this sequence took all night to fix.

Although I was certain this dream had no effect on reality, it was still good practice to learn how to go back into dreams multiple times and control their outcome without rippling the present timeline. But I was still paranoid other people could enter my dreams and alter their outcome.

After the strange Christmas party dream, I had dream that Rachel and I were at a Halloween party on an old Navy ship, the U.S.S. Little Rock. Several of her high school girlfriends were there and they were all dressed as eighties rock stars—big hair, make-up, high heels, and leather-clad outfits. Rachel had a few drinks and was starting to get loose. I wasn't sure exactly where this dream fell in relation to her brother Jeremy's skydiving accident, so I just took a chance and blurted it out. Luckily, this dream took place about a week before the accident.

"So is your brother still planning on going skydiving?" I asked.

"Ugg. Don't remind me. I am totally freaked out by that."

"Yeah, I am, too."

"Well, I know you are. You've already told me you have a bad feeling."

"Do you think we can change his mind?"

"No," Rachel responded. "I think he's determined to do it, and he is fairly stubborn once he makes up his mind."

"When is the jump?" I asked.

"This Saturday. And that reminds me, he's actually going to that Sexy People Party tomorrow on the corner of Main Street and Northrup Place."

"Really? That's invite only."

"I know. I think that is the only reason they invited me, to be honest," Rachel said somewhat disappointingly.

"But you know, I have a plus one, Larry. Do you want to go with me?"

I wasn't invited to the party because I wasn't deemed sexy enough by the swingers that hosted the party, and under usual circumstances, I'd have said no. But since Rachel's brother Jeremy was going to be there, I figured I may be able to convince him to not do the jump.

"Sure. Why not."

"Oh my god, I'm surprised you said yes, Larry. That is totally not your scene."

"I know, but I'm going to convince your brother not to do the jump."

I had to go to the bathroom, which was inevitably a sure way to wake me up and end the dream. I tried to stay asleep when I was peeing by leaning on the shower curtain rail, but the stream seemed to go on forever. I went back to sleep and tried to focus on getting back into the dream. After several more erotic dreams with Rachel, I found myself at the party.

Rachel's brother Jeremy was kind of strait-laced and clean cut. I think I freaked him out a bit. After all, I wasn't the type of person he'd associate with.

A group of us broke off into one of the bedrooms. I was trying to tactfully bring up the skydiving, but the conversation in the room seemed to be focusing on penis size. Several of the people were speculating on the size of some of the male professor's penises. While the conversation was going on, this smallish kid kept rubbing into me. At first, I thought it was just because the room was overcrowded, but I soon realized he was hitting on me. I rotated around the room over to Rachel.

"Hey, put your arm around me."

"Why?" Rachel asked.

"Because that guy is hitting on me and I want him to know I'm straight."

Rachel complied. She was getting freaked out as well. Apparently, this party was just an excuse for an orgy.

Jeremy then approached Rachel and me. "Oh my God, are you guys together?"

I could see Jeremy was kind of a knucklehead. "Sure. Why not," I said casually. Rachel giggled a bit.

"So how long has this been going on? Wait until I tell mom."

Rachel giggled. "No, don't you dare. They'll make a big deal."

"That's right, Larry," Jeremy went on. "Soon, you'll be invited to Sunday dinners. He laughed."

I decided to change the topic. "What about you, Jeremy. I hear you're going skydiving tomorrow."

The whole room was paying attention now. And he seemed to gloat in it.

"Yeah, that's right. I'm pretty stoked."

"Are you nervous at all?"

"Not really. The instructor goes with you the first time."

"Are you sure you really want to do it? I mean, is it safe?"

"Yeah man. And I don't want to hear all the statistics about the chute not opening. My sister already tried that angle. And she also told me how you are psychic and had a bad feeling. I don't want to hear it."

Just then Todd chimed in. "You're a psychic, Larry? Do tell."

The room of people converged around me and Jeremy slipped out of the room. I was going to have to do something more extreme to prevent him from doing the jump.

Jeremy left the party with some girl at the end of the night and they were both were intoxicated. He peeled out of the driveway in his red mustang. It occurred to me he shouldn't have been driving, but he clearly was a risk-taker. Then the idea hit me. I'll call the cops. He'll be put in a holding cell overnight and will most likely miss the jump tomorrow. This was a tough decision but was the only solution I could find. He'd have some legal issues with the DUI, but at least he'd still be alive. I hoped.

I called the cops but woke up from the dream. I quickly fell back asleep but dreamt of Dina floating in a river. I woke up to the radio of my alarm clock, but when I turned it off, the sound kept playing. I called Dina and told her about the dream I had of her, but then I woke up again. I was once again dreaming within a dream.

# 22

Year 2020

Melanie Merriman was waking up from her dream. Bryce Patrick and Harold Mitchell were standing over her.

"Nice work, Melanie," Harold Mitchell proclaimed.

"What exactly did she accomplish, Mr. Mitchell?" Bryce asked abruptly.

"Melanie can explain it best. Go ahead Melanie."

As Melanie stood up, Bryce couldn't help checking her out. She was about 5'9", had blonde hair, and an hourglass figure.

"I'm currently working in a dream from year 2000. Martin and his team have still not figured out our entire evacuation or when it takes place."

"Who else is on the team?" Bryce asked.

"Well, we already knew about Dina Lawrence, but it seems there's only one other person involved. His name is Scott Saxxon."

Bryce and Harold looked at each other.

"Oh shit," Bryce blurted out.

"What's the problem?" Melanie asked.

Patrick answered. "Dr. Scott Saxxon. I should have known he was involved. He's been working on the colony since the seventies. Do we know where any of these people are in present time? Maybe we can extort them."

"No sir," Mitchell responded. "They're ghosts."

"You can thank Saxxon for that. Things just became more complicated."

Melanie responded. "Well how should I proceed?"

"We'll need the three of them alive for questioning. Find out what they know and who they told and then eliminate them. But be extra cautious with Saxxon. He's a clever son of a bitch."

Melanie complied. "Agreed. It will be in the year 2001. Six months have already gone by in the dream I was just in."

Mitchell chimed in. "That is correct. A significantly more amount of time goes by in the dream than in the present time. In Melanie's case, she was asleep for six hours, but six months actually went by in her dream."

Melanie continued. "I also was able to hack Martin's chip in 2000. I put a virus in his chip that will project random images. There will be so many images in his dreams, he'll not be able to differentiate what is real or what is dream. He will probably lose his mind before I have to kill him."

"Good. So how much longer in *present* time do we have until this situation is resolved?

"Maybe another week," answered Mitchell.

"You'll have to do better, Mr. Mitchell. We can't jeopardize the project. And the chaos is getting worse in the streets."

# 23

The next morning, Dina called me with an update on Jeremy.

"Well, the good news is Jeremy is still alive. The bad news is that he was arrested for DWI. He was almost twice the legal limit."

"Yeah, I couldn't think of anything else to do."

"Did you tell Rachel?"

"No, but I just talked to her. She has no recollection of us having sex in the dream, but she remembers the party."

"Hmmm. Interesting, Larry. It seems our theory of you not benefiting from these dreams is still holding up."

"I know. That's too bad. If the first time with a woman could be in a dream and both of us remembered it, it would certainly take the pressure off when we did it for the first time in real life."

"I suppose! Then again, it might not be as good in real life for either of you."

"Maybe. Hey, did you see the image of you floating down the river?"

"Yes, I did. But I quickly deleted it. This has been my new protocol for any dreams you have of me. I don't want to know my future."

"Yeah, but, what if you are going to be in danger?"

"I don't want to know," Dina screamed.

"Yeah, but you are interested in others. How is that any different?"

"It is different. I'm a scientist. I have to take my personal life out of the equation."

"I suppose, but I'd stay away from rivers if I were you for a while."

"No, Larry. I'm not going to stop living. And you shouldn't either."

I then went on to tell Dina about another dream I had about another girl I went to high school with named Kristi. Kristi was a straight edge girl, very smart, and was captain of the tennis team. In the dream, she was crying and asking me why I didn't love her.

Dina brought the dream up on the monitor and watched it. It started with me asking Kristi a question.

"What do you mean?" I asked.

"I asked you to prom junior year and you turned me down," Kristi responded.

I searched my memory but had no recollection of anyone asking me to prom.

"Are you sure it was me, Kristi?"

"Yes. Don't you remember? I sent my friend Tina over to you to see if you were interested."

"Yes, I remember Tina asked me if I was going to prom in French class. I told her no, I thought prom was stupid, but she never mentioned your name."

"You're lying."

I tried to reason with her, but I ended up waking up. I fell back asleep and then dreamt Kristi killed herself. A quick internet search revealed she was still alive in the present, which meant the suicide hadn't taken place yet. I was still unable to go back into the past and resurrect the dead, but I was certain I could prevent a death, given the little girl at Niagara Falls, the mother on the train, Jeremy, and Gina—well, somewhat, Gina. The next day, I went to Dina's lab to get another hit of psilocybin to see if I could go back and prevent Kristi's suicide. Dina was re-reviewing the dream when I arrived.

"Larry, why didn't you go to the prom with that nice girl?"

"I swear, I didn't know she wanted to go."

"Oh, you knew she liked you. You just didn't want to go."

"Probably, but I had no idea this could have led to her suicide."

"Come on. You really think it is was your rejection that led to her suicide some ten years later?"

"No, but maybe that was just one of the straws in the timeline that broke the camel's back. I have to go back in and say yes."

"You could but think of the consequences. This might change the space-time continuum big time. I mean, your life and Kristi's life may be totally different if you agree to go to that prom. Remember what happened with Michelle? And Raja?!"

"Yeah, you're right, Dina. Well, maybe I could just talk to her?"

"You might make things worse. And besides, we don't even know when, or if, she's going to kill herself. Your premonition dreams are hovering around the seventy-five percent range. So, there is a small chance she won't even do it."

After some convincing, Dina agreed to help in the name of science. I brought my high school yearbook and a bunch of old photos. We scanned in the images and I took the hit of psilocybin. We seemed to be getting better control of the dreams, because this one worked on the first try. I was in the dream and it was the day Tina came over and asked me if I was going to the prom. Instead of saying no, I said, "I don't know. I don't have a date."

"Oh really?" Tina responded.

"Why, are you going?"

"Yes, I'm going with Craig."

"Hmmm. Maybe I'll ask Kristi?"

"Oh, no. She already has a date. Besides, I don't think you're her type."

It was then I realized that Tina had some beef with Kristi, and this was her way of getting back at her. I stumbled through the distorted halls of my high school and tried to find Kristi. I saw her talking to this dim-whit football player named Vito who seemed to be hitting on her. Vito was a typical aggressive, "over-testosteroned" alpha-male. He used to knock people's books out of their hands, punch people randomly in the hall, and start fights on a weekly basis.

"What are you looking at, Martin, you skinny stroke," Vito yelled at me.

My dream then shifted to another time shortly after this when we were in the swimming pool for gym class. Vito was punching people in the pool and splashing people with water. He was also making crude remarks to the females in the class, including Kristi. "Hey Kristi, too bad you can't pad your swimsuit like you do your bra." I swam by him and he punched me in the kidney. I lost my temper and dragged him away from the edge of the pool into the deep end. I noticed Vito couldn't swim very well. I held him under the water and pushed him down with my feet. I thought he was going to retaliate and kick my ass, but he didn't seem to be moving. I grabbed him by the hair and pulled him up. He was crying like a baby.

"What the fuck, Martin. I was drowning. You almost killed me!"

The gym teacher blew his whistle. As I climbed out of the pool, I could see Kristi smiling at me. I winked back at her.

122

Later that day, or later in the dream, Kristi came up to me.

"Hey Larry, that was awesome what you did to Vito. That guy is a dick."

"I know, and apparently he doesn't swim too well."

"Hey, by the way, did Tina talk to you about going to the prom?"

"She did, but it looks like I'm suspended for almost killing Vito. They said I can't participate in any functions for the rest of the year and that includes prom."

"Oh, did she mention me at all?" Kristi asked.

"No. But when I brought up the prospect of possibly asking you, she told me I'm not you're type."

Kristi freaked out. "What? That bitch! I knew I couldn't trust her. She's mad at me because I didn't go to her party last week. But I'd have totally gone with you."

"Yeah, that would have been fun. Oh well, maybe next year."

Kristi seemed relieved but somewhat disappointed. "Yeah, or maybe we could get together this summer?"

"That sounds good."

I woke up from the dream and saw Dina looking at the images.

"Well, this is an odd case. The only difference thus far is that Kristi is living in North Carolina. Before your dream, she was living in New Jersey."

"Oh, so maybe it was New Jersey. Maybe that's why she commits suicide?"

"Funny, Larry. But we don't know. Since we don't know when exactly she kills herself, we're just going to have to play this one out."

"Can't we isolate the image of when I saw her kill herself. Is there anything in the background that can identify a time?"

"Unfortunately, no. I already checked."

"But it is cool that one event of me not rejecting her, lead to another sequence of events that ultimately makes her end up in North Carolina instead of Jersey."

Dina didn't seem to share the excitement.

"I'm not sure, Larry. I don't think we knew enough about this one to get involved. I mean, we just altered this woman's life."

"Yeah, but we might have saved her."

"We don't know that. If we did, great, but in the future, I'd suggest we don't mess with space-time unless it is a more well-defined life or death situation."

"Fine. But what defines well-defined? Is the meteor collision well-defined?"

"I don't know, Larry. I think we should talk more with Saxxon about this. After all, he's an environmental psychologist. Maybe he'll have some insight into the ethics of all of this."

# 24

During the summer, I had a strange dream of a beautiful Russian blonde named Heidi getting attacked in a dingy room. I had never seen her before, but the dream was as clear as day. A few weeks later, one of my classmates named Jim was getting married and was having a bachelor party up in Niagara Falls on the Canadian side. All the guys were five to ten years younger than me, so maybe they were looking to me to be a responsible voice to keep them from getting too crazy. Against my liking, we ended up at a strip bar. The young bucks crowded around the stage and I receded off to the side bar to get a drink. A gorgeous blonde approached me. It was Heidi from my dream a couple weeks prior.

"Are you lonely?" She asked.

"Yeah," I responded timidly.

Indeed, her accent sounded Russian.

"You come in back with me. I give you lap dance," she responded.

"Well, I don't have much money. And that's not really my thing."

"How much you have?"

"Trust me. Not enough. But I can buy you a drink."

The woman giggled. "Okay, but I have to make money, so only one drink."

I ended up talking to Heidi for quite a while. She bought another round of drinks. I decided to ask her about her career.

"So how did you get into this business?" I asked.

"What business?" She responded with a sly smile.

"I don't know, the adult entertainment business?" I responded.

Heidi responded in her broken Russian accent. "You make it sound so formal. I'm in school studying to be nurse. This is just to pay bills."

"Oh, really? Where are you in school?"

"University of Toronto."

"Do you enjoy it?"

"Sometimes."

I could see Heidi was somewhat sad. She went on.

"Some nights, money good. I make up to thousand dollars in tips. Other nights, it's not tips and just drunk, mean men."

"Well, what do you do for tips?"

"Haven't you ever been to a bar like this before?" Heidi inquired.

I glanced around the room and saw several of the other floor dancers taking men into the back room. It was a busy night. There was a fraternity in the bar from a nearby college. I knew what went on, I just wanted to hear it from her.

"Of course, but I know some of the dancers do more than others."

"I always keep clothes on," Heidi responded. "But I do give massage. With hands only, though."

"Do you wear latex gloves?"

"She laughed. No, silly. I don't think clients would like that."

Heidi finished her drink and tried to persuade me one more time.

"You sure you don't want to come in back with me? I give you a free dance."

"No, I'm good. But really, be careful. There are a lot of creeps in here tonight."

Heidi giggled again. I could see she may have been through far worse. I imagined her exiled from Russia during the Cold War. I wondered if she was here on her own will, or if she was an enslaved in a sex ring in exchange for citizenship. Anyway, I watched Heidi out of the corner of my eye for the rest of the night. She kept looking up at me and smiling every time she came back from the back room. After about forty-five minutes or so, I noticed Heidi hadn't come out of the back room. This was a long stretch of time seeing she would usually do around three songs of lap dances per client. I walked into the back room but didn't see her on any of the semen lined couches. There was another door in the back of the lounge that led to a long hallway. At the end of the hallway, there was a rickety staircase leading to the upper level. I could hear the screaming as I ascended the stairs. Heidi was practically passed out on a sketchy mattress. There were three frat boys having their way with her.

One of the frat boys yelled at me. "Hey man, what the fuck? This is a private room. Get the fuck out of here, perv!"

I looked at Heidi. She was gagged and her mascara was running down her face because of the tears.

"No. Get the fuck off her, pal, or I'm calling the cops."

The frat boys taunted me.

"Pal? Okay Pal? What are you going to do about it?"

One of the guys seemed to not want to be a part of it. He slowly receded against the wall. One of the guys pulled up his pants and came at me, but he was so drunk, he tripped on his pants and fell on the floor. I put my boot on his face and grabbed the guy on top of Heidi. He was quite muscular and far stronger than me. He charged me and slammed me to the ground. The other guy got back to his feet and pulled out a syringe, probably the same syringe they used to drug Heidi. In the meantime, Heidi was able to get loose. She jumped on the guy with syringe and was able to turn it on him and jam it into his jugular. Blood rushed out all over the floor. I was able to get loose from the guy on top of me and started swinging Rocky Balboa style. I knocked the big guy to the ground. He was about to charge me again, but the frat brother against the wall yelled out. "Guys, someone else is coming. Let's get the fuck out of here."

Two of the other women down the hall heard the commotion and came in the room. The one lady pulled a gun and started firing.

The three frat boys ran out of the room, giggling and yelling profanity as they fled.

"Dude, she's shooting at us!"

The other ladies tended to Heidi. I offered to call the cops, but they said that was out of the question given their line of work. They took Heidi to the attic level where there was a full apartment where several of the ladies seemed to be living. They put Heidi in the shower and tended to her wounds. When she came out, she looked like the innocent girl next store—no makeup, high heels, fish net stockings, or shiny silver dress. She was dressed in a loose pair of sweatpants and a hoodie. She didn't seem stressed.

"Thank you, Larry. I knew you were good soul."

"No problem, but you need to get to a hospital. You need to get a sexual assault forensic exam and get started on post-exposure prophylaxis."

"I go in morning," Heidi responded. "I'm okay. He had condom on."

"I know, but what about the needle and all the blood?"

127

Another one of Heidi's co-workers chimed in. She was American and seemed like this was not new to her. I assumed she was the madam of the operation.

"We'll take care of it sweetie. We've dealt with this before. We have someone we go to that keeps everything off the record. You know she is here illegally, right?"

"Well, I kind of assumed that."

"Right. And they will send her back to Russia if we report this."

"Well, you can't let those kids get away with it. Look, I know the Greek letters they were wearing on their hat. I'll track them down for you."

The madam chuckled a bit. "We have someone to take care of that as well."

In the background, another woman yelled out. "Yup. He's already on it."

Heidi thanked me again. She gave me a hug and kissed me on the cheek. She also gave me a card with her number on it.

"You call me sometime? We can get coffee or something?"

"Yeah, that sounds good. Are you sure you're okay?"

"I'm okay. Tough Russian. Now go home and get some sleep."

Before I left, I decided to use the bathroom. Due to the fight, I had blood on my hands, and of course, I had small cuts on my hands from all the shop work in architecture school. I totally freaked out. This incident totally triggered my existing obsessions with diseases and germs, which all started before graduate school when I found out my girlfriend was getting around. Every what-if scenario went through my head. I was totally paralyzed. I ended up driving back to Rochester to talk to my family doctor. He said this was a low risk scenario to contract any disease, but we would still have to run tests to be safe. Unfortunately, the testing window went out to six months for a conclusive result. So, for the next six months, I went for monthly full-panel blood tests. I totally became obsessed with blood-borne diseases and retroviruses. I spent hours in the computer lab reading papers on transmission, prevention, and cures to diseases. It was at that point I realized I should have gone into medical research. I was a complete nervous wreck and could barely function in school. To make matters worse, all my dreams were about me dying or contracting a disease from the blood incident. Dina tried to assure me these were just intense fears that were surfacing, but I didn't believe it. I thought something terrible was going to happen. In addition to terminal illness dreams, I also saw several dreams with mass destruction, but I was so focused on my health, I ignored them.

And then in September of 2001, the attacks on the World Trade Center and the pentagon happened. Was this what I was seeing but ignored? Could I have prevented this from happening if I wasn't so focused on myself? Dina once again reassured me. She said the images of destruction I was seeing were too unclear to determine if they were the 911 attacks. I didn't believe her, though. I think she was just trying to prevent me from going off the deep end.

The doctor gave me a high dose of Klonopin to deal with the anxiety. Because of this, I was unable to take any psilocybin to go back into dreams. The Klonopin was stronger than any other licit or illicit drug I had ever taken. I thought it was crazy that weed was illegal, but this stuff was legal. When I turned my head, the room would rotate slowly and come into focus about five seconds later.

Despite being totally zoned out, I somehow managed to complete my thesis. I stayed at the university after I graduated to conduct research with Saxxon. I also finally made it to the six-month mark to get my last round of blood tests, but still didn't believe it, so kept testing for another six months. Fortunately, everything came back clean. However, my OCD elevated and was completely out of control. I now saw infected fluids everywhere I looked and would have daily freak outs. I wore gloves as to not touch doorknobs or gas pumps for a fear there was blood on the surface. I sealed up cuts on my body with several layers of epoxy and tape. I avoided crowds so I wouldn't have to shake hands or get sneezed, spit, or coughed on. I wouldn't step on cracks or walk through high grass for a fear of stepping on needles. I stopped eating in public because of the way the chefs or wait staff handled the food, cups, or utensils. I was afraid to sit on chairs for a fear of something soaking through my pants. I stopped dating, dreaming, having fun … I stopped living. Eventually, I decided not to leave the house. Dina and Saxxon were both concerned. Even though both were trained in psychology, OCD and anxiety orders were not their specialty. Dina found a colleague who was based in

Albany that I began seeing for therapy. We tried a variety of cognitive behavioral therapy and exposure and response prevention techniques, but nothing seemed to work. I also tried a slew of drugs, including antidepressants, benzodiazepines, anti-psychotics, various supplements, and a range of illegal drugs, but nothing helped. Most of the drugs skewed my entire equilibrium. I was tired but couldn't sleep, hungry but couldn't eat, and had no sex drive or interest in dating. I had no interest in living. The only thing that seemed to get me out of the spiral when was I started dreaming about the blonde on the dock, but I had no idea who she was or if she was from the past, present, or future.

The medication and state of depression further decreased my ability to dream. The drugs would knock me out and interfere with my REM sleep. Our research on the end of the world came to a halt. The only things I would see were germ or disease related, and I couldn't tell what was real or not. On one particular night, a friend of mine from undergraduate was in town and I decided to meet him out for a drink. I reached for my beer and took a swig, and then realized the beer belonged to some sketchy guy with bad oral hygiene. I had a panic attack and passed out on the ground.

During my blackout, I had a series of strange dreams, the first being that I was playing coed Division 1 basketball for Syracuse University with Dwayne "the Pearl" Washington, Kobe Bryant, Olympic runner Allyson Felix, and Dan, my best friend growing up. Jim Boeheim put me in off the bench and I lit it up with twenty-seven points, getting the team into the tournament. Bill Clinton congratulated us at the end of the game. The second dream I remember was attending a Buffalo Bills game with Jerry Garcia who gave a speech at halftime about how he was sober. I never knew what to make of these random dreams and if they required further attention or if I should try to go back into them. At one point, Dina did warn me about over-analyzing every dream. Sometimes, dreams were just dreams, or as Dina put it, an "abstract montage of my memories, fears, and desires."

I woke up sometime later in a laboratory facility. The mysterious blonde-haired woman I had been dreaming about was standing over me. I smiled at her, she smiled back, but then a man in a lab coat injected me with something and the room went black.

130

# 25

Melanie Merriman's plan seemed to be working as conceived. Three months had gone by since she captured Larry Martin in 2002 and quarantined him in a hidden laboratory with Harold Mitchell and two other scientists. The lab was being funded by millionaire Ned Beaumont. Beaumont's team stole software developed by Swiss engineers that could manipulate dreams. The software, named OC17 by the Swiss, could connect to a chip inserted in a subject's head. When the subject would fall asleep and enter the dream cycle, the dreams could be projected onto a monitor. The goal was to be able to re-enter dreams that took place in the past to control and change the outcome, ultimately changing the present, and to capitalize on dreams that took place in the future. Before Melanie from the year 2020 told her 1998 self about Larry, she was only one of four people that the software seemed to work on. Her boyfriend, Matthew Brennan, realized the potential of the dreaming ability and brought her to Harold Mitchell about a year before her future-self visited herself in 1998.

It seems the Swiss discovered that the software only worked in people with an extremely over-active basal ganglia and/or abnormal brain functional connectivity in the hypothalamus. Since Harold Mitchell was a neurologist, he was able to gain access to thousands of medical records with the help of a computer hacker supplied by Beaumont named Douglas Lynch. Melanie had an overactive basal ganglion that caused extreme anxiety and body dysmorphic disorder. Mitchell offered her relief from her mental suffering in exchange for access to her dreams. Over the years, Harold was only able to find a dozen or so people with this abnormality. Out of these twelve, he was only able to keep four that were useful. The other eight mysteriously disappeared. Each of the "dream makers," as they became known, was given a number. Since Melanie was the first recruit, she was referred to as Dream Maker Number One. Dream Maker Number Two was a guy in his thirties named Justin, Dream Maker Number Three was a young girl about sixteen named Claire, and Dream Maker Number Four's name was Bryan.

***

I later discovered that I became Dream Maker Number Five. After running several tests, Harold determined that I was rare. I had both an overactive basal ganglia and abnormality in my hypothalamus, which made my dream sensitivity exceptional.

Apparently, Beaumont's immediate goal was to make more money by being able to predict future market trends, outcomes to sporting events, or whether certain investments in the present would be lucrative in the future. I also discovered his strong desire to go back and change things in the past that didn't suit him. One of the most disturbing things Beaumont was trying to change was the abolition of slavery in 1863. Beaumont was a known white nationalist and was openly racist against non-white citizens. His ultimate goal was to create an all-white society of people with "superior" genes.

Mitchell and Merriman gave Larry a high dose of psilocybin to prevent hemorrhaging and seizures when in a past dream state.

"It seems the only thing coming up are dreams of you, Melanie. Has he met you?"

"No, we never met. I uploaded a love fantasy of myself into his chip. This way, he'll trust me and any premonition dreams warning him about us will be wiped out."

"Really? What about me?" Harold said with concern.

"You're on your own, Harold. You'll have to concoct a scenario to upload where he trusts you."

Just then, a dream of an older man dying from lung cancer appeared from Larry's dream on the monitor.

Wait, what's this?"

Melanie did a quick facial analysis on the man in the dream.

"Ahh, that's his uncle, Edward Martin."

In the dream, Ed was in hospice surrounded by a medical staff.

"There's your in, Harold. Project yourself as one of the doctors."

"Brilliant," Harold exclaimed.

Harold was able to take images of himself and montage them onto the doctor's face in Larry's dream.

"We'll first need to get him to go into the dream about our space colony to see what else he knows. Then we need to wipe that memory from him altogether." Harold explained.

"That should be easy. Don't we have renderings of the space colony and a computer simulation of the meteor shower with the nuclear missiles?"

"Indeed, we do, Melanie. Let's upload the images."

"Won't Lawrence and Saxxon be able to see these dreams as well?" Melanie asked Harold.

Just then, Doug Lynch popped his head up from his computer.

"That shouldn't be a problem. I'm going to alter the images before they're transmitted to Ms. Lawrence's terminal."

Lynch went on. "See, this is what Dina Lawrence will see. Instead of travelling to our space colony in his dream, it'll just be Larry watching the movie *Moonraker* on an airplane. He'll fall asleep on the plane and wake up and think the space station was just a projection from the movie." Lynch went on. "Also, when she tries to view Larry's dreams, we'll be able to triangulate her location."

The uploaded images started to work. Larry was on one of the evacuation shuttles headed to the space colony.

"Wait, why is he on the escape shuttle?" Melanie asked.

Harold hypothesized. "Well, maybe we end up keeping this guy alive in the future after all."

"Well that makes sense," Melanie responded. "People with this dream sensitivity are rare. But it's funny, I've seen this exact scene before. It actually looks like one of my dreams."

"Really? Hmm. Interesting. We'll have to explore this later," Harold responded.

Larry's dream continued. Out of the window of the space shuttle, he could see nuclear missiles being launched at the meteors. But it seemed way too low in the earth's atmosphere. He then saw the meteors collide into Earth and suddenly, it was just one huge cloud of smoke. The shuttle then went on and boarded the space station. The station was a toroidal design that looked like a giant wheel rotating around a central axis.

Lynch chimed in. "It looks like he knows."

"Knows what?" Melanie asked.

"About the nuclear war heads," answered Harold. "But do you think he knows what we're doing with the missiles?"

"Not sure," answered Lynch. "Let's see what he does."

Larry ran off the space shuttle and tried to find someone in charge. He ran up to one of the officers.

"What happened? Did Earth survive the impact? Did the nuclear missiles work?"

The officer responded. "Mr. Martin, please get back in line. You'll be briefed about the status of Earth at your first orientation."

Larry went back into the line. A young girl standing behind him also seemed curious.

"Hey, did you see those nuclear missiles strike the meteors?"

Larry answered. "Yes, but it looks like they detonated as the meteors collided with Earth."

The girl responded, "Yes! That's what I thought as well. Wouldn't that make the destruction worse?"

"Yeah. I think so. What the hell is going on?"

Back at the lab, Melanie, Harold, and Doug were watching Larry's dream unfold on the monitor. Melanie chimed in. "Yeah, I think he knows. They are definitely responsible for releasing the information to the public."

Lynch was irritated. "All right Mitchell, he's seen enough. Wake him up!"

In the dream, Mitchell projected a security guard overhearing Larry talking to the young girl. The security guard zapped Larry with a stun gun. Just then, Larry woke up in the lab.

***

I woke up and didn't know where the hell I was. Two creepy guys and the beautiful woman who was recurring in my dreams were standing over me. I also saw three others asleep in recliners next to me. I recognized one of the guys in the dream I had of my uncle on his death bed but was unsure what he was doing in the room and something didn't look right on him. His face was more distorted than it was in the dream. I went to get to my feet, but realized I was strapped to the bed.

"What the hell are these straps? Who the hell are you?"

I started to get agitated. In addition to my OCD, I also have a fear of entrapment. I always had to sit in the back of a room near an exit and had to have my back to the wall in restaurants. I also quit flying in the early nineteen-nineties. Flying is four of my fears—heights, entrapment, germs from the recycled air, and crowds of people. Dina told me she would work on this with me some time once we figured out how the world was going to end.

Just then, the beautiful blonde walked over towards me and sat on the corner of the bed. She put her hand on my head and gently stroked my hair.

"Hey Larry. It's me, Melanie. Do you recognize me?'

Just then, I had an image of swimming out to a floating dock in a lake. I remember checking Melanie out on the beach. She looked like an angel and I knew she was way out of my league. Then, she followed me in the water and swam out to the dock. We talked for about two hours. We had so much in common that it was surreal. I was a bit skeptical, but I went with it.

"Yes, I recognize you. I have been seeing you in dreams at a barn and on a floating dock. And you were the one who picked me up after I passed out at the bar."

"Indeed. And I had the same dream, and that's why I brought you here."

"Where's here? Where are we?"

"This is a laboratory where we study people with dream sensitivity. Until now, there were only four other people we have found with this ability." Melanie responded.

"So how did you find me?"

"Like I said, I dreamt of you on the dock as well. I ran a facial recognition on you and was able to track you down."

"Really? You can see things before they happen as well?"

"Yup."

"And what about dreams that take place in the past? Can you go back into them and change what happens?"

"Well, we're working on that."

"So why am I tied down? Why are you monitoring my dreams?"

Harold chimed in. "Mr. Martin, we're here to help you and in the process, you can help us, too."

I had been fiddling with the straps and just pulled my arm free. Melanie went to tie it back down, but Harold interrupted her.

"No, you can leave him free, Melanie. I don't think he will go anywhere after we explain to him what we're doing."

"What are you doing and how is it that I can help?" I asked

"Mr. Martin, our organization is a private research company funded by Ned Beaumont. Our purpose is to prevent disaster. We're utilizing the same hardware that Ms. Lawrence put into your head. We're trying to locate more people like you and Melanie that can interact with the hardware."

"How did you know about Dina?" I asked somewhat suspiciously.

"We were able to track her through your OC17 chip."

"So, can I call her and let her know about this lab?"

"No. That won't be necessary. We've already sent someone for her. She should be here shortly."

Just then, Doug Lynch came up and whispered in Harold's ear. "Harold, we found Dina Lawrence."

"Ahh. Great news. Mr. Martin, your associate Ms. Lawrence should be here momentarily."

Later that evening, Melanie suggested to Harold that she take me outside to get some fresh air. After all, I had been in a dream-induced coma for about three months. Harold agreed. The facility was located on the western end of Martha's Vineyard in Aquinnah and escape would be quite difficult, especially given the fact that they could track exactly where I was because of the OC17 chip in my head. Beaumont's security team also controlled the ferry, so any attempt to board would be fruitless. Melanie and I walked along the beach. The warm misty air and the sound of the ocean was therapeutic for me, but my distrust of Melanie and this science experiment prevented me from truly enjoying it.

Melanie was quite bright. She grew up in Madison, Wisconsin and had a variety of degrees in sociology, psychology, and computer science. She was an accomplished violinist and pianist, had strong knowledge of the arts, was an avid reader, and had a love for birds. It blew my mind that a person so bright could be brainwashed by a guy like Ned

136

Beaumont. Melanie was a progressive feminist, and Beaumont was a sexist. She believed in science, where Beaumont often mocked or ignored it. I decided to just be blunt.

"So how did you end up working for a fascist like Beaumont?"

"A fascist?" she responded defensively. "Why do you think he's a fascist?"

"Ahh, are you kidding me? Where do I begin? He fires or frames people who don't agree with him, he has purchased several news agencies and is running false propaganda, he's an admitted white supremist, and he's vowed to completely close our borders to immigrants if he is ever elected president. Is that enough?"

Melanie chuckled a bit. "Yeah, he is a fascist, isn't he?"

"Well, yeah. So why are you working for him?"

Her laughter quickly ceased. "Oh, it's a long story."

"Try me."

"First of all, I don't consider what I do working for Beaumont. I work for an agency funded by Beaumont."

"Potato, po-*tah*-to," I responded.

"No really. The research we are doing is cutting edge. I mean the ability to alter past events and manipulate future events using dreams is amazing. We can prevent wars and disasters, discover cures to diseases, and save people from harm or even death. Truly, you of all people should appreciate this, Larry? After all, there are only five of us thus far who have this ability."

"I agree. But it's *our* ability. Beaumont and his team are using our abilities to help them make money so they can build a space colony for the elite and watch the rest of us die in a meteor collision."

Melanie laughed. "Are you sure about that Larry? You ever think we may have programmed that dream into your head?"

"Bullshit! I've been having these visions long before I met you."

"Are you sure about that? After all, I was sent back in time through a dream to see what you knew. How do you know we didn't hack your chip? And even so, do all of your dreams come true?"

"Actually, yes, most of the bad ones come true. I think I'm around ninety-five percent."

"Ha. More like seventy-five percent. And what makes you think the space colony is a bad thing even if it is or isn't true? I mean, after all, we would be saving humanity, right?"

"Yeah, but at what cost? Beaumont is hand-picking the make-up of his colony. It's all white, Christian, neo-Nazi, super-models."

"Even if that was true, which it's not, you have to think realistically. Not everyone can be saved. They only can choose so many people. There has to be a cut-off."

"So, you're okay with a Hitler-esque colony?"

"That is not what I—" Melanie stopped herself. I think she realized she was admitting this whole thing was true. I continued.

"What about the nuclear warheads?"

"What nuclear warheads?" Melanie seemed genuinely confused.

"Come on. You've seen what I've seen. Beaumont and his team are going to pretend to implode the meteors with nuclear warheads, thereby looking like heroes. However, the real plan is to make the destruction worse and more widespread to ensure that all the human race is wiped out. Oh, I've seen it!"

"That's ridiculous," Melanie responded. "I've never seen anything like that."

Well, you better look again."

Melanie shrugged off the conversation. "I'm over-heated. I'm going swimming."

Melanie took her dress off and stripped down to her underwear. "Are you coming in?"

"I don't like the ocean. I only swim in lakes."

"That's right. I forgot. You watched *Jaws* too many times in college, right?"

Just then, I remembered Melanie might know more about me than I anticipated. After all, our brains were connected for the past three months. But I didn't remember dreaming about sharks in the past three months. How did she know that?

"Hey, I didn't have any shark dreams since we met. How did you know?"

Melanie was up to her waist now and couldn't hear me because of the crashing of the waves. I decided, what the hell. Even if this woman was evil, how many chances do I get to swim with underwear-clad, beautiful blondes? I dropped trow and headed into the ocean. Melanie giggled.

"It looks like the water is a little bit cold, huh Larry?"

I looked down and realized my penis was sticking out through the slot in my boxer shorts and it wasn't my best showing. Indeed, the cold water had done its part.

"Right, there's a bit of shrinkage there, huh?"

Melanie laughed. "Oh, don't worry, I've seen it before, there's nothing to worry about."

Again, where did she see me naked before?

We swam in the ocean like two giddy school kids. I almost forgot I was being held prisoner to help in the annihilation of humanity.

Our beach strolls and naked swims became a regular thing. However, every time I tried to take things a bit further, Melanie would fade away and I would be left alone. One time, we were holding each other in the ocean. I kissed her and slowly moved my hands over her, and she started doing the same to me. Then suddenly, we were both clothed on the beach and she was acting very distant. It's like I was in a movie and someone was fast-forwarding the sex scenes. It was very frustrating, to say the least.

# 26

Dina Lawrence was in her lab when the images came up on the monitor. She quickly picked up her cell phone and dialed Scott Saxxon.

"Scott, I found Larry. He is in a dream right now!"

"Really? Where is he?"

"Well, I'm having a difficult time triangulating his signal. It keeps bouncing all over the planet."

"Hmmm. That doesn't sound right. What are the images that you are seeing?"

"He is on a plane and he is watching the film *Moonraker*," answered Dina.

Saxxon interrupted. "On a plane? Larry Martin? Is it a nightmare that he is having?'

"No. He seems quite relaxed. His vitals look good."

"Dina, something is wrong. Larry hasn't flown in a plane since 1997. If he was dreaming about being in a plane, he'd be panicking!"

"Holy shit! You're right. He mentioned that was one of his fears when we first met."

Just then, Dina's monitors turned blue and her computer was locked.

"Scott, my computer just crashed."

"Dina, get out of there. Get out of there now!"

A team of three mercenaries busted through the massage parlor in the back of Dina's lab. The lady at the desk tried to smooth talk one of the men, but he threw her across the room. Dina could hear the raucous. She gathered a few things and ran out the front door.

Another three mercenaries were staked out in the front and ran after her. The mercenaries on the inside grabbed all of Dina's equipment and torched the lab. The lead hit man tapped his earpiece to contact Bryce Patrick.

"Mr. Patrick, Ms. Lawrence is on the run. Should we take her out?"

"Negative. We need to question her to see who else knows about the project."

Dina ran to Devil's Hole in the Niagara Gorge and frantically stumbled down the steep trail. When she arrived at the gorge, the mercenary team had her surrounded. There was a helicopter in the air. She considered jumping into the river, but the Whirlpool rapids were much too treacherous. She put her hands in the air and surrendered. Just then, another mercenary pulled the trigger and hit Dina just above the heart. She fell backward into the Whirlpool rapids and floated down the river toward Lake Ontario.

# 27

Back at his office in Hayes Hall, Scott Saxxon logged into a satellite that he used to use when he worked for NASA. He zoomed the camera of the satellite over the building and just as he expected, he could see a team approaching the building in standard tactical formation. Saxxon pulled his hard drive and slipped down a back staircase that led to a tunnel beneath the building that connected to the Buffalo Metro light rail tunnel. Saxxon jumped onto the train and could see another team of three mercenaries surrounding his Pontiac Fiero in the parking lot. Scott jumped off the Metro and ran down the side streets several blocks to get back to his house in the Elmwood neighborhood. As he was running, he dialed his wife's cell phone and told her to get out of the house and head to the rendezvous point.

As Scott approached his house, it was eerily quiet. No lights were on and there was little action in the neighborhood. He entered the house from the back door and quickly grabbed a pre-packed camping backpack. But out of the corner of his eye, he saw a trail of blood. He walked into the living room. He was too late. The mercenaries had killed his wife. Saxxon's eyes filled with tears and he couldn't breathe. Suddenly, a loud noise and flashing lights came from the sky. It was a helicopter. Several armed mercenaries came up his driveway. Saxxon ran through his backyard and jumped over the fence. He cut through several other yards and ended up on the Elmwood strip. He slipped into a strip bar and ran toward the bathroom. The team followed him in. It was like they were tracking him. Even though he worked for the government, he never had a locator chip injected, so it couldn't have been that. To be safe, he took off all his clothes and threw his watch into the toilet. He then put on one of his wife's disguises that he had in his backpack and hid the backpack in the ceiling tiles. Much to his luck, it was a "stripper" disguise. He went into the dressing room at the strip bar and sat down amongst a group of women. No one seemed to notice that he was out of place. Many of the strip bars in the area allowed anyone off the street to strip on certain nights. It was like an open-mic night for strippers. Luckily, this was one of those nights.

The swat team entered the dressing room but were confronted by several bouncers from the strip club. This bought Saxxon more time. Saxxon heard one of the mercenaries say, "Pull out. He ditched his tracker in the bathroom and he's not in the bar." His disguise must have been better than he thought. He went back into the bathroom and grabbed his pack. But Saxxon was still curious as to who planted the tracking device on him.

Saxxon waited out the swat team on the streets. This required him to go on stage and perform. Luckily, there were several drag-queens stripping that night, so he fit right in. He did so well, he thought he might have a lucrative backup career as a cross-dressing stripper if his professor gig somehow went awry. He then slipped out the back, hailed a cab, and headed for Niagara Falls.

When he arrived at Dina's lab, he could see from the outside that the place had been torched on the inside. All of Dina's equipment was destroyed and the massage parlor in the back was abandoned. Since the lab was modelled after the Kiva in Baldy Hall at the University at Buffalo, Scott knew all the secrets — including the hiding places. He cleared off the debris in the back of the circular room under one of the seats and lifted the floor tile. As he suspected, there was an external hard drive hidden under the floor. Scott set up his laptop and triangulated the signal from Dina's cell phone. It was moving quickly and was headed up the river to Lake Ontario. He also plugged in the hard drive to see what was on it. He could see Larry's dream files and the OC17 software, but he knew he shouldn't activate the software since it could be tracked.

Scott stole a car from the street and drove as fast as he could toward the cell phone signal. He drove past Lewiston towards Youngstown, New York. He then saw several sheriffs, state troopers, and rescue vehicles at one of the houses near the outlet of the Niagara River and Lake Ontario. It seems some kids were fishing in the river and found a body. It was quite common for bodies to be found in this location, especially in the spring when all the ice melted. Niagara Falls was still a popular place for people to commit suicide and often their bodies would be chopped up in the Robert Moses Power Plant's turbines. However, the body being pulled out of the river seemed to be intact. Scott snuck up into the scene and was able to get a good view. He was shocked to see it was Dina. Just as he was going to approach the scene to identify the body, the team of mercenaries showed up again. Holding back tears, Scott took a bunch of photos and slipped into his stolen car and drove away.

# 28

For the next few months, I had dreams that were not in my sub-conscious. They were not past events nor were they fears or desires. They could have been future events, but I usually had some connection with or knowledge of the event. These dreams were completely different, such as the stock market, political outcomes, sporting events that I didn't even watch, relationships between people I had never seen, and visions of places I had never been. I knew Harold Mitchell's team was manipulating my dreams, but there was not much I could do about it. I tried to manipulate a few outcomes, but the cocktail of hallucinogens they were using prevented me from controlling the dreams. The only thing familiar and pleasant in any of the dreams was Melanie. She seemed to either be with me or in the background somewhere. I really wished Dina would contact me to analyze this, but strangely, I hadn't heard from her. She wasn't retuning my emails or phone calls.

Harold also gave me a tour of the technology and how it interacted with the dream makers. Harold's system seemed to be much more advanced than what Dina and I were using. In addition to the five of us dream makers, Harold had a team of animators that could computer generate entire scenes and implant them into our OC17 chips. This was like what Dina and I did by scanning still images and video clips into the system, but much more advanced. Often, Harold's team would create a scene and it would become part of our dreams, but we were unable to alter anything in the dream if it was in the past and unable to change an event in the future. Harold discovered that we could not alter the past or future from the artificial implantation animations unless we had either dreamt the scene before on our own or had an actual memory of the event. This was why they couldn't just go back in time and kill me sometime before I had the end of the world dream or just prevent me from being born in the first place. Harold's findings about personal gain also seemed to hold true with the other dreamers. However, since the gain was for Beaumont, Harold was still able to capitalize on the dream makers' premonitions. I also was able to overhear Harold and Doug when they were working on a way to tweak the chip so they could view things from the dream makers even when they were awake. This freaked me out, to say the least. It was a real-time monitoring system and a way to ensure we didn't expose Beaumont's plan. Everything we did and saw could be monitored. It was like a George Orwell nightmare come true. Luckily, they couldn't get it to work. They were experimenting with it on Claire, which was even creepier seeing she was only a sixteen-year old girl.

Melanie and I continued to walk along the beach and swim in the ocean. We also took long walks in the meadows, went hiking, bowling, and went to see live music. It was amazing how similar her taste in music and film was to mine. One night, we went to see a jazz trio in Martha's Vineyard. We went to the back of the room to get away from the crowds and sat down at a secluded table in the corner. We started talking about past relationships—things we like and things we didn't like. A piece of her hair was out of place, so I decided to fix it. I ended up putting my other hand on the other side of her head and kissed her. This time, the images didn't cut out. She looked shocked when I pulled away.

"Sorry," I said. "Was that weird?"

"No, but we can't. We just can't."

"Why not?"

"I have to tell you something, Larry, but you'll probably hate me."

"Well, I'm not even sure I like you yet. But what is it?"

"I'm kind of engaged."

"Engaged? What the hell?"

"You didn't know I was engaged? I thought you knew?'

"No. No. I didn't know."

"And what did you think this ring was for on my left hand?"

"I never saw a ring. Believe me, the first thing I do is sweep for a ring."

"Who is the guy anyway?"

"His name is Matt. We met in graduate school."

"What does he do for a living?" I inquired.

"He works for Beaumont. He's his personal advisor."

"Sounds lame."

"You're just jealous, Larry."

"Yeah, you're damn right I'm jealous."

"Stop berating me, Larry. You're starting to frighten me."

Suddenly, I heard the voices of the scientists from the lab but couldn't see their faces.

"This is getting out of control. Wake her up!"

Suddenly, Melanie vanished in thin air, and I was sitting in the club alone.

\*\*\*

Melanie woke up from her dream chair in the lab. Harold Mitchell was standing over her and two other figures were looming in the background. One was Bryce Patrick, and the other was Melanie's fiancé, Matt Brennan. Matt was a graduate of Harvard Law and was responsible for drafting the evacuation plan and the selection criteria for the inhabitants of the colony. His family owned the pharmaceutical giant named after his surname, "Brennan." They had considerable wealth and political influence. Matt initially financed and organized the entire dreamer research program shortly after he discovered Melanie had abilities. He utilized the dreams to nearly triple his fortune and eventually teamed up with Ned Beaumont to further enhance their vision of a new society, which would ultimately be used in the construction of the space colony, the space shuttles, and ten resorts that would be used as holding areas to shuttle people to the space colony.

At least half of the colony were friends, family, or business colleagues of Beaumont, Brennan, and Bryce Patrick. They considered scaling back the population, so it was just this group, but they still needed medical staff, engineers, astronauts, facilities staff, and agricultural specialists to grow and supply food. At one point, Beaumont proposed just taking a thousand people and bringing vials of sperm and eggs with select DNA, but being the juvenile he was, he thought it would be more fun to make it a game where people competed for a spot. Beaumont was the host of several reality TV shows. One of the shows pitted people against each other in a series of physical and mental challenges. The winners would be given a free residence at one of Beaumont's ten resorts and free voyage to a future hotel in space that Beaumont would advertise on the show every week. Advertising the space colony as a "hotel" was a great way to hide the true intention of the project in plain sight.

Since the show started, Beaumont had twenty years until the meteor collision to accumulate a pool of people to fill the other spots on the colony. Matt Brennan was in charge of screening the applicants. Every year, they would get close to ten thousand applicants to be on the show. The applicants were required to provide their birth certificates, resumes, photos, copies of their medical records, results from an IQ test, and transcripts from high school and college. Since the show included physical challenges, Beaumont and Brennan were able to bend the law so that those selected to be on the show had to undergo more extensive medical tests. The tests screened for disease and any genetic abnormalities. Two hundred and fifty people were selected each year, so over twenty years, the remaining five thousand people would be selected. Obviously, there would be some attrition. Some people may not have chosen the free residence, the space trip, or both. But Beaumont loved this. Each week on the show, he'd review all the people who dropped out or refused to live at one of his resorts. He'd publicly berate them, call them names, or fabricate entire stories that would defame their character. So essentially, remaining at one of his resorts became a whole separate competition that was continued after people left the show. Those that stayed were obviously rewarded both financially and with public praise.

Brennan's criteria for the colony was simple: they had to be white/Anglo, Christian, English speaking, straight, good looking, and disease and genetic abnormality free. Higher education was not required. In fact, Beaumont preferred people to be less educated and less intelligent than himself—especially the women. He despised intelligent women. Although Beaumont claimed he was a genius, his real IQ was only around ninety, which is considered low average. Thus, people at that or lower were preferred. He figured he'd have enough "smart" people in his medical and engineering division.

*** 

Melanie's relationship with Larry concerned Matt. He began to yell.

148

"What the hell is this, Melanie? You were only supposed to get him to trust you, not get him to fall in love with you!"

"It's not my fault," Melanie responded.

Harold Mitchell piped in. "She's right. Actually, Mr. Martin is jumping into her dreams."

Matt Brennan was getting more angered. "Wait. They're sharing dreams?"

Harold brought up the playback from Larry's dream on the space colony and several of Melanie and Larry's beach dreams.

"Indeed, Mr. Brennan. And it looks like they are more than friends. What is going on Ms. Merriman?"

"Wait, this is bullshit. You told me to get him to trust me, so I did." Melanie tried to explain.

"So, does that include naked swims in the ocean?" Matt responded.

"I'm afraid Mr. Brennan is right," Bryce Patrick chimed in. "Ms. Merriman is becoming too much of a risk. She and Mr. Martin seem to be connected in their dream state. He sees what she sees, and she sees what he sees."

"What do you suggest we do, Mr. Patrick?" Harold Mitchell asked.

"Merriman is off the project."

Matt interrupted. "Wait a minute. That is my goddamned fiancé you're talking about."

Matt grabbed Melanie by the arm. "Now look Mel, this is serious. They could expel you from the colony. You've compromised the whole mission. I can save you, but I just need to know one thing: Do you love Larry Martin?"

Melanie looked at Matt and her eyes welled up. He grabbed her tighter and shook her. She pulled her arm away from him and told him the truth.

"If I said no, I'd be lying."

Matt pushed her away.

"Wait! But it's not like that," Melanie explained. "I still love you, Matt. Yes, I love Larry, but it's more like a brotherly-love."

"What the hell does that mean? You shouldn't have any feelings for him. You're a goddamned scientist ... start acting like one!"

149

Melanie regained her composure. "You know, you're right Matt. I wasn't being objective."

"No, you weren't. You totally flaked out. You better hope Bryce doesn't get you expelled from the project, or worse yet, get you kicked off the colony."

"Come on. They still need me."

"Don't be so sure, Melanie. Bryce is paranoid. If he thinks you are leaking pertinent information in your dreams, who's telling what he'll do. I'm going to have to smooth talk him."

"Well, I'll stop communicating with Larry in my dreams. That's it. No more connections."

"Yeah, but he's the one jumping into your dreams, Mel. How can you prevent that?"

"I'll have Harold program in a block."

"I hope that will work, because otherwise, your boy Larry is fish food."

"Don't say that Matt! He's, he's ..." Melanie couldn't finish. Matt interrupted.

"He's what? Don't say any more, Melanie. Let me see what I can arrange with Bryce and Doug."

Matt stormed out and locked Melanie inside the room. On the other side of the glass, Melanie could see Matt talking to Bryce Patrick and Doug Lynch, but couldn't hear a thing since she was in a soundproof room. She carefully studied their lip movements. She thought that maybe she could see it more closely in a dream and determine what they were saying. Then, the three of them noticed her watching and turned off the light.

"Matt, we have a situation with your fiancé," Bryce Patrick exclaimed. "I just briefed Beaumont and he wants to fire her from the project."

"Wait, no. You can't fire her. She'll lose her place on the escape shuttle. Can't we just wipe her memory or program in a virus so they can't see each other's dreams?"

Harold chimed in. "We're one step ahead of you, Mr. Brennan. Any time Larry thinks of or sees Melanie in a dream, we have programmed a fear response in Mr. Martin. Over time, the fear will force him to avoid Melanie in any dreams."

"Will it work?" Bryce asked curiously.

"In theory, yes."

"Well, good. It looks like you lucked out, Mr. Brennan. But if this doesn't work, we'll have to resort to other measures."

Matt looked concerned but shook it off. "It will work, Bryce."

After Bryce left the room, Matt took Harold aside.

"Harold, I wonder if we can tweak things in Melanie's dreams a little more."

"I'm not sure I understand, Matt."

"Well, even though she doesn't claim to love Larry, I want to make sure she doesn't."

"Ahh, I know exactly what you mean, Mr. Brennan. You want me to make him a jerk?"

"Exactly," Matt responded excitedly. "Can it be done?"

"I'll get to work on it right away. I agree it will be extra insurance that these two don't communicate."

# 29

For the next few months, Melanie and I were placed in separate rooms. Any time I started to dream about her, I'd get nightmares that would wake me up out of my sleep. It was usually ghosts standing over me, but I also had several of being chased and not being able to scream or run, falling out of a building, drowning, getting buried alive, or getting hit by a bus. My contamination OCD would also enter my dreams. Like the time in the bar before I passed out, I'd drink out of bottle and realize it was someone else's or I would get spit on in public. The list of incidents was endless, and they didn't seem to stop. Eventually, any time I had a dream about Melanie, I'd try to avoid it and change the course of the dream. I must admit, I missed her. I missed our rendezvous on the beach, even if they were fictional dreams designed to get me to trust her. Even though she was engaged to a member of Beaumont's crooked cabinet, I realized that I had feelings for her, whether they were fabricated in the dreams or not. And I was convinced she felt the same about me.

One night, I dreamt I was back in my undergraduate days. It was a Saturday night and I was out with my girlfriend Natasha, a Russian gal from New Jersey. We were at a local college bar named PJ's. The bathroom was horrible. It was just a long trough with no partitions. I had to urinate badly, but it just wouldn't come out—total stage fright. I swear, bathroom design could be a thesis project. Privacy, acoustics, accessibility, ventilation, and sanitation in most bathrooms need to be addressed. You shouldn't have to physically touch a seat to move it up and down. You should press a button and the seat should go into the wall and be sterilized. Anyway, I ran outside to the back alley and found a quiet spot to take a squirt. Two thugs cornered me on my way out of the ally and wanted to sell me hash. To prevent getting mugged, I bought the hash. I tried to get back into the bar, but the bouncer wouldn't let me back in. Suddenly, I had the urge to go to the bathroom again but this time it wasn't just urine. There was nowhere to go, so I frantically ran up to Hayes Hall on the south campus at the University at Buffalo. I entered the building and ran into the basement where the bathrooms were located. Suddenly, my urge to go to the bathroom was gone, and I heard footsteps of someone approaching. The hall was dark, but I knew that parted hair profile well. It was Scott Saxxon.

"Scott? Holy shit! Am I glad to see you."

Then I remembered I was in the past, so of course he was alive.

"Hurry. Get into the film developing room."

"What?"

"Just get in. No time to explain."

Scott turned on one of the developing lights. It had a reddish glow.

"What the hell is going on, Scott?"

"Do you still have to take a crap?"

"No. Strangely I don't. How did you know I had to go?"

"Because I set all this up."

"Set what up?" I asked.

"Well, that's where it gets cool. I was able to get a hold of some of Dina's files on your dreams that she kept on a hard drive. I figured out how to hack into your chip. This is from some of the imagery you dreamt of back in 1993. I couldn't find your signal for four years but then yesterday, out of the blue, your signal was loud and clear."

"I have to say, this is a pretty accurate rendition on a typical night in my college years. I hated the bathrooms at the bar, so I used to walk up here and go," I responded.

"So where exactly am I in real-time, Scott?"

"Well, that is where I am having some difficulty. They keep scrambling the signal. I'm getting readings all over the world. Do you remember anything when they took you?"

"No."

"Larry, in 2002, you were kidnapped by a white nationalist group led by millionaire, now billionaire, Ned Beaumont. Do you remember?"

"No."

"Okay, what is the last thing you remember?"

"Well, I was at a bar with a friend of mine from undergraduate that was visiting. I drank out of someone else's beer bottle, had a panic attack, and passed out on the floor. Then Melanie picked me up and took me."

"Who's Melanie? Is she the blonde you keep dreaming about?"

"Yeah. And I think I kind of dig her, too."

"Oh boy. Look Larry, I know she's sharp, but she's part of Beaumont's group. She kidnapped you, brought you to their lab, and they have been extracting information from your dreams for the past four years to help them make money, fix the elections, and help them with their supremacist colony in outer space."

"Yes, I know. They are somehow able to prevent me from controlling the dreams. But wait a minute, four years? What year am I dreaming in?"

"2006. Four years have gone by since the black-out."

"Holy shit," I responded, shocked by the passage of time.

Scott answered grimly. "I'm afraid so. Time flies while you are in a dream state."

Scott went on. "And this Melanie, I think she might be responsible for …." Scott suddenly stopped talking.

"For what?" I asked Scott.

Then Scott continued. "Larry, we don't have much time, but I have some more difficult news. Dina, your family, my wife … they are all gone."

"What? What do you mean?"

"Beaumont's team killed them all."

"No! I didn't see any of this. It can't be. Are you sure?"

I started crying inconsolably. Scott started crying as well. He put his hand on my shoulder to console me.

"Yes. They know we expose their entire scheme sometime before year 2020 and are ensuring they eliminate anyone we may have told that could compromise their plan."

"And when do we actually expose them?" I asked shakily, still in shock from the deaths.

"I don't know. But they are definitely manipulating the past at some time in the future," Scott answered.

After about twenty minutes of sobbing, I looked at Scott with great determination.

"Goddamnit Scott, I'll bring them back. I'll go back in a dream and bring them back. Dina, your wife, my family—all of them!"

"The last I checked, you haven't been able to raise the dead, Larry. Has Beaumont's team been able to figure out how to do that yet?"

"No, but Melanie and I together may be able to figure it out." I was still in shock. But Scott continued.

"Look, Larry, I know you're in shock, but we don't have much time.

"Wait, Scott, won't they be able to see this dream?"

"In theory, no. I coded a virus into the dream, so they should be seeing a different image on their monitors."

"I hope you made it a good one."

"Oh yeah. It's an orgy dream with Donna. They'll see a loop of her uncrossing her legs when she had no underwear on. That should keep them distracted. But we don't have much time. The Beaumont group will figure out that I hacked in a few minutes. You need to try and get outside their lab. That may descramble the transmission somewhat."

The image of Donna un-crossing her legs briefly gave me some relief from the panic attack I was having about learning of the deaths.

"I'm not sure I can get out, Scott. They have me bunkered down pretty tight."

"Well, what about Melanie? Can you convince her to help you?"

"Actually, they just separated us. They figured out that the two of us could jump into each other's dreams, so I guess that jeopardizes their plan somewhat."

"Wait, what? Holy shit Larry, you can share dreams with her? This is huge!"

"It was. But I think they programmed a virus into my dreams. I'm getting nightmares every time I see her face."

"Interesting. They are trying to simulate avoidance by capitalizing on your fears. Larry, you need to fight through those fears and get back into her head. This may be the key to ending this whole thing."

"What do you mean, ending it, Scott? Isn't the meteor collision inevitable?"

"No. We may still have a chance to mitigate it."

"How?"

"I'm working on that. But you need to get back in this woman's head. We may be able to use her if we can see her dreams just like they are using you."

"And maybe we can figure out a way to bring back Dina, my family, and your wife. Two heads in a dream are better than one."

"Maybe, Larry, but don't get your hopes up."

Just then, the dream ended, and I woke up in the lab. Harold and Doug were monitoring me at their stations and chuckling somewhat. I decided to make a joke.

"You could see right up her skirt, huh?"

Both men laughed. Saxxon's virus worked. They only saw Donna in my dream.

Harold let me take a bathroom break. I strolled down the halls, but the place was locked down incredibly tight. There were guards at every corner, cameras on the ceilings, and absolutely no windows. We must have been several stories underground. I was amazed Saxxon was even able to find the signal. But, when Melanie and I woke up from our bar dream, they must have disconnected the scrambler and gave Scott the window to find the chip in my head—the chip I wish I could pull out.

After my bathroom break, the guards escorted me to the cafeteria. Much to my surprise, Melanie was getting herself a cup of coffee. I walked over to her, but the guards grabbed me and pushed me away from her. I yelled her name. She pretended not to hear me. The guards escorted me to the other side of the cafeteria. Melanie walked by and put her hand on her boob and scratched it in a circular motion. This was something I used to do to try and pick up women in college. I used to scratch my own breast in hopes it would illicit some strange sexual attraction. It was totally stupid and never worked, but now Melanie was doing it to me. How did she know about this? Anyway, I took it as a code that she may have been on my side. I smiled back at her. Just then, the guard smacked me in my face with a night-stick. I could hear him say, "Quit looking at the broad," right before I blacked out.

***

Melanie went back into her private room. Melanie's room was a full, plush apartment with a kitchen, bathroom, hot tub, and a balcony. The room was on the ground level of the bunker above the lab portion.

Every time Melanie dreamt about Larry, she'd either see a disturbing image of him or she would wake up. The most common image she saw was of Larry strangling her. There were also ones of him as a misogynist, doing whatever it took to take advantage of women. The only image that seemed accurate was the one of Larry rubbing his own breasts. That's something Larry would do, she thought. Larry as a sexist womanizer made no sense, however. Melanie began to wonder if this was how Harold, Doug, and Matt decided to keep her from dream-communicating with Larry. After all, she was the first to implement this technique, seeing she was programming dreams into Larry's head. Melanie contemplated the dreams she had with Larry, or more specifically, which dreams were hers and which were his, and who jumped into the other one's dream. She didn't buy this evil perception of Larry and was upset that she was programmed to think so.

Matt then entered Melanie's room and interrupted her contemplating.

"Well, it seems our plan is working. We have prevented Larry from entering your dreams. You're lucky, you know, you could have lost your spot in the evacuation."

"Yeah, but at what cost? I'm not dreaming of anything lately."

"Nothing?" Matt said.

"Well, just nasty images of Larry. Was that part of the deal, Matt? To make me not care for him?"

"I don't know what you're talking about, Mel, but you're starting to sound psycho."

"I sure hope you're not manipulating me, Matt, because if you are—"

Matt cut off Melanie. "What? What are you going to do, Melanie? Do you realize they will kick you off the evacuation shuttle if they think that you are still communicating with Larry? Do you want that?"

"No, but I also don't want my dreams manipulated."

"It's for your own protection, Mel. You have a soft spot for this guy that could get you killed."

"So, these negative dreams are being fabricated?"

"I don't know. Harold and Doug built a block whenever you have a vision of Larry. Maybe that's just where your mind is going. I mean, you know nothing about this guy."

"I'm not stupid, Matt. I know you're threatened."

"Fuck you, Mel, fuck you. I'm not threatened by anything. Larry Martin is an insignificant low life. If you want to risk everything, then go to him. I don't give a shit. You'd be nothing without me anyway. I know of a hundred more women that would beg to be on that shuttle, and I'm their ticket."

"I think it's the other way around, Matt. I'm the one with abilities."

"Wrong. You're replaceable, Mel. You think you're special because of your dreaming ability, but you're not the only one out there. Harold has identified at least twenty other potential people with the same ability. So you're not special. Beaumont, Bryce, and I are the ones who decide the makeup of the colony. Not you. Remember that."

"Yeah, but I'm the one who can alter the timeline, so you remember that, you spineless prig."

"Is that a threat, Melanie? Because if so, I'll have Harold program your dreams into a state of horror that you can't even imagine."

"Get out of here, Matt, get out of my room."

After Matt left, Melanie went up to the mirror and looked at the spot where the OC17 chip was injected into her head. She knew how to take them in and out but needed an extraction gun. But if she removed the device, she wasn't sure if Beaumont's team would still need her. She wondered if she really wanted to be a part of this anymore. She fell asleep and dreamed she was floating in the air above Larry's apartment in Buffalo. Then, she was in a circular room with Larry and Dina Lawrence. She realized she was dream-sharing with Larry.

\*\*\*

After being knocked out by the guard, I woke up back in the lab. My head hurt, and I fell back asleep. I was dreaming I was back in the past in the circular lab with Dina in Niagara Falls. It was the night I was trying to warn her that I saw her floating in a river in a previous dream, but this time, I knew how it ended. I tried to tell Dina about her fate, but she didn't want to hear it. She closed her ears and sang loudly so she couldn't hear me.

"Larry, I don't want to know my fate," She explained.

The dream started getting hazy. I thought I was going to wake up, but then Melanie appeared.

Dina looked at her.

"You? What the hell are you doing here?" Dina asked.

158

Melanie responded, "Dina, I know you don't know me, but you need to listen to Larry."

"Wait a minute, you two can share dreams?" Dina asked inquisitively.

"Yes. But just shut up and listen to me. You are going to get shot and end up in the Niagara River."

Just like that, I was out of the dream and three creepy ghosts hovered over me. This was part of Harold Mitchell's program to block Melanie and I from dream sharing. I remembered what Saxxon said, so instead of freaking out and waking up swinging at the ghosts, I decided to talk to them. It turns out, they were a family that lived in my apartment back in 1841. I used to see them in my sleep all the time when I was home. Harold and Doug must have grabbed the images from my dream bank and used them to illicit fear when I saw Melanie.

As I talked with them, they weren't so scary. The women ghost then suddenly turned into Melanie.

"Larry?"

"Melanie?"

"How did you … it doesn't matter. We don't have much time. They will see we are communicating again."

I grabbed her by the side of her head and kissed her, but she quickly disappeared. A moment later, I woke up in the lab with someone kissing me. I looked up, and it was Melanie. Harold and Doug were not in the lab as it was three in the morning, but it looked like Melanie had knocked out the guard on duty.

"Larry, just shut up and listen to me. I'm taking your chip out."

Melanie put the gun in my head and pulled out the OC17 chip.

"Now take mine out."

"Are you sure? How do I—"

"Just point and squeeze the trigger right here," Melanie shouted.

Suddenly, the alarms went off on the system. I couldn't get Melanie's chip out in time.

"Oh shit! Our chips were armed. They'll be here any minute …"

Before Melanie could get another word out, the guards arrived at the lab. She kissed me and gave me a key, some wire cutters, and directions on how to get out of the lab. She then whispered in my ear, "You'll survive if you jump."

"Go, Larry. Get out of here."

"But what about you?"

"Don't worry. I'll tell them you attacked me. Now go. I'll be fine."

I ran to the backdoor and went through a maze of hallways to a freight elevator. I ran across a field but came to a security fence. I cut through the fence with the wire cutters Melanie gave me and ran down a road. I came to the edge of a cliff about one hundred feet above the ocean. I was suddenly surrounded by helicopters.

I could hear one of the mercenaries in the helicopter on his headset, "We've got Martin surrounded, what should we do?"

Another voice on the other end responded, "We still need him alive. Bring him in."

Just then, I saw Matt Brennan's head pop out of one of the helicopters with an assault rifle. I contemplated jumping but was unsure if I would survive the fall. Then I remembered what Melanie whispered to me. Was she telling the truth? I analyzed the cliff. I jumped from higher places than this. My best friend and I used to jump off a platform into a quarry in Rochester, New York when were in high school that was about the same height.

As I was contemplating the jump, I heard the shot go off. I couldn't tell if it hit me because I fell backwards over the cliff. I hit the water, and everything went dark.

Bryce Patrick yelled into the headset. "You were supposed to bring him in alive, Matt!"

"He was too much of a threat. Besides, we have everything we need from him."

"Then so be it. I hope Beaumont sees it that way, for your sake, Matt."

Melanie watched the whole thing from the monitors and hung her head in tears.

# 30

The helicopters hovered and every so often, Matt Brennan would shoot his AR-15 into the water. I was a strong swimmer. My mom used to say that I knew how to swim ever since I was born. I must have inherited it from her. When she was a teen, she swam across the Niagara River about two miles upstream from the falls and made it all the way across before getting to the rapids. Anyway, I was sure they'd either shoot me or spot me since there was nowhere to hide. But I was able to hold my breath long enough for them to give up. I learned this trick from an older relative of mine who dropped out of society in the mid-1980s. He used to periodically show up at our house every summer. He would swim in our above-ground circular pool and was able to circle the perimeter six times under water without coming up for air. He slowed his heartbeat down and was able to get into a meditative state. I thought it was bullshit at the time, but I remember practicing it frequently after that. Anyway, the technique seemed to be working and the helicopter left. Then again, maybe they were running short on fuel. I looked at the horizon and could no longer see land. I didn't even know which way to go.

It was an overcast, foggy day, so I couldn't use the sun to guide my direction. I started swimming but began to lose hope after about fifteen minutes. I was stranded in the middle of the ocean. The first thing that ran through my head was sharks. I had watched *Jaws* one too many times and had Quint's speech memorized about being attacked by sharks when the USS Indianapolis sunk. I knew I could float on my back for hours, but it was starting to get dark and the waves were picking up.

I contemplated death at this point. The death of my family, Scott's family, and Dina was too hard to bear. Then I thought about the eight years I wasted in architecture school, the amount of debt I incurred from student loans, my OCD, anxiety, and depression. Yes, there was Melanie, but most of that was fabricated. My only true friend that was still alive was Saxxon, but without the chip in my head, he had no way to find me now. Then I thought about the end of the world. Even if I did survive this ocean, the meteors were going to hit in 2020 anyway, so what was the point of living?

I was out of energy. The waves were just too powerful. One wave hit me so hard, I swallowed water and was pushed under toward the ocean floor. Then, the wave pulled back and I was suddenly pushed back to the surface and slammed into a large wooden object. Much to my surprise, it was a large fishing vessel.

The crew on the boat pulled me aboard.

"Holy shit! We caught a human," one of the crew shouted.

The captain of the ship's name was Art. He was a tall, skinny guy with a goofy voice. His first mate was his brother-in-law, Jim. I could tell right of way that Jim was "the bad cop" and Art was the "good cop." There were three old-timers named Wayne, Jack, and an Italian who didn't speak English named Franco, and three younger guys named Bennett, Chris, and Joe. The crew only worked on the fishing vessel for the winter. In the summer, they all worked as greenkeepers on a golf course in Rhode Island with the same hierarchy, Art being head greenkeeper and Jim being the head foreman.

I decided not to tell these guys that I escaped from a white nationalist lab that was extracting my dreams to help them make money for a supremacist colony in outer space to escape mass Armageddon on Earth from a meteor collision. Somehow, I didn't think that story would fly with this group. They asked what happened and why I was in the water. I had to think quick. I made up a story of my kayak capsizing because of the waves. They didn't believe that I would be out that far on a kayak, but I explained I was training for a race across Nantucket Sound. I had no idea if such race even existed, but they seemed to accept the story.

*** 

I worked golf course maintenance during high school in the summer months, so I was able to use some of the lingo to gain their respect. They only had a couple more weeks of fishing and said I could work with them on the golf course in the spring if I wanted. Seeing I had no other options, I accepted the offer.

Jim was a total prick and used to break our balls if we made a mistake. He would say things like, "It looks like they didn't teach you how to use a chain saw in college, huh?" One day, Jack's machine dripped hydraulic fluid all over one of the greens and burnt out the grass.

Jim yelled at him and said, "Hey Jack-off. Man, the better part of you dripped down your father's leg, didn't it?" Wayne hated Franco because he was Italian and used to call him "Wapp" and "Guinea." Things really became strange when the golf pro in the pro shop started sleeping with Art's wife, who was the gardener at the golf course. The two of them would sneak off to a deserted cabin on the thirteenth hole. Art didn't seem to have a clue. One day, we were all gossiping about it and Jack came to the pro's defense.

Since the course abutted city property, the prostitutes used to use our compost piles as places to bring their Johns. Every day around three o'clock, I'd dump the grass out of my green's machine buckets and stumble upon a young girl giving a guy a blow job or having full blown sex on the compost pile.

I was still having premonition dreams while I worked on the golf course. Without the chip in my head, I felt a strange dichotomy. On one hand, I felt free that no one could see my dreams; on the other, I felt a bit naked—kind of like leaving the house without your cell phone. Most of my dreams were insignificant. For example, one night, I dreamt Bennett tipped over the Cushman watering vehicle. The next day, it happened. I also dreamt Art's son lost his arm in a hiking accident. A few months later, it happened. He was hiking alone and became trapped between two boulders. After five days, his only choice was to cut off his own arm. I still dreamt of Melanie. I saw her in great pain, crying herself to sleep every night. Every so often, I'd search for Saxxon, but my efforts usually came up empty. The technology and public information had been greatly expanded since I had been held captive, but I was still unsuccessful in my search.

I worked on the golf course for about two years. Then one night, I dreamt about Melanie. She was getting married to Matt on a farm in the country. The dream was as clear as day. I could make out several of the mountains in the background, and when I woke up, I sketched them out. One of the mountains clearly looked like the hump of a camel's back. Using the computer in Art's office, I was able to find the mountain I was looking for. Fittingly, it was Camel's Hump in Vermont. Without the

163

OC17 chip in my head, I was unable to figure out the timeline of the dream. I didn't know if this was in the past, present, or future. The next day, I put in my two-week notice at the golf course and headed for Vermont.

# 31

Year 2008.

Scott Saxxon was contemplating the last six years of his life living in exile from the university and hiding from the government—the same agency he used to work for back in the seventies. His wife and Dina were both killed, and he hadn't been able to trace Larry since he hacked his chip two years prior. He assumed Larry was dead, but always had a small glimmer of hope that he was still alive somewhere. Saxxon knew the meteors were going to hit in 2020, but he was so depressed, he wished they would drop today.

Scott went into exile shortly after Dina and his wife were killed. Beaumont had all the government agencies looking for him. The university had assumed he was dead. Since he could no longer teach his course about the annihilation of earth as an open classroom exercise, Scott began recruiting former students who took his course to form a secret futurist society. He could only find four people he could trust: Todd, Sam, and Rachel from Larry's class, and Margaret Shade—the professor Larry defended from getting lambasted. Todd was now a dean at another school of architecture, Sam was a practicing architect, Rachel went into horticulture, and Margaret left academia to work as a structural analyst. It was a small team, but it was enough to sift through the hundreds of projects Scott had accumulated throughout the years dealing with the end of the earth. The proposals included outer space, underwater, and subterranean colonies. The makeup of the colonies had a range of proposals, including colonies made up predominately of women with vials of sperm for procreation, colonies consisting of one dominate race or religion, and more ethnically and racially diverse colonies. Scott would meet with the group once a month in a remote cabin in the Adirondacks.

Todd found one design somewhat compelling. It was an underwater colony on the floor of Lake Champlain and coincidentally, it was a design Larry did when he took Scott's course back in 1994. Todd never really thought Larry was a good designer, but this project was different. Or maybe he was just feeling nostalgic about his missing friend. Todd was convinced the project could be constructed on a smaller scale, but they needed an exorbitant amount of funding. If only Dina and Larry were still around, they may be able to get that funding through one of Larry's dream premonitions. Then again, Larry's clairvoyance never really could be used as a personal benefit, but this was different.

Larry structured the professional makeup of his underwater colony similar to a college or university, which made sense seeing most college campuses are like small cities. He used the University at Buffalo as a model and took the percentages of faculty and staff working in both the academic and administrative units and applied it to the labor distribution in the underwater colony. The largest category was medicine, followed by the sciences, engineering, agriculture, horticulture, the social sciences, education, architecture, planning, athletics, and the visual arts. He also looked at the breakdown in the administrative units, particularly the physical plant, police, public safety, and facilities management departments, to determine how many people would be needed to maintain and manage day to day operations in the colony. Like a college, many people would have dual roles in their respective field and in the daily management of the colony.

Larry also took an inclusive approach to the ethnic makeup of the colony to ensure all groups were represented. He took a snapshot of the current demographic world percentages and applied it to the population in the colony. He first broke down major divisions, such as Asian, Black, White, Hispanic, Latino, American Indian, Pacific Islander, and Other. From there, he placed all one hundred-ninety-five countries into one of the main categories. Recruiting people from all over the world may have been difficult. Seeing colleges were diverse, Larry toyed with the notion of having a lottery or just selecting an entire college for the makeup of the colony as long as its demographics were similar to the world demographic breakdown. However, Larry feared that depending on the college, there could be disproportionate amounts of certain groups. There was no real conclusion and it seems Saxxon marked him down a few points.

As far as gender, Larry took the same approach as the ethnicity percentages. Larry also was inclusive of sexual preference and had percentages for straight, gay, bisexual, and asexual, which was ahead of its time seeing the paper was written in 1994. Larry didn't talk about religion in the paper in any great detail and was marked down a few points. He stated that ensuring the ethnic and professional makeup would be difficult enough and whatever religions those colonists preferred would be accepted.

As far as the political structure, Larry proposed using the structure and makeup of the United Nations as a model, which would include a general assembly, a security council, and economic/social council, the secretariat, the international court of justice, and the trusteeship council. But as Scott noted on Larry's paper, the UN had close to 38,000 staff, so he'd have to figure out how to scale that down to the colony.

Todd thought Larry's design wasn't half bad either, even though it would need considerable work if it were ever to become a reality, especially the technical pieces. Larry once again used the footprint of the University at Buffalo's spine on the north campus as a guide but put glass domes over all the structures. He mentioned a nuclear reactor for power and had limited discussion on the actual construction of the colony, which made sense seeing he was only a sophomore in college when he wrote the paper.

Larry's evacuation plan of Earth seemed a bit nefarious, but it may have been a necessary evil to prevent mass hysteria if people found out the truth about the meteor collision. The people involved in the design and construction, which made up about a thousand people, along with the other nine thousand inhabitants, were told the underwater colony was a resort. The resort would be hiring people to work in each of the professions Larry defined by looking at college administrative and academic structure. A hiring committee would then examine the applications and choose the remaining people. In essence, it really wasn't a lie. The people just didn't know they'd be living there permanently for ten years and that life on the surface of the earth would be destroyed.

*\*\**

Every morning, Scott would wake up and turn on his system to see if he could trace Larry's signal. He also would go through all the dreams he had on file for Larry to see if he could find a clue or another way to stop the destruction of the earth. Scott browsed through all of Larry's dreams, including Donna's infamous leg cross, the murder of Raja, the orgy, Rachel's brother Jeremy's skydiving accident, the little girl he saved from falling into the Niagara River, Cindy's rape, Fred Knight's cancer, Gina's overdose, Michelle, Kristi, Diane, and of course, the end of the world. One of the most reoccurring dreams Larry had was of Melanie. Scott noticed Larry was dreaming about Melanie long before she hacked into his chip. These were most likely premonition dreams, but none of them indicated any kind of harm from her—they all seemed to be pleasant dreams. Since Larry mentioned he was able to share dreams with Melanie, Scott thought that finding Melanie may be able to lead him to Larry. However, seeing he didn't have the codes to Melanie's chip like he did for Larry, hacking into it would be difficult. If Scott was going to find her, he'd have to do it the old-fashioned way, but in six years, he couldn't find any clues—until today.

In 2012, Wanda Rice became the first female and the first African American president elected in the United States. Ned Beaumont took it upon himself to disparage President Rice any time he was given any press. He called her names like "Amazon woman," "black mamba," and "President burnt Rice." He went as far as fabricating a story that she was not a United States citizen and posted altered photos of her engaging in sexual acts. One day, Beaumont was holding a fundraiser dinner at one of his hotels in Atlantic City. It was unclear what the fundraiser was for, but there were rumors that Beaumont was going to make a run for the presidential election in 2016. The press had extensive coverage of the event. At one point, the press cornered Beaumont and asked him about his intentions to unseat President Rice. Saxxon was disgusted at the prospect and went to turn off the television but became focused on the group of people that were with Beaumont during the interview. Beaumont was with a large group of people, including his wife, his two sons and their wives, and several other couples. Saxxon was hardly surprised at the beauty of all the people in his circle seeing this was consistent with what Larry saw in his dreams regarding the make-up of the space colony. Scott then suddenly became mesmerized with one of the young ladies. He knew he knew her from somewhere. He quickly went to his computer and clicked through Larry's dream images on his computer, glancing manically between his computer and the television. And then he found the image. The woman was Melanie. Saxxon searched out articles about Beaumont's inner circle. He discovered the woman's name was Melanie Merriman and she was engaged to one of Beaumont's chief advisors and fixer lawyers named Matt Brennan. There was a ribbon cutting ceremony for one of Beaumont's new casinos in Atlantic City planned for the following day. Saxxon fired up the Pontiac Fiero and headed for Atlantic City.

Saxxon knew he had to be cautious. In the past ten years, any attempt he made to expose Beaumont's plan to destroy the human race and create a white-supremacist colony in outer-space had been foiled. He wrote anonymous op-eds to newspapers. Seeing Beaumont owned several of the media outlets, most of the articles were not published. One small paper decided to run Scott's piece, and a day later, the business was burnt to the ground and a letter was found from a supposed disgruntled employee who claimed to fabricate the whole "end of the world" story to discredit Beaumont. Saxxon still had a few contacts in Washington from his NASA days. He told them about Beaumont's plan and over the course of a month, they all turned up dead. Luckily, they were still unable to find Saxxon. He had years of experience and several tricks up his sleeve on how to stay off the grid and how not to leave a digital footprint. So, going to this ribbon cutting ceremony was like entering the lion's den. If he was spotted, he'd be killed. But Scott figured it was worth the risk. After all, this woman may be the only one who knew how to find Larry, and if Larry was dead, she might be the only hope in exposing or altering Beaumont's plan.

Getting into the event was going to be difficult, especially seeing the only disguise Scott had was the same drag-queen outfit he used to get away from Beaumont's team of mercenaries in 2002. He put it on and headed towards the event. There were quite a few people in the lobby trying to get a glimpse of Beaumont and some of the celebrities that were attending the ribbon cutting, so it was easy for Scott to blend in. Scott patiently waited for the event to conclude. About an hour before the event was scheduled to be over, a tall, attractive blonde exited the ballroom. It was Melanie and she was alone. She was headed toward the elevators.

Scott slipped into the elevator.

"Exciting event, huh?" Scott said in his female voice.

Melanie responded half-heartedly. "Yeah, real exciting. That's why I stayed to the end."

"Oh, I thought it goes on for another hour?"

"Yeah," Melanie said like Scott should have known.

Scott giggled. "Ohhh, I see what you mean."

"I've never seen so many sexists and bigots in one room," Melanie responded.

"So why were you there, my dear?"

"Long story. And complicated."

"Complicated, huh? Is it more complicated than being able to change past, current, and future events by going into a dream?"

"What? Who are you?" Melanie shouted.

Saxxon took off his wig and face mask. Melanie recognized him but motioned for him to stop talking. She then started rambling about the food at the fund raiser, and how crappy it was. As she was rambling, she wrote a note, folded in a half, and handed it to Saxxon. Saxxon opened the note.

*They are watching and listening to everything I see. Get out of here now. 09J3-7T72-8K75-1W89.*

The elevator doors opened, and Melanie ran frantically back to her room. There were guards all over the floor. They charged the elevator toward Saxxon. The doors were just about closed, and the guards reached in and halted the elevator. They entered the elevator and took Saxxon to the roof.

One of the guards called Bryce Patrick from his cell phone.

"We have Saxxon. Do you want him dead or alive?"

Bryce was in bed with two women he courted at the ribbon ceremony. He put the phone down, kissed one of the ladies, and then picked the phone back up.

"We don't need him. He should have stayed dead. Throw him off the roof and make it look like a suicide."

The guards approached Scott.

"Not your lucky day, Saxxon. You should have stayed in hiding."

The guards dragged Scott to the edge. Scott tried to resist, but he was overpowered. After all, he was not in the best shape after years of working in the ivory tower. Scott closed his eyes, and then heard two pistol shots from a silencer on a gun. The two guards dropped to the ground. Scott turned around. It was Dina Lawrence.

# 32

Scott was speechless. He grabbed Dina and hugged and kissed her.

"Dina? Is it really … it is you! But how? Ten years ago, you were shot and fell into the Niagara River. I saw it with my own eyes."

"Wrong. Ten years ago, I was shot, but thanks to Larry and the blonde woman, I had a bullet-proof vest on. I know, I usually didn't listen to any of Larry's premonitions, but with the two of them yelling at me, I had no choice. That Kevlar is great stuff. I did end up in that goddamned river, though. Man, that river is cold. I floated downstream and pretended I was dead to fool the mercenaries."

"Wait, so both Larry and Melanie warned you?"

"Yeah. They warned me back at the lab." Dina paused and then figured it out. "Wait a minute, so that was a dream. Larry and Melanie warned me in a dream. Duh. I would have known that if Larry still had the OC17 chip in his head, and you would have seen both timelines, too. He must have had the chip removed somehow. Either that or Beaumont's team is hacking us." Dina went on. "So the two of them were sharing a dream?"

"It appears so," Scott answered.

"Wow. So that was what must have been missing. We tried to bring Raja back to life from a past dream, but it always failed. Maybe the power of them together can raise the dead?"

"Maybe. Hopefully. You know the mercenaries also took out my family and Larry's family, right?"

"Yes, I read about that. I assumed you and Larry were dead, too."

"So how did you find me, Dina?"

"Well, I figured you would be spying on Beaumont, so for the past ten years, I've been to every public event this asshole has hosted. It's been torture. He's something else."

Just then, the roof door opened, and more guards came rushing out. Scott and Dina jumped over an alley to the adjacent building. They ran down the stairs and out to a side street. And there was Scott's Fiero.

"I see you still have the same car, Scott. I guess some things haven't changed. How many miles does this thing have?"

"250,000."

"Holy shit. And it's a Pontiac?"

"I know. It's a total enigma."

Scott fired up the Fiero, but Beaumont's team was right behind them. As they were being chased, Scott and Dina tried to catch-up.

"I'm assuming Larry is still alive, seeing he brought me back from the dead and everything?"

"Most likely," Scott responded. "But I don't know where he is. Beaumont's team captured him in 2002 and held him prisoner for four years. I was able to triangulate his signal in 2006 but have not been able to find him for the past six years."

"Damn it," Dina responded. "They probably extracted all the information they needed from his dreams."

"Yeah, probably. But if he can share dreams with Melanie, she may be able to help us find him."

"I know. I had to brush up on my coding a bit. But there's just one problem," Scott replied. "Beaumont's team is monitoring her chip. If she dreams about Larry, they can see it. As a matter of fact, I think they can track her at all times."

"You mean even when she is not dreaming? Like a real-time camera in her chip?'

"Exactly. But she gave me this code in the elevator. It is like the one Larry had in his head that I was able to hack."

Dina examined it. "Indeed. And nice work with the computer, Scott," Dina answered half-joking, half impressed.

"Do you think we can hack it without them seeing us?"

"I'm not sure, but we'll have to try," Dina said.

Beaumont's team was gaining on the Fiero.

"I'm being out horse-powered. I'll have to outmaneuver them."

Dina giggled. Scott was a nerdy professor, but he was talking like Han Solo.

"Okay, do what you have to do!"

Scott drove to a nearby freight-rail yard and was able to lose the SUVs amongst the maze of rail cars.

"Let's try to jump the train" Scott said.

"Sure, but you know you're going to have to abandon the Fiero, right?"

"I know."

Scott turned, faced the Fiero, and took his baseball cap off. He was almost brought to tears. Beaumont's team was closing in. Dina grabbed Scott's arm.

"Come on Dr. Saxxon, we don't have much time."

Scott and Dina jumped aboard the freight train.

# 33

I picked up an old 1999 Jeep Cherokee with a straight six under the hood. It was much better than my old Cutlas with the front seat removed. I was considering staying in Vermont regardless of how the Melanie situation was going to turn out. I was an avid skier before graduate school and wanted to get back into it. I had been to Vermont quite a few times when I was younger to go skiing with my cousin, so I was familiar with the geography. For the next four years, my cousin let me stay in an apartment over his carriage barn while I conducted my search for Melanie's wedding.

I was able to narrow down the list of venues to three after driving around Camel's Hump State Forest. I tried to get a list of the wedding parties, but none of the venues would divulge such information. In my dream, the leaves on the trees were starting to change a bit, so I assumed the wedding was going to take place in late summer or early fall. I just didn't know which year. Hell, it may have already happened for all I knew. I really wished Dina was still monitoring the OC17 chip that Melanie removed from my head. For the foreseeable future, I'd just have to crash weddings at three different venues.

Luckily, I had another vivid dream about the wedding. I was at the reception and was able to get a good look at the wedding cake. It read, "Melanie and Matt, 2012." Seeing it was August, the wedding was most likely going to be held within the next few months. After scouring several online newspapers, I was able to narrow it down even further since many couples published wedding announcements. In addition to the Vermont newspapers, I also searched the papers in Melanie's hometown in Madison, Wisconsin and in Matt's hometown in Poughkeepsie. Since Matt was now a recognizable public figure working with Ned Beaumont, their wedding would most likely not be advertised. All three venues were also public inns with hiking, swimming, and cross-country skiing. The venues all posted when certain activities or areas on the property would be "closed for a private event." Crossing this with the list of published wedding announcements, I was able to narrow it to six potential days.

To pass the time, I started hiking extensively on different sections of the Long Trail. After hiking, I'd hang out at a local bar at the base of Stowe called Melfi's. The bar had live music on the weekends and the vibe was mostly ski-bum locals waiting out the summer for the snow to fly. One night, a Grateful Dead cover band was playing, and the keyboard player got into a fight with his girlfriend and had to take her home. While he was gone, the guys in the band asked the audience if anyone knew how to play keyboards to fill in on the song until the other keyboard player returned. Even though I hadn't played live since before graduate school, I decided to jump on. It felt good to be back on the stage. I always felt more comfortable on the stage than I did in the audience. When the other keyboard player returned, I headed back to my bar stool. A bunch of the locals applauded me as I walked by and the bartender, named Marcus, came over and bought me a drink. Marcus, another bartender, and the owner of the bar had a band and were looking for a keyboard player. I told them I'd think about it. Playing in a band is like dating five people all at once and it's just as difficult in finding a good match, but I had a feeling I would jive with these guys. Like me, they all seemed to be self-taught and didn't take themselves too seriously.

After one too many free Jack and cokes given to me by Marcus, I almost forgot that I had to go and crash one of the six weddings I had narrowed down. The venue was about thirty minutes from the bar. I probably shouldn't have been driving, but then again, I may have not had the courage to crash the wedding without the booze.

The venue was up a windy dirt road in a secluded meadow. There was a giant round barn on the property where the reception was taking place. Even though I was under-dressed for the event, I don't think anyone noticed, as several of the guests were drunk outside of the barn and smoking cigarettes. When I walked in, I pretended like I wasn't surprised to be there. I used to use the same trick when using the bathroom in a hotel lobby that I wasn't staying at. If you walk with authority and don't look around aimlessly, it made it seem that you were staying in the hotel, thus the receptionist wouldn't question you. I went up to the bar and grabbed a drink. I scoped the room but could not see the bride or groom. Suddenly, I was surrounded by a bunch of drunk, blow-hards that were philosophizing with each other. I never liked crowds. I always had to sit in the back of the room and near a door in school, restaurants, and movie theatres. The wedding party was entering the room and blocking the only way out.

The DJ started announcing the wedding party. Since I never met any of Melanie's friends, I still didn't know if this was her wedding or not. I started to convince myself it was, though. I thought to myself, "Yeah, look at that woman, a smart, arty type, that would be someone Melanie would hang out with." Then the DJ announced the bride and groom.

"Ladies and gentlemen, let's give a huge warm welcome to Mr. and Mrs. Ganim!"

The bride and groom entered the room. Damn. I was at the wrong wedding.

The next two weekends, I had similar results. However, both weddings had signs up indicating who was getting married, so I didn't have to endure the awkwardness of entering the room. For the first weekend of October, there were two weddings booked on the same day that I had to check out. I once again made the mistake of stopping in at Melfi's where talk of joining the band led to several more free drinks. Both weddings were at the same time, so I asked Marcus which one I should go to first. He thought I was crazy to even be crashing a wedding in the first place.

"So, what are you going to do, say something when they ask if anyone feels these two should not be married?"

"I might!" I responded. Marcus was laughing hysterically. "Well, have another shot and good luck."

Dan Melfi, the owner of the bar, overheard some of the conversation. He said that one of the venues used to be a brothel.

"Yeah, back in the 1920s, the bootleggers that would cut through Smuggler's Notch used to go there. They would trade booze for sex."

One of the locals at the bar chimed in.

"Yeah, rumor has it, it is still a place the prostitutes meet their Johns."

"Huh, well I guess I'll check that one out first," I responded.

Melfi chimed in. "Yeah, just don't get hooked on it. When I was living in Vegas, I got hooked on the massage parlors. And they used to get freaky—whip out toothbrushes and shit!"

Marcus was in disbelief. "What?" "How many deep are you, Melfi?"

Melfi had at least three gin and tonics while I was sitting there. He started laughing. "Hey barkeep, how about a couple of slices for me and our new friend?"

I woofed down the slice and headed to the former brothel. When I pulled in, I could see the talk at the bar was completely inaccurate. This place was posh, totally high end. I thought this had to be the place. I walked in and tried my method of not looking surprised, but it didn't work. A bunch of guys approached me.

"Hey. Can I help you?" One of them asked.

"Oh, no. I'm just looking for the restroom."

"It's down the hall. But were you invited to this wedding?"

"Yup."

"What's your name?"

When I was a kid, my buddy Jim always had an alias that he used for when he got caught doing something nefarious. I remembered Jim's alias word for word.

"Rick Button."

"Okay, let me check the guest list. Are you from Vermont, Rick?"

"Yes. I live at 85 Marble Drive. 555-8545."

"Why are you giving me your phone number?"

"Ah, just habit, I guess."

"Well, wait here, Rick. I don't see you on the guest list. Are you friends with the bride or the groom?"

"The bride."

The guy questioning me went and found the bride. It wasn't Melanie.

"Yeah, I don't know this guy. Who the hell are you?"

I apologized. "Oh, man, I'm sorry, I'm at the wrong wedding."

The guys in the wedding started surrounding me. I decided to comment on the bride's glasses, as they were similar to mine.

"Hey, by the way, nice frames."

One of the guys in the wedding party then mocked me for the comment. He repeated what I said using a dumb-sounding voice.

"Uhhh, nice frames." He and his friends started chuckling. I don't know if it was the booze from Melfi's, the frustration about Melanie, or just my state of mind, but this triggered me somehow.

"Hey, I wasn't talking to you, pal."

178

Then one of the other guys mocked my use of the word "pal." This was the second time I was mocked for saying "pal."

"Pal? Pal? Who even says that anymore?"

I fired back. "You have a problem with the word pal? You know where I come from, people get their teeth knocked out for talking trash like you are."

"Oh yeah, tough guy. And where do you come from?"

"Hey, if you want to take this outside, I have no problem with that," I said.

"Just get the fuck out of here, asshole," One of the guys in the wedding yelled.

"Yeah, that's what I thought. You bunch of pussies!"

I made it back to my car and peeled out. I could see the wedding party flipping me off and hear them yelling profanity at me. As I headed to the other wedding venue, I was pulled over by the police. Apparently, the wedding party saw my plates and called the cops on me. The cop gave me all the sobriety tests and I seemed to pass them. However, when I refused to do the breathalyzer citing my contamination fears, he cuffed me and brought me to the station saying I was resisting arrest.

The next morning, the chief of police came into my cell and asked me a few questions. He seemed to be a nice guy. I told him the truth—how I was crashing the wedding of an old girlfriend to try and change her mind but ended up at the wrong venue. He seemed to find this story entertaining and decided to let me go.

"Hey, before you leave, you know there was another wedding up the road last night, right?"

"Yes, I think that was the one I was supposed to be at."

The officer chuckled. "Well, you didn't hear it from me, but that venue has overnight accommodations. I think most of the wedding party is still there this morning."

"Thanks officer, but it's too late now."

As I left the station, I decided to still check out the venue. As I pulled up, the entire wedding party was out on the grounds taking photos. It rained the day before, so they must have been getting some shots with the better weather. And then I saw them. Melanie and Matt holding each other for a picture. The sight made me sick. It felt like I was getting repeatedly punched in the stomach. And the whole crew was there — Matt Brennan, Bryce Patrick, Harold Mitchell, a bunch of other white supremacists, and Ned Beaumont himself.

I drove the Jeep up to the loop of the inn. I wanted Melanie to see me. I needed to see her reaction. I circled the loop a few times until the pictures were over and I was within her field of view. She looked happy, which made me feel even sicker. I thought back to the conversation we had at the bar on the island when she said she would be lying if she said she didn't love Matt. So maybe she really loved him. Maybe this was all a fantasy in my head. I decided to drive away. In my rearview mirror, I could see her staring at the Jeep. But then a large Chevy Suburban with tinted windows was blocking my way out. It was Beaumont's security.

Two armed men stepped out of the car and drew their guns.

"Get out of the car," one of them yelled.

But I had confidence in the Cherokee. I put the 4-wheel drive on and headed off-road into a field. The guards started firing their guns. They hit the car several times, but the Jeep held tough. Two more *Suburban's* approached me in the field. One of them struck me on the driver's side sending me down a steep hill. The Jeep plowed through the woods and I ended up upside-down on a main road. I somehow managed to get out of the car, but the *Suburban's* were approaching me from the direction of the inn. I started running down the road and another car was coming at me from the other direction. The car was an old Pontiac and I thought that's too much of a piece of shit to be one of Beaumont's cars, so I ran toward it. The Pontiac sped up, but the *Suburban's* were quickly approaching. The Pontiac then slammed the brakes inches from me, and a man opened the window.

"Get in, Larry!" It was Scott Saxxon.

# 34

Saxxon put the pedal to the metal, but the *Suburban's* were gaining. I was shocked to see Scott. Since I escaped from Beaumont's lab on the island, I had been looking for him but couldn't find him. Instead of asking obvious questions, I asked about the car.

"Where's the Fiero?"

"I'm sorry Larry, I had to abandon it down in Atlantic City. But I found this P6000 and it was the closest thing I could find. You know me, I'm sentimental about my cars."

"I've been looking for you, Scott, where the hell have you been?"

"I've been off the grid. I've been on the run ever since I hacked your chip. Beaumont's team was able to trace the hack back to me. I had to abandon my house, my job, everything."

Scott went on. "Then, I saw Melanie on TV and approached her at a ribbon cutting ceremony for one of Beaumont's casinos. I figured if I could find her, it would lead me to you."

"So how were you able to find her in Vermont?"

"She gave me the access code to her OC17 chip, so we hacked it."

"We? Who else is in on this?"

"Oh yeah, I forgot to tell you, Dina is alive."

"What? How?"

"Well, do you remember sharing a dream with Melanie about Dina?"

"Of course. We told her to wear a bullet proof vest. It worked?"

"It seems so. Unless Beaumont's team cloned her and it's all a trap."

"Can they do that?"

Scott chuckled. I could tell he was joking. "No. I don't think so. Not yet anyway."

"So where are we headed?"

"I have a friend from college that is now a professor at the University of Vermont. He gave me the keys to an abandon seismograph room underground near the geology building. It's a perfect hideout and there's enough space for us to get to work."

"Get to work on what?"

"Larry, we still have to try to defend against the meteors and to prevent Beaumont's plan from happening."

Just then, I could see Scott had lost the *Suburban's*.

"I don't know, Scott. It seems like a lose-lose situation. Beaumont has too much control. He owns the press and has corrupted all the intelligence agencies. And either way, the meteors are going to hit and there's not enough time to build our own defense system. And Melanie is married to that asshole and is good as gone anyway."

"Ahh. That's what this is all about. The girl."

"She was the one, Scott. I saw how happy she looked with Matt. What's the point? Let the meteors hit."

"Jesus, Larry. Here's the deal. She still has her chip in her head, but Beaumont's team is now monitoring her when she is awake, too. So, we don't know what she is doing to survive."

"Huh. That could be why she ignored me at the wedding."

"Why, did she see you?" Scott asked.

"Yeah, I think so. I circled the loop a few times and she seemed to look over but quickly turned away."

"Right, because they see what she sees."

"Well, can we block what they see on her chip?"

"Dina is working on that as we speak."

We pulled into the university and headed down to the old seismography room. The space was reminiscent of Dina's lab in Niagara Falls. It even had a circular sitting area in the center. I walked in and Dina ran to me and gave me the longest and hardest hug I have ever had.

"Dina, I can't breathe!"

"I'm so happy to see you," she said.

Scott chimed in from across the room. "She looks pretty good for being dead, huh?"

"Yeah. About that—what was it like being dead?"

"I only have a vague recollection of dying. It was kind of like falling asleep and just waking up the next day. Your dream, with the help of your crush Melanie, altered the timeline."

"Wow!"

Scott chimed back in. "Exactly, Larry. With the two of you combined, we may be able to bring more people back—your family, my wife—we may be able to prevent the meteors from even hitting. We may be able to save the world!"

I could see Scott was getting excited. "Have you been able to get into her chip?"

"Apart from being able to triangulate her signal, no, we haven't been able to actually get into it. The encryption is highly sophisticated, and if they trace it to us, we'll all be dead."

Scott chimed in and said, "Right. And if Larry and Melanie are killed, there will be no hope of bringing us back."

# 35

After all the commotion during the wedding pictures, Melanie went back to the honeymoon suite at the resort. Matt was also in the room doing some work on his laptop.

"Ahh. There's my beautiful bride."

Matt walked over to Melanie and began caressing her. They then started kissing, and soon he was on top of her on the bed. As he thrust himself upon her, Melanie glanced over at the laptop and was able to read what Matt was working on. She knew Harold Mitchell would not be watching them in real-time since Matt would turn off her OC17 chip when they were having sex. The screen displayed the following:

*The public will be told the space structure will be a luxurious hotel. Contestants from Beaumont's reality show will compete for voyage to the hotel and be led to believe that their stay is only temporary. In the event the meteor collision is made public, the people will be told that several space defense platforms will also be constructed with laser-based defense against the meteors.*

Matt continued to thrust, but Melanie needed to see more. She reached her hand over to the laptop to scroll down. The text went on:

*The on-orbit assembly of components of the colony will be performed by separate teams at separate locations in space to prevent them from being able to visualize the whole. The final low-orbit assembly of those major components into the overall colony configuration will be performed by a single team which upon completion, will have to experience some fatal misfortune so the plan won't be made public.*

Melanie continued to scroll down and saw a map of ten of Beaumont's resorts that would double as launch sites for the 10,000 people selected to be on the colony. Another map showed the potential sites of the meteors and there was another layer that showed where the nuclear bombs were targeted for. Oddly, the two did not line up. As she further examined the map, Matt realized she wasn't into the sex.

"What the hell is wrong with you, Melanie? You're just lying there."

He looked at her and saw her face was turned toward the laptop.

"Wait a minute, were you reading what was on my screen?"

"I couldn't help it, Matt. You are keeping me in the dark with the evacuation plan."

"The less you know, the better."

"Can you tell me why the nuclear war heads are not targeting the meteors?"

Matt slammed the laptop down.

"How can you even see that? You don't know what you are looking at Mel."

"Oh really, I think you forgot my background and forgot what I did see before you blocked my dreaming ability. There are no plans to save humanity. Beaumont *is* planning to annihilate humanity, isn't he?"

"You don't understand, Mel. There is no way to save everybody and we're doing them a favor, so they won't suffer when the meteors do hit."

"So, Larry was right. I can't believe it. I thought he was crazy. He was right."

"What did you just say? I thought we agreed never to mention his name?"

Just then, there was a knock at the door. It was Harold Mitchell. Matt walked away from the bedroom and toward the door.

"Is there trouble in paradise?" He said sardonically.

"No, no problem. My wife is just having a hard time accepting reality."

"Yes, I saw she was reading our evacuation plan."

"Wait a minute, I thought the chip was turned off?" Matt said with anger.

"No Matt, you forgot to turn it off."

"So you watched, you pervert!"

"Get over yourself, Matt. I'm only concerned about what she saw on the screen."

"What do we do about it?"

"Let's get Beaumont down here. Have him talk to her directly. He has a way of persuading people."

Mitchell called Bryce Patrick on the phone.

"Bryce. It's Harold. We have a situation. The girl knows. Is Mr. Beaumont still in his room?"

Harold hung up the phone. "Okay, we can go up."

185

Harold, Matt, and Melanie walked over to the suite where Beaumont was staying. His wife went into Burlington to do some shopping which explained the prostitute that was leaving Ned's room when they arrived. Ned answered the door in a silk robe.

"Come on in. Oh, what a beautiful couple. It was a great wedding. Probably the greatest I've ever been to."

"Thank you, sir," Matt replied.

"So, what is the problem?"

"Well, it seems my wife stumbled upon the evacuation plan."

"And?" Beaumont said casually.

"Well, she's having a difficult time accepting it."

"Ah. Come over here sweetheart. What seems to be the problem?"

"Well, I was under the impression that we were going to try and prevent the meteors from hitting. But based on what I saw, it looks like we are intentionally wiping out more people!"

"I know sweetheart. It was a difficult decision, but my analysts told me there is no other way. They say it is impossible to destroy all the meteors. There are too many of them."

"We're just going to kill the remaining survivors?"

"That's the thing, sweetheart. They have no chance of surviving. We are just going to end their suffering. It's really the humane thing to do."

Matt put his arm around Melanie and tried to console her in a condescending manner.

"I told you, Mel. We have all been working on this. All our scientists tell us the meteor collision is inevitable. Those who don't die from the immediate impact will be sickened by the radiation from the meteors and die a slow, painful death. We are trying to prevent the suffering."

"I don't believe there is nothing we can do. We have eight years until the impact. Can't we build more colonies? More fall-out shelters?"

Beaumont signaled to Harold Mitchell to illustrate the evidence. Mitchell set up his computer and a projector and projected the images on the wall. He showed a simulation of all the meteors and ran several scenarios.

"As you can see, trying to destroy all the meteors simply isn't possible. We are showing forty-four meteors with radii larger than a hundred miles, the largest being the size of Texas and another one

186

hundred or so less miles wide. Much of these will get broken when they enter the atmosphere, but given the size and velocity, there could be thousands of pieces scattered around the globe. To give you a perspective, a chunk just ten feet in diameter will emit enough radiation to infect a ten-mile radius. Just think what one of the hundred-mile diameter chunks will do."

Melanie still seemed to have hope. "Well, we have to try something. We can divert them into the ocean, or we can move people away from the impact, or we can build more missile defense systems."

Beaumont responded. "There is just simply not enough time. We will just be able to complete the colony before the first impact, and even that is pushing it."

Melanie interrupted. "What if we had more time? Yes, that's it. I can work with the other dream makers and go back in time and warn ourselves earlier so we can better prepare."

Harold Mitchell was shaking his head. Bryce gave Matt a sinister look, motioning him to control Melanie. Beaumont interrupted.

"You are very noble, Melanie. Sure, we can try that."

Bryce cut off Beaumont. "But sir, that won't—"

Beaumont cut off Bryce. "Don't interrupt me, Mr. Patrick. If the lady thinks she can get us more time through her dreams, let her try."

Matt looked at Melanie. "What do you think, babe? Does that satisfy you?"

"Jesus, Matt. This isn't about me. This is about humanity."

Beaumont concluded. "After your honeymoon, we'll get you back in lab with the other dream makers. Sound good?"

"Yes. Thank you, Mr. Beaumont."

After Matt and Melanie left the room, Bryce Patrick started yelling at Beaumont.

"With all due respect, sir, how can you allow this? She could compromise our whole plan."

"Mr. Patrick, do you think I'm stupid?"

"No, of course not, sir, but—"

"Don't worry, after the honeymoon, she won't be questioning the project anymore. Isn't that right, Mr. Mitchell?"

"That's correct, Mr. Beaumont."

# 36

After the wedding, Melanie and Matt went to one of Beaumont's private resorts in the Bahamas. On the first night, Melanie dreamt of Larry. It was the first dream she had of him in over two years, which she thought was unusual. She did remember a few dreams where she started dreaming about him, but the course of the dream was either changed or she woke up with a crippling headache. But this time, she saw him clear as day. She wondered if she was sharing a dream with him or if it was her mind seeing a past, present, or future vision of him. In the dream, they were sitting next to each other on the stairs of a carriage barn. Larry handed her a heart-shaped rock he found along the lakeshore.

"Oh boy," Melanie exclaimed. "I'm going to need a double vodka-tonic after that."

"Oh, like you didn't know," Larry responded.

"Well, I kind of knew, but now it's official. And now it's awkward."

"Why is it awkward?"

"Because, I'm married, Larry. It's too late!"

Then Melanie's dream shifted. It was in the future sometime near the meteor strike. It was mass hysteria. People were looting, screaming, killing each other; there were fires, explosions, and cars being driven into buildings. The screens showed mass chaos throughout the world. She was in Times Square and the news was being displayed on the outdoor screens: "President Beaumont's so called "meteor defense system" being constructed in outer space turns out to be an escape colony for 10,000 people."

Then Melanie was with Matt.

"See, this is what will happen if people know about the escape plan."

Melanie woke up briefly but fell back asleep and was back on the stairs next to Larry. Larry was explaining what Beaumont's plan of exasperating the meteor collision with nuclear weapons to ensure no humans survive. Then she woke up in a cold sweat.

Melanie had similar dreams throughout her honeymoon. Several showed people suffering after the meteors struck. She was starting to believe Beaumont was doing the right thing.

\*\*\*

Back in the lab outside of Washington, Ned Beaumont, Bryce Patrick, and Harold Mitchell and his team were watching the monitors.

"Great work, Harold. Great. Do you think she's buying it?" Beaumont asked.

"Based on her vitals and her reactions, yes, she is believing it. And why wouldn't she? After all, her dream prediction rate is around ninety percent."

On the last night of the honeymoon, Harold had one special finale he was going to upload into Melanie's OC17 chip. The dream showed Larry, Scott, and Dina doctoring audio and video showing Beaumont's plan of nuclear enhancement.

After seeing the images, Melanie started to think Larry, Scott, and Dina might be some extremist left-wing conspiracy group that were trying to discredit Beaumont. But then the dream went black. Melanie was then back in Vermont at a park near the lake. She could hear voices but couldn't see anyone.

Then Larry emerged out of the lake.

"Larry! Wait, they can see you. They are still monitoring my dreams." She could hear Larry's voice, but his lips weren't moving.

"Don't worry. Dina and Scott just hacked your chip and are blocking Beaumont's access, but we don't have much time until they figure it out."

"Wait, are we dream-sharing right now?"

"Kind of. This is a simulation Scott and Dina built. They uploaded video of me for you to see, but I'm currently not dreaming. I'm speaking with you in real-time. Look Melanie, we can still save the world, but we must do it together. We need your help!"

"Save the world? We can't, Larry. I saw what happens when we try to do that. People will suffer more. Beaumont's genocide is the humane thing to do."

"What? No! We have a plan to save millions of more people, Mel."

"You're wrong, Larry. I've seen the destruction of the meteors. Billions of people will suffer from the radiation alone."

"No, Mel. That is not what I've been seeing in my dreams. We may have the ability to launch our own technology to destroy some of the meteors. We can also construct shelters underwater that will resist both the impact and the radiation. But without the chip in my head, we need to work together."

"So, you just want me for my dreaming abilities? You're as bad as Beaumont."

"Well, no, that's not it. I love you, Melanie! Sure, we can't do this without you, but even if there was no way to save the world, I'd still be reaching out to you. I don't want to go on without you."

"Larry, we talked about this. I love you, too, but I also love Matt and we're married now. It's too complicated, Larry."

"Come on, do you really love him? How do you know they are not manipulating your chip and forcing you to love him?"

"You mean like you, Scott, and Dina are doing to me now?"

"Well, that's different—"

"No, it's no different. Beaumont is manipulating me, and you are berating me. The things you have been saying to me, the way you have been treating me."

"Mel, that's ridiculous."

"Goddamnit. I am not ridiculous. And quit calling me Mel. Only Matt can call me that."

"Okay, fine."

"You have been berating me for the past two years. And I am so angry at myself for backpedaling and making excuses. You can't just joke about that! Ask any woman. They will all agree underneath, even if they laugh on the surface. It's not a nice thing to be biologically weaker, in fact, it's very scary. You must be aware of yourself a little and what you sound like when you say certain things. If you think I'm crazy, fine. But what I'm saying is, it is irrational that I would take you seriously, yes, but not irrational thinking that you shouldn't have said it in the first place. If you talk that way to everybody, I can see why nobody loves you."

I looked over at Dina and Scott and shrugged.

I covered the microphone transmitting to her chip. "What the hell is she saying?"

"They're onto us, pull the connection," Dina shouted.

Scott disconnected the entire system and frantically pulled the chord out of the wall.

"But what the hell was she talking about?"

Scott responded. "Larry, it looks like they have been feeding false dreams into her chip. It looks like they're making you appear as the villain in all of this."

"So she doesn't know what's true?" I asked.

"It seems that way. You must let her go, Larry. We'll have to do this without her." Scott said ambivalently.

# 37

Todd, Sam, Margaret, and Rachel eventually joined us in the old, underground seismology room at the University of Vermont. Ever since Scott convened them shortly after Larry disappeared, they had been reviewing numerous student proposal's from Scott's Environmental Behavior and Design class and cherry picking the best ideas on how to sustain the planet in response to the meteor collision.

Since we only had an eight-year time frame until the meteor collision and limited funding, the team decided to focus on the design and construction of a laser-equipped space drone. Saxxon assumed a new alias, Kyle Reardon, and began teaching his class at the University of Vermont. Once again, Saxxon conducted the end of the world scenario in the course as to hide the reality in plain sight. To ensure the students wouldn't freak out if they discovered the meteor collision was really going to happen in eight years, Scott changed the end of the world scenario to a nuclear holocaust, which, in some respects was also true since Beaumont's team planned to enhance the meteor collision with nuclear warheads to ensure the annihilation of the human race. In addition to the three sites students could choose to develop—outer space, under water, and underground—Scott also added a fourth category of missile defense. Since the course could be used as a general education requirement, Scott recruited engineering students to enroll in it.

Over the next four years, Scott continued the course and recruited students for the research and development of the drone laser. He was also able to recruit some of his old co-workers from his days of working at NASA in the seventies. One particular friend, Sherman Miles, provided most of the funding for the project. Sherman was an engineer on the Space Shuttle missions but retired shortly after the Challenger disaster in 1986. Distraught from the disaster, Sherman went into exile and became severely depressed. Luckily, a group of college students lived in the downstairs apartment under Sherman and were instrumental in bringing back his will to live. He made fake IDs for them to sell to their classmates and they soon became the largest fake ID distributer in the Georgetown area. One of the students was a marketing major and decided to develop a penis enlargement stretching device for his senior thesis. Naturally, the student asked Sherman to help him with the design. Sherman was able to create detailed three-dimensional design drawings of the product that were so convincing, the marketing professor encouraged the student to pursue a patent. Sherman and the student made about twenty million dollars in the first year after the product was patented. It certainly wasn't rocket science, but at least Sherman was wealthy. Anyway, Sherman was happy to once again be working on a worthy project and something more closely aligned to his expertise. He graciously funded the drone laser research. It was difficult to tell if he was passionate about saving the human race or if he just felt guilty for making millions off a product that didn't even work.

It was good Sherman showed up. Since my dreaming ability precluded me from personally benefiting from anything I saw happen in the future, Dina and I could not seem to profit off any of my dreams. She tried to get another OC17 chip for me to make the task easier, but Beaumont's team had closed down the manufacturing of the chips, so we had to analyze the dreams the old-fashioned way. I had one dream that spring that showed the Boston Celtics defeating the Los Angeles Lakers in the championship, but judging by the bad outcomes of my other two sports dreams, including both the Buffalo Bills loss in 1991 and the Buffalo Sabres loss in 1999, I was a bit hesitant to try this scheme again. But we decided to test fate anyway and figured it might work if Dina placed the bet. Dina placed the bet online and the Celtics won. However, when Dina went to collect her winnings, she was shocked to see that there was a glitch in the online betting interface and her bet never went through. "I told you," was all I said. So yes, it was good Sherman showed up when he did.

## 38

As planned, Ned Beaumont was able to utilize the dreams from the dream makers to win the 2016 election. In addition to Melanie and Larry, the other three dream makers also saw Beaumont's opponent originally winning the election. Beaumont's team was able to pinpoint key districts where he lost from the dreams. They then hacked into the electronic voting machines and altered the counts. Although his opponent won the popular vote, the altered counts in the specific districts, particularly in Wisconsin, allowed Beaumont to get enough electoral votes to win the election.

But even without the fix, Beaumont was still able to conjure twenty million votes. Even though some of his support came from capitalizing on people's fears by convincing them that white Americans would eventually become the minority if nothing was done to deport immigrants and close down the borders, many of his supporters also found him charismatic and entertaining. His reality shows and the game show that he hosted prior to running for president were popular and in general, people liked his smooth, no-nonsense approach to speaking. Although the liberal left considered him a misogynist, many of his female supporters found him handsome and somewhat charming. As an independent, he ran on a promise of obliterating the partisan divide in Washington. Since he was independently wealthy, he said he was immune to being swayed by campaign contributions from wealthy lobbyists. In his first two years in office, he revoked most - if not all – of the policies of his predecessor, whether he agreed with them or not. Beaumont did not actually believe he was racist or xenophobic. He justified expunging immigrants and closing the borders with decreasing crime, decreasing unemployment, and preserving natural resources. And he wasn't the first one in his family to have aspirations of a homogenous society—his father and grandfather before him also believed in this structure. It seemed that in his mind, he really believed these policies would make society a better place and the economy more productive.

Although he spoke his mind, Beaumont despised negative publicity and being questioned and lambasted by the press. Luckily, he owned one of the largest media companies and was able to manipulate the news to his benefit. He declared all other media companies the enemy of the American people and, with the help of the dreamers being able to see the future, was eventually able to control all of the headlines and subsequently put all the other media organizations out of business. This was one of the reasons Saxxon couldn't get the story out about Beaumont's plan to wipe out civilization.

To make matters worse, he was able to appoint three of his personal friends who shared his beliefs to the Supreme Court, all of who agreed to pardon the president of any crimes he committed in the past or would commit in the future.

On the space colony, he would convince the survivors that he indeed was attempting to save the earth, but that the other evacuations did not happen before the collision. After ten years, it would be safe to repopulate the earth. Beaumont and his successors would still rule, but this time, it would be all their handpicked people. Beaumont would forever be known as the "savior of the planet."

# 39

On the night of Beaumont's State of the Union address, Melanie Merriman was in her hotel suite near the National Mall in Washington D.C. with her two children. William was now four years old and Lila just turned two. Beaumont's team of doctors had been running extensive testing on the two children seeing they may have inherited Melanie's dreaming abilities. It was discovered that Lila was showing signs of autism, so Matt had arranged a consult with some of the doctors. As she watched Beaumont's speech, she realized how much she despised him. How could she ever have condoned this plan, she thought? She thought about her last encounter with Larry. Something was wrong. Maybe Larry was right. Maybe her husband and Harold Mitchell were altering her dreams. Her gut told her Larry was an honest guy; her heart told her she loved him. So why all the distrust of him? Melanie put the kids to bed and decided to go through some of her memorabilia. She found a joint of cannabis and a song that Larry wrote for her when they were on the island. She smoked the joint and slowly read the lyrics of the song:

*Madison Wisconsin*
*it will always make me cry*
*because when she swam up to me*
*I thought she was an angel from the sky*

*she likes picking berries*
*she has a guidebook for the birds*
*a mysterious rock collection*
*a myriad of words*

*she plays classical piano*
*guitar with perfect pitch*
*but if I try and praise her*
*she'll call herself a bitch*

*She sold the teddy bears with zeal*

# Dream Makers

*she fed the ghosts a meal*
*she thought the wooden ducks were real*

*guilt of 1000 Catholics*
*too much lacquer on her plate*
*but when my crush comes crashing down*
*she gladly bears the weight*

*she nearly swam across the entire lake*
*her long fingers gently glide*
*she whipped my ass in bowling*
*rolled a 149*

*she knows the periodic table*
*I saved the poem she made*
*she stopped chewing gum*
*around the 7th grade*

*her hands dampen like the dew*
*odor-eaters for her shoes*
*on The Point, she'll never lose*

*her diet consists of glue and paint*
*built a table made of wood*
*she believes a man should keep*
*his natural hanging hood*

*a thong for feeling sexy*
*like her snazzy bowling shoes*
*she has not thrown up*
*since 1982*

*she noticed my hanging hook rug*
*she wants to shave my beard*
*I can always tell her stories*
*she never thinks are weird*

*speaks French to fight her fights*
*thinks that driving really bites*
*she's fond of men in tights*

*what would Desdemona say?*
*with your brother you should stay*
*we're not related, its ok*
*under the stars we can lay*
*bird nerds always like to play*

*On the stairs she must conceal*
*a crocus not concave*
*even though my name is Larry*
*she thought I was a Dave*

*we walked the farm late at night*
*I placed a flower in her hair*
*and when the fog rolled in so thick*
*we decided to walk bare*

*I dreamed I kissed her in a pool*
*at first she held her breath*
*then I tried one beardless night*
*and this I don't regret*

*she saw the future in her dreams*
*we were dancing, kings and queens*
*I laid my head between her knees*

*she kiniports my heart at night*
*she pensed my mind to boot*
*I wish we could just run away*
*or hide below the root*

Melanie couldn't tell if it was the weed or an actual revelation, but she realized Larry was writing about things in her life long before she ever implanted herself into his OC17 chip in 1998. The more she thought about it, the more she remembered about him. She dug through more boxes and found some old journals where she used to log her dreams before Matt discovered her ability and started the dream maker program. And then she confirmed her suspicions: she had been sharing dreams with Larry since she was a young girl. She passed out on the floor and found herself freezing on a ski slope at Whiteface Mountain. Her hands were frost bitten, as she only had on hand-knitted mittens.

***

Time passed quickly. Each day I woke up and felt I had wasted another day. I knew the end of the world was coming and figured I should be living each day like it was the last, but I had no desire to do anything and didn't really see the point. I hated Beaumont and his cabinet of comic-book villains and especially hated Matt Brennan. I dreaded seeing them on the news and turned the radio off whenever he spoke. The guy was so eerily like Hitler but sadly, he had support of at least half of the country. I also made the mistake of looking at Melanie's Facebook page. It seemed she and Matt had two kids. Melanie hated kids. I couldn't figure out how Matt convinced her to have them in the first place. Was he brainwashing her through the chip? Did he trick her somehow? Or worst yet, did she really love the guy, and did she change her mind about kids? Anyway, I had to somehow let it go.

One night, I took two Ativan, drank four glasses of bourbon, took a bunch of pulls off my vaporizer, and by habit and mistake, took a sleeping pill. I had many strange dreams throughout the night, which was somewhat relieving seeing I hadn't had any premonition dreams in about six years. I had a dream I was in the sequel of the movie *Smokey and the Bandit*, but this time, I was driving a rig full of marijuana from Colorado to Massachusetts. Ryan Reynolds was driving the Trans-Am and I remembered asking why Burt Reynolds was missing. I also dreamt that Rachel was pregnant, and that Sherman was killed in a car accident. I woke up and wrote the dreams down so that I could bring them back to

Scott and Dina for analysis. When I fell back asleep, I dreamt of Melanie sporadically, but decided to ignore her. First, I saw her at a bowling alley with one of her friends. She saw me lurking in the distance and told me to meet her at a concert in Lake Placid known as *Snoe Down*, which was hosted by the band Moe. Melanie was very competitive at the bowling alley. I could see she would be upset if she lost. Luckily, her friend wasn't a very good bowler. The dream then shifted to Whiteface Mountain in Lake Placid. I saw Melanie on one of the steeper trails stuck in some deep snow. She wanted me to teach her how to ski, but I was still bitter that she married Matt, so I let her go off on her own. She had hand-knit mittens on, and it was ten below zero with the wind chill. She had severe frost bite on her fingers. I could see she was in trouble, so I grabbed a spare pair of gloves and headed for the trail where Melanie was stranded. I warmed her hands and guided her to the bottom of the mountain.

"What were you doing on the upper mountain?" I asked.

"I don't know. I don't ski, Larry. This is your dream."

"Right. But I wonder when this is?" I asked.

"Well, judging from the outfits, it's definitely not the present and I hope it's not the future."

"Ahh, right, I remember. I came up here in year 2000," I said.

As I was reminiscing about the ski trip, Melanie took out a piece of paper, wrote something, and handed it to me. She motioned for me to read it under my jacket. I opened the note and it read:

*Did you forget, Harold will be able to see this dream, stupid.*

I motioned for the pen and wrote her a note back. Amazing that the OC17 technology's weakness was good old fashioned, junior-high style, hand-written notes.

*We're in the past before you were recruited into the dream maker program. If we run away together now, we can prevent everything that's happened.*

Melanie looked at me with sad eyes and shook her head no. I was about to try and convince her, but then saw one of the dream makers Bryan out of the corner of my eye on a chair lift above us.

\*\*\*

200

Back at the underground lab at the University of Vermont, Dina yelled to Scott.

"Scott! I'm in! I hacked into Melanie's chip."

Dina brought the dream up on the monitor.

"It looks like she's in one of Larry's dreams at Whiteface Mountain."

"Damn it! He knows better. Beaumont's team will be able to see this, too. Can they figure out where Larry is physically located?"

"No, not without the chip in his head," Dina responded.

Back at Beaumont's lab, Harold Mitchell and Doug Lynch were viewing the dream from Melanie's chip.

Harold called up Bryce Patrick.

"Mr. Patrick, we have Larry Martin and Melanie in a dream in year 2000. I can send in another dream maker have him wipe out Martin, which should eliminate our threat in the present. What should I do?"

"This could have other impacts, right? I mean, what if this changes Melanie's course and she never ends up meeting Matt and then the Dream Maker program would never be initiated."

"Well, that could be true, but since we are tethered to Melanie's timeline, we'll still remember the old timeline and can thus still create the program. We wouldn't need Brennan to start it this time," Harold answered.

"Interesting, I'll have to check with Beaumont," Bryce replied.

"We don't have that much time. I need a decision now."

"Fine. Take him out," Bryce responded as he hung up his phone.

I grabbed Melanie by the hand and began skiing down the trail. Seeing she was a beginner, I had to straddle her from behind to prevent her from falling. We made it about fifty feet, and then I heard the gun shot. I fell on top of Melanie. I could see her crying, but then everything went dark.

Harold dialed up Bryce Patrick again.

"Martin's been eliminated."

"Great. Did it work? Are you able to ascertain the threat to us in current time?"

"I'm looking at the timelines now. Martin is indeed still dead. It looks like Saxxon and Lawrence are no longer doing dream research. They are both back at their old jobs."

"Excellent. And what about Merriman?"

"Hmm. Ahh, well, it looks like she is institutionalized."

"Like in a mental institution?"

"Yes," answered Harold somewhat melancholily.

"Can we fix that somehow?" Bryce asked.

"Not without going back into that dream, and then we could end up missing Martin," Harold responded.

"Okay. Is Matt still tethered to Melanie's timeline?"

"Indeed."

"Shit. He'll be aware of all this. I'll break it to him," Bryce answered.

***

Dina and Scott watched the shooting unfold on the monitor. Dina put her hands over her face and Scott fell to one knee, dropping his head. When he looked back up, Scott was in his office at the University at Buffalo and Dina was back at her lab in Niagara Falls. Scott quickly dialed Dina's number.

"Where the hell am I?"

Dina was still crying.

"Yes. This is the first time we have been physically displaced as a result of altering the space-time continuum. Do you remember being in the underground lab?"

"Yes. But then I passed out or fell asleep or something."

"Exactly. Me, too. I then I woke up back in my old lab."

Dina went on. "The timeline was reset. After Larry was killed, none of the events over the past twenty years took place. Larry never comes to me for help, we never get chased by Beaumont's team, I never get killed and brought back to life, Larry is never abducted, oh, the list goes on and on."

"But we both remember Larry in the old timeline. How is that possible? He didn't have a chip to tether to."

"Well, luckily, I was able to tether us to Melanie's timeline right after I hacked into it, otherwise, I'd have no memory of Larry. You would still know him because you knew him before the year 2000 when he took you undergraduate course."

"Well, we can fix it, right? We can go back into the dream, right?" Scott asked in a worried tone.

"Not without Larry. Or someone else with dreaming ability."

"Are we still inside Melanie's chip?"

Dina further examined the altered timeline on the monitor.

"No. In the new timeline, Melanie never meets Matt, never enters Beaumont's Dream Maker program, never gets an OC17 chip implanted, and eventually ends up at a mental institution after having Larry die on top of her."

"Can we find her?"

"Already did. The institution is in Madison, Wisconsin."

"What about the Dream Maker program? Beaumont's annihilation of Earth? Did this impact any of that?"

"Unfortunately, none of that was impacted. Beaumont's team must also be tethered to Melanie's timeline like we were, so they also retained all of their prior knowledge."

"Holy shit. It's a good thing you hacked that chip. Does Beaumont's team know that we know about both timelines?"

"No, I don't think so. But we need to make him keep believing we don't know," Melanie explained. "Without Larry in the picture, they may think our threat is eliminated."

"Well, it kind of is. All our research, our defense laser, it's all gone. And we only have two years until the meteors collide."

"I know. Our only hope is Melanie Merriman. We have to go find her at the institution before Beaumont does. I mean, I'm sure her husband will be looking for her."

"Right. I'll meet you in the front of Hayes Hall in an hour. And Dina, hear this, the Fiero is back!"

"Great. That's the only good thing that came out of all of this."

# 40

Scott and Dina drove through the night and made it to the mental institution where Melanie had been committed to after Larry died on top of her in the dream at Whiteface from year 2000. Luckily, they were both psychologists and were able to get passes to tour the facility, but just to be safe, they didn't tell the staff they were there to see Melanie. The facility was posh as far as institutions are concerned. Several of the residents were outside walking in the gardens, which were impeccable as Scott noted on the way in.

As they walked toward Melanie's room, there were several men outside the door. Scott grabbed Dina.

"It's Beaumont's team. They beat us here."

"Shit. They can't see us," Dina exclaimed.

Scott and Dina slipped into the adjacent room. Luckily, the resident in the room was passed out. Scott then took out a small listening device that enabled him to hear into the next room. Dina looked at him in a funny way.

"From my NASA days," Scott responded.

The two huddled over the device. They could hear the conversation. Matt Brennan, Harold Mitchell, Bryce Patrick, a woman named Heather, and one of the doctors were in the room asking Melanie questions. Melanie was catatonic and not responding. As the group convened in the hall, Scott and Dina kept listening.

"Do you think she remembers us?" Matt asked Harold.

"In theory, she should remember both timelines. But it seems she suffered some kind of break down, so she may not know what is real and what isn't," Harold explained.

"Well, we probably should get her out of here just to be safe," Bryce added.

The unknown woman, Heather, chimed in. It seemed she was Matt's new love interest.

"So then what? Are you going to go back to her?" She said in disgust.

Matt put his hands on the side of Heather's face and kissed her.

"No, of course not, I'm with you now. This is just a precaution."

"So how do we get her out of here?" Bryce asked.

"Well, Matt still has the paperwork from the old timeline proving she's his wife. As far as this institution is concerned, they are still married. They can sign her over to him," Harold responded.

Matt approached the doctor to inquire about the release, but the doctor didn't seem to comply.

"Well, Mr. Brennan, she's been here for eighteen years and you are the first visitors she has had. Can I ask where you've been?"

"Well, she disappeared on us when she went away on a ski trip. We just found her whereabouts yesterday," Matt responded.

"Well, Mr. Brennan, besides not speaking, her cognitive abilities have been quite intact. She still seems to be able to make medical decisions for herself, so unless she gives the word, we have to comply with her wishes," the doctor explained.

Matt started getting angry, but Bryce interjected.

"That's fine, doctor, we'll be back in a couple of days to check on her. Maybe she'll remember more then."

As the group exited the facility, Matt was still angered.

"She's faking it. She remembers us. Maybe she doesn't want to come with us?" Matt said.

"Well, we'll have to come back tonight and kidnap her," Bryce responded.

As the doctor escorted the four out of the facility, Saxxon and Dina slipped into Melanie's room.

"Melanie. It's me, Dina Lawrence. And I'm with Dr. Scott Saxxon. Do you remember us?"

Dina went on. "Melanie, we were friends with Larry Martin. Do you remember him?"

Melanie didn't respond.

"Set up the projector. Show her the videos," Scott exclaimed.

Dina played back the video of the dream from Whiteface Mountain. Saxxon started reciting the previous timeline from the past eighteen years. Scott could always get out a lot of content in a small amount of time. It was one of the reasons he was such a great lecturer. The audio from the video amplified down the hall, and soon a team of nurses and security stormed the room. Saxxon and Dina jumped out of the window and were chased by security. As the security guards cleared the room to chase down Scott and Dina, Melanie whispered to herself, "Larry, look out!" Melanie began convulsing as all the memories from both timelines came rushing into her head.

"She's convulsing," Yelled one of the nurses.

Another nurse came in and injected a sedative into Melanie's IV and she slipped into a deep sleep. And it seems she jumped right into the images from the ski trip that Dina had projected.

"Larry, look out!"

I turned and saw the rifle pointed at me from Bryan on the chair lift. I hit a small mogul and did a three-sixty with Melanie in my arms. I could never do that in real life and remembered this was a dream. Then I remembered I could fly in my dreams. We crossed another intersection and I was able to get enough speed to jump through the air. I used my swimming motion to glide to the base of the mountain. But it seemed that Bryan had some abilities in his dream as well as he was able to project himself from the chairlift and ended up right in front of us. I ran up and used a flying knee to knock the rifle from Bryan's hand. We both fell to the ground. I was able to grab the rifle, but he grabbed Melanie and put a knife to her throat. He completely shielded himself with her so I couldn't get a clean shot. Just then, Bryan disappeared from the dream. He must have woken himself up in fear of getting killed.

Melanie and I hugged each other. Melanie looked at me with sadness in her eyes.

"Larry, I'm going to wake up. I have to go back to my life in 2018."

"No! Why? We have a chance to change all this. Look, just stay with me right here in my arms. We're changing the timeline as we speak."

"I thought of that, Larry. But don't forget about Justin, Claire, and Bryan—they can manipulate the space-time continuum just like us. Harold is tethered to my chip and my timeline. If we change things now, they'll also be aware of the altered timeline. And they have this dream recorded. They'll just keep sending in one of the three until they get it right."

"True, but we're the only two that can dream together. We can out manipulate all of them."

"Not with the chip in my head, Larry."

206

"Well, figure out how to take it out. You took mine out."

"I can't. They monitor me in real-time."

"And even if we could beat them ... my kids, Larry. I must get back to my kids. If we alter the timeline in year 2000, I may never have met Matt, and never have had William and Lila. I don't want to erase that."

"Yeah, about that, I thought you hated kids?"

"I do hate kids. But Matt wanted them, and I figured it was now or never."

"Well, okay, forget Matt, we can make new kids, Melanie. I'll have kids with you."

"Come on Larry, it's not like changing towels. These are my kids that I love, that exist in another timeline, and are irreplaceable. What is wrong with you?"

"You're right. I am being crass. But Matt, Melanie? Come on. Do you really think he's the one for you?"

"It's not so black and white, Larry."

"Ugg. So why did you even stay with this dream? Why not wake yourself up?"

"Because I missed you. And I wanted to tell you that you were right about Beaumont's plan. They are going to make the meteor collision worse by using nuclear warheads."

"Why did you ever doubt me? I mean, you saw what I saw."

"I didn't know what was real and what wasn't real. I think Harold is manipulating my dreams."

"Not just Harold, Melanie. I'm sure Bryce Patrick and your husband are involved as well."

"You're wrong about Matt, Larry. I've spoken with him about all of this. He agrees that Beaumont is out of his mind."

"He's just telling you what you want to hear. And what do you think they'll do when they see this conversation?"

"I know. I'm in a lose-lose situation."

Melanie kissed me on the lips and whispered, "I love you." She then disappeared from my dream.

# 41

I woke up back in 2018. I was happy to be alive, but still distraught that Melanie didn't run away with me in the Whiteface dream from year 2000. Her love proclamation to me was bittersweet. I was doubting our relationship would ever come to fruition in the "non-dream" world.

I poured myself some cereal and heard knocking at my door, which made me skeptical since I never had any visitors. I looked out the window to make sure it wasn't any of Beaumont's hit men and I wondered if Melanie had set me up. Much to my surprise, it was two undergraduate students that were working in our lab. They were taking Saxxon's course and researching past proposals and had some questions about the underwater colony I designed in 1994.

"Hello Mr. Martin. My name ith Buth. Jamth Buth."

He had a thick Scottish accent and a bad lisp. I think he meant to say, "James Buss."

The young woman also introduced herself. "Hi. I'm Lorie."

"We are studenths een Scott Saxthons cloth," James muttered.

Lorie interrupted. "Yes, in Scott Saxxon's class. He said he called you to let you know we were coming."

"Ah. My phone's broken." I replied. But really, I couldn't afford the data plan anymore and the service was cut off.

James started talking again, but for the life of me, I couldn't understand a word he said. All I could make out was "theven forty theven."

Lorie went on. "Yes. We are looking for a full set of drawings for the underwater colony you designed. We only have the sketches you submitted with your paper. Like James said, we are particularly interested in drawing 747."

"I might have a set in the back room. They're all hard copy. This was pre-digital. What do you need them for?"

"James thinks he figured out a way to engineer a component you designed. Isn't that right James?"

"Yith."

James went on and explained how he was also doing a structural analysis of the project for another engineering class he was taking.

I dug the drawings out of the back room.

"Saxthon ees going to be pumped," James exclaimed.

"Will you be coming back to the lab anytime soon, Mr. Martin?" Lorie asked me.

"I doubt it."

"Scott and Dina miss you and could really use your help. They said something about a project called *Nike Jesus*?"

*Nike Jesus* was the original title Saxxon used for the project in his course, but he hadn't called it this in about twenty years. In recent times, Scott and Dina used this in code to refer to the actual meteor collision that was going to occur in 2020. Sadly, these students had no idea. They just assumed all this was for a class project.

Two days later, I saw the headlines on the news. "Feds raid underground lab at the University of Vermont—arrest several undocumented researchers."

I knew Beaumont was a white supremacist and that he vowed to expel all the illegal immigrants, but why would he care if the human race was going to be wiped out in a couple of years anyway? That is, unless he found out about the lab. I wondered if Melanie had set me up or if Harold figured out a way to triangulate my location even without the OC17 chip in my head. But then again, I didn't tell her about the lab. Maybe the students were followed, though, I thought.

# 42

Luckily, the lab was equipped with an extensive array of security cameras. This allowed Saxxon, Sherman, and Dina to evacuate the laser and about half of the research staff before Beaumont's team raided the complex. When Saxxon saw the team of mercenaries approaching the lab, he sent an encrypted text message to all the researchers. However, at least fifty of the researchers, mostly students in Saxxon's class, were taken to one of the new containment facilities Beaumont's cabinet employed to detain illegal immigrants. Although some of these people were from foreign countries, many were indeed U.S. citizens, which uncovered the grim truth that the government was using these facilities for anyone that challenged their authority. Sherman once explained how a source from inside the government told him Beaumont had a team of people dedicated to social media surveillance. Any negative talk about Beaumont, his policies, or his administration was flagged, and action would be taken to either frame or arrest these "rebels" or to detain and/or kill them. Although I was skeptical of this theory when he first told us, it was seemingly more and more plausible with this lunatic leading the country.

Saxxon and Dina had the drone laser in the back of an old van and were headed toward the mountains. Todd, Rachel, Sherman, Sam, and Margaret were all off site when the raid occurred.

"Where are we headed, Scott?" Dina asked.

"There's an abandoned ski resort just south of here. I used to go there as a kid. It has an old lodge where we can bunker down until we reconvene the team."

"How in the hell did Beaumont find us? I thought that lab was contained … that no signals could get in or out."

"It was. That's what concerns me."

"You think it was someone on the inside?" Dina asked in a concerned tone.

"It must have been." Scott responded solemnly.

"But who?"

"That's what we'll have to find out."

# 43

Matt Brennan was in a hotel suite at the Hilton when his phone rang.

"Matt, it's Bryce."

"Bryce, why are you calling me so early?"

"Did I interrupt something? And why are you at the Hilton and not in one of Mr. Beaumont's hotels?"

"You know why."

"Ahh, but you know Ned won't divulge your indiscretion. Hell, he cheats on Mrs. Beaumont all the time."

"Yeah, but I'm just being safe."

"I hear you. Cover all your bases. Well, anyway, the man wants to see you about a matter ASAP. How fast can you get here?"

"Twenty minutes. What's it about?"

"He didn't specify, but he said it's about your family."

"Oh shit. What has Melanie done now? I'll be right there."

A young man popped his head up on from the king-sized bed in the hotel suite. It was Justin from the Dream Maker program.

"Who's calling you this early, Matt?"

"Shhh. They'll hear."

"So, you don't have time for a morning quickie?"

"No. You better get dressed and get back to the lab."

"But look at what you're leaving me with."

Justin stood up completely naked and displayed his erection to Matt.

"Maybe tomorrow," Matt responded.

Matt walked down the west wing of the White House and was greeted by all the familiar faces. Bryce Patrick was waiting at the door.

"Come on in, Matt."

President Beaumont was seated at his desk and was reading over some material. In addition to Bryce, two other of the president's cabinet members were in the room—the Secretary of State and the president's doctor.

"Have a seat, Mr. Brennan."

Beaumont then put down his pen.

"How have you been, Matt?" The president asked.

"Not bad, sir. Yourself?"

"How's your beautiful wife?" The president responded.

"She's great. She's been busy with the kids."

"Ahh. The kids. That's what I have to talk to you about. It's come to our attention that your youngest, the girl, has some mental issues. Is that true?"

"Well, they're still running tests, sir, but—"

"I've seen the test results. That's why I asked Doctor Hess to be in the room. Dr. Hess, would you indulge Mr. Brennan."

"Certainly, sir. Mr. Brennan, after an intense psychological evaluation, we've found your daughter to be in the autism spectrum."

"Oh, yes, my wife thought this might be the case. Is there anything we can do?"

"Well, certainly. We can get her started with a specialist," Hess responded. "There are some new experimental treatments they can try."

"Well, great! Thank you."

Beaumont interrupted. "We will certainly do everything we can, but you do realize the real dilemma here, don't you Matt?"

Matt thought about it a bit, and then it sunk in.

Bryce interjected. "We'll make sure she's treated well for the next two years, Matt."

"And after that?"

"I think you know the answer to that, Mr. Brennan. After all, you were the one who devised the list of conditions that would preclude an inhabitant on the colony," Beaumont replied.

"True, but with all due respect sir, there has to be exceptions."

"No exceptions."

"But what if we can fix her?"

"No exceptions, Mr. Brennan." Beaumont responded even louder than the first time.

"You want me to sacrifice my own daughter?"

"It's for the good of the colony. We can't have any imperfections in the gene line."

"My wife will never go for this."

"Well, that's her choice. She can stay back with the girl if she wants. But we would hate to lose your wife. She has been a valuable asset with her abilities and all."

"I'll have to discuss this with her, of course."

"I understand," the president said. "Just don't take too long. The longer you drag this out, the harder it will be."

"Yes, sir," Matt answered.

Bryce then escorted Matt out of the office.

"What am I supposed to do, Bryce?"

"Well, what do you want to do?"

"Honestly, I never cared for the broad in the first place. I only had the kids to prove that I was—" Matt stopped himself.

"That you were what?" Bryce asked.

"A nice guy."

"Ahh. Kids don't make one nice, Matt."

"I know that. But what am I going to tell Melanie? She'll never go for this, and I need her to prove that I'm—"

"Nice?" Bryce answered.

"Yeah, something like that."

"Well, what if you didn't have to tell her anything?"

"What do you mean?"

"Matt, we have access to a brilliant team of scientists and three other dream makers that can alter the space-time continuum."

"Are you suggesting we erase Lila from existence? I don't know about that. Can that even be done?"

"Let's go talk to Harold." Bryce responded.

# 44

I received the coordinates from Saxxon to the old abandoned ski resort. I was almost going to ignore the message, but I looked out of the cupola of my carriage barn and saw a strange van parked on the street outside. Saxxon was serious—Beaumont's team found me. Luckily, I was prepared for just such an incident. My car was parked on the adjacent street at a tailor shop. I even had the shop's decal painted onto the side to enhance the decoy. I climbed out of the hopper window in the rear of the barn and made it to the car. Just as I pulled out, a train was approaching from the north. The train went off the rails and crashed into the carriage barn—my apartment was no more. I had always predicted this to happen since the tracks were only about twenty-five feet from the apartment, but this was way too much of a coincidence. Then I saw two men with large crow bars get out of the van to sift through the rubble. I slipped out of the tailor's office in the disguised vehicle.

I headed south toward the rendezvous point Saxxon sent to me. I was familiar with the abandoned resort as I once skied there as a kid when it was open. Even though much of the vegetation was overgrown, you could still make out where the ski trails were once located. The towers were still in place where the chair lift had stood, but the chairs and cables were all gone. The lodge was an octagon shape and was still actually very cozy. There was a large fireplace in one corner that was already lit by the time I arrived.

"Larry!"

Scott and Dina ran over to me and hugged and groped me like that hadn't seen me in years.

They squeezed me so hard I started to giggle. Dina kissed me on the mouth!

"What is all this?" I said as I chuckled.

"What do you mean? You died, silly."

"Oh, you know about that? But how?"

"Dina was able to hack into Melanie's OC17 chip and tether to her timeline," Scott answered. "So yes, we watched both iterations of the Whiteface dream."

"You know, I never did ask Melanie how she brought me back."

"Well, we visited her in the altered timeline in the mental institution and showed her a video of the dream. She must have been able to get back into it after we left."

"Wait, a mental institution?"

"Yes, after you were killed in the first dream, she ends up there for eighteen years."

"See Larry, she does love you, so quit acting so depressed." Dina said.

Dina continued, "Once again, it seems you two dreaming together can raise the dead—even yourself, apparently."

"So, I assume you saw that I asked her to run away with me in year 2000. Are you pissed about that?"

"Yeah, a bit. I mean, if we hadn't tethered to Melanie's timeline and you did run away, we would have never met," Dina said.

Scott chimed in and said, "And I would have known you, but only from my undergraduate course. All of our current effort to mitigate the end of the world would not exist."

"Yeah! Did you think of that, Larry?" Dina shouted.

"Well, yeah, of-course. I would have tracked you down in the new timeline. I swear."

"Yeah, I bet you would have," Dina said sarcastically. "Ahh, but don't feel too bad. The things you do for love, right? Besides, we would have found you in the altered timeline even if you didn't look for us."

"Well, it's all water under the bridge now," Scott interjected.

"So, what happened? How did they find the lab? Did they track me through Melanie?"

"Unlikely," said Dina. "Without the chip in your head, there is really no way to track you. And besides, even if they could, there was no mention of the lab in the dream."

"Well, maybe there's a mole? Hey, two of your students came to my barn the other day looking for drawings of my underwater colony, maybe it was them?"

"Lorie and James? No. It wasn't them. Trust me."

"Who, then?"

"I'm not sure. Dina is reviewing the surveillance videos to see if she can find any clues."

"What about the rest of the team?"

"They're being held in a containment facility near the Canadian border," Scott answered.

"That's sugar coating it. It is a concentration camp. Beaumont is worse than Hitler," Dina chimed in.

"Can we get them out?"

"We're not sure yet," Scott answered. "But in the meantime, we have to get our team re-assembled. The laser is almost done."

"*THE* laser? You mean there is only one now?"

"Unfortunately, we were only able to save one. The rest of the material was either destroyed or confiscated in the raid."

"In the best case scenario, how much of the world will we be able to save with one laser?"

"Not much," Scott said grimly. "But it's better than nothing. Even if we can save 10,000 people here on Earth, it will be worth it."

# 45

Bryce Patrick and Matt Brennan arrived at Harold Mitchell's lab. Harold was already briefed by the time they arrived.

"Okay Harold, so what are our options?"

"Well, thanks to the camera that we implanted in Melanie's head, we have all the footage of when you and Melanie conceived Lila in 2014 and we know the exact time and date."

Bryce started cheering like an immature schoolboy. "All right, crank up the video."

Harold went on. "We can implant this footage into both Melanie's chip and into one of our dream maker's OC17 chip. We'll have Bryan go into your room in 2014 and, well, interrupt."

"Interrupt?" Matt asked.

"Yeah, just try not to kill him when he pulls you away, Matt."

"With all due respect, can we use Justin?"

"Well, sure, any of the three will do. Why Justin?"

"Well, after Bryan's failed attempt to kill Larry at Whiteface, I figured we would try someone new."

"Fair enough," Harold agreed. "But we'll have to wait until Melanie falls asleep for this to work," Harold explained.

"You can monitor when she's asleep?" Asked Matt.

"Of course. We can monitor all our Dream Makers' actions, Mr. Brennan. The chip is a real-time feed."

"Right, I forgot," Matt replied.

About an hour passed and Melanie fell asleep. Harold brought the video up of the night Lila was conceived on the monitor to review any details that could better help Justin.

"I'm uploading the scene into both Justin and Melanie's OC17 chips," Harold explained as he executed the commands.

The scene was then visible on the monitors. Bryce started getting giddy like a schoolboy.

"Wow, Melanie is really hot, Matt!"

"Enough. You don't have to tell me," Matt answered.

In the dream, Matt was fussing with his smart phone in the bedroom.

"What are you doing with the phone, Matt?" Bryce asked. "Wait a minute, are you filming it?"

"Yes, but if I knew you were monitoring Melanie's chip, I wouldn't have had to."

"Hmm, that's interesting," Harold noted.

"What?" Bryce asked.

"It looks like someone else is on the phone."

Matt had to think quickly. "Oh, that is just a little porn I was using to get in the mood."

Harold zoomed in on the phone but couldn't enhance the image enough to decipher it.

Harold began the upload into Justin's chip.

"As we know, Justin may not be able to alter the dream since this is not a dream he dreamt of nor an event that he actually witnessed. But we'll see if it works."

"Fine, let's just get on with it," Matt yelled.

I fell asleep in the ski lodge next to the fireplace. I first had a dream that Matt and Harold were in a room manipulating a past event by uploading imagery into one of the dream makers at the lab. It seems they were trying to reverse Melanie's first pregnancy with Lila because of her autism. I walked up behind Harold, Matt, and Bryce and saw the interior of Melanie and Matt's penthouse. I could see Melanie on the bed and could see Matt facetiming someone on his phone. Matt then placed the phone on the dresser facing the bed. Then Justin suddenly appeared in the room.

"Jesus Christ! What the hell are you doing here, Justin?" Melanie yelled as she pulled a sweatshirt over her night gown.

Justin tried to play it cool.

"Oh, I am so sorry, I'm here to see Matt, actually."

Matt was confused as to how Justin could be in two places at the same time.

"Justin, what are you doing here? How did ..."

Just then, Melanie saw the phone angled on her on the dresser.

"Matt, what the hell is this?" She grabbed the phone and was stunned to see Justin on the other end.

"Melanie, I'll explain, just hand me the phone," Justin said in a condescending fashion.

Melanie started figuring things out.

"Wait a minute. This is a dream. But how did you get this footage? Harold! I know you can hear me, you freak! What is this? Justin, why did they send you?"

Just then, Justin jumped on Melanie to grab the phone. Melanie went to swing at him, but he vanished in thin air. Harold must have woken him up in the dream.

"Matt, what the hell is going on here? How and why was Justin on the phone and in our room at the same time?"

As Matt tried to fabricate an answer, Melanie began scrolling through the phone. She could see several correspondences with Justin. She scrolled through the photos and videos. There were several intimate videos of she and Matt, Justin by himself watching she and Matt, Matt and Justin together, Matt with another woman, and Matt, Justin, and several others together.

Matt lunged at Melanie and grabbed the phone. Melanie threw it at him. Then Melanie woke up back in 2018.

***

Justin woke up back at the lab in 2018.

"Did it work?" Matt inquired.

Harold examined the altered timeline.

"Well, yes and no," Harold replied.

"What do you mean?" Asked Matt.

"Well, Lila was not born, but it looks like you and Melanie are divorced."

Matt's vision suddenly went out of focus. He could hear Harold talking, but couldn't make out the words. Then, everything seemed to be back in focus.

"That's right, I'm with Heather now," Answered Matt.

"Ahh, yes, that's why you just blacked out. The memories from the past two years in the new timeline were just catching up with you. Are you okay with this, Mr. Brennan? I can send Justin back in and try and fix it if you'd like."

Matt looked up at Justin, who seemed disappointed in the outcome.

"No. It's fine. I have to get home to Heather and William."

Matt stormed out of the room and Justin went after him.

"Where the hell is he going?" asked Bryce.

"Good question. Let's check the new timeline."

"Hmmm, that's odd," muttered Harold.

"What?"

"Well, I no longer have a location on Melanie's chip!"

***

Melanie woke up in a panic since she didn't recognize the room she was in. And then her memories caught up with her from the 2014 dream in her old penthouse. She remembered the images of Matt with Justin and another woman who she now realized was Heather. She remembered confronting Matt about it, Matt admitting to his infidelity, and making a deal with him—her silence in exchange to have the OC17 chip removed from her head. If Beaumont knew about Matt's pansexuality, he'd be banned from the space colony. Ironically, it was Matt who defined the criteria for the inhabitants of the colony. What a hypocrite, she thought. She remembered Matt showing up with the gun-like device to remove her chip and being injected with something and passing out. As she looked around the room, she also then remembered Matt bringing her to one of Beaumont's rehabilitation clinics. She then heard some voices in the hall and a series of doors unlocking.

Matt then entered the room with William holding his hand and a doctor from the clinic. William ran to Melanie and gave her a big hug.

"Mommy!" William yelled.

Melanie hugged William.

"Where's your sister?" Melanie exclaimed.

"Why don't you go play down the hall for a while Daddy talks to Mommy. Here's some money—there are some vending machines in the lobby."

"So how is she doing, doctor? Does she still think someone went back in time and stole her daughter?" Matt asked in a disbelieving tone.

"She does, Mr. Brennan. We still can't get to the bottom of these delusions. But it seems she is making progress on her sexuality. Our latest tests seem to indicate that she prefers monogamous relationships with men, so the therapy is working," the doctor said with much certainty. "But yes, these delusions are concerning. She'll have to stay here until we can get to the bottom of this."

"Of course, doctor," Matt said diplomatically.

The doctor left the room. Melanie then remembered Lila was never born.

"I take it that memory just caught up with you?" Matt asked.

"Yes, but I still don't know why you had to prevent her conception? Why couldn't we have just hidden her?"

"Beaumont knew about her autism. There was no way she'd be deemed fit to be on the colony. This was the best way, otherwise, she'd have been left on Earth to die. Did you want to have to make that choice, Mel?"

"It wasn't your call. She was my daughter. I loved her," Melanie shouted.

The doctor overheard the commotion in the room and peaked his head in.

"Is everything all right in here? I can give her more valium, if necessary."

"No, we're okay. But thanks, doctor."

Melanie then started to laugh. Wait a minute, is this one of Beaumont's gay-conversion clinics?"

"Indeed, it is Mel. It seems your infidelity caught up to you."

"My infidelity? I think you have that backwards, dear."

Matt pulled out his phone and scrolled to several videos. It seems he doctored the footage of the sex videos of him, Justin, and Heather—his face and Justin's face were replaced with Melanie and Larry. He also showed her a video of her dream with Larry at Whiteface.

"And they bought this?" Melanie asked.

"They did. But you should be happy. Things could have turned out worse."

"Worse? How can this get any worse? My daughter is gone, and my pansexual husband has me locked in a clinic."

"Well, Beaumont and Bryce suggested that you be eliminated and not because of your infidelity, but because of your continued communications with Larry Martin. They didn't appreciate your insubordination in the Whiteface dream. I pleaded for your life and convinced them this therapy would help. You should be thanking me."

"Thanking you? And how's that, Matt?"

"Well, you still get to see your son. And if you quit acting crazy, you still may be able to be on the colony. And don't forget, thanks to me, that damned chip is no longer in your head."

"You only took the chip out so Harold and Bryce won't find out about you and Justin. It was only a matter of time until I dreamed about that again since those images are ingrained in my head. And what makes you think I still want to be on the colony? I'd rather stay here and die."

"Well, your son will be on the colony with me. With you committed, Beaumont wants William to take your place in the dream maker program."

Melanie's face turned blank.

"That's right Mel, Will is coming with me whether you come or not. Look, this doesn't have to be a fight. Just stop talking about Lila and denounce Larry Martin. The doctors will give you clearance, and we can make this work."

"I don't see how," Melanie responded.

"Well, that's up to you, Mel."

Without the chip in her head, Melanie realized she could just go back and change things again and Harold Mitchell would never know. However, it was a double-edged sword. She had to conjure up the dream all on her own. It had been a while since her dreams were not monitored and controlled by the dream maker program. If she could just get back to the dream from 2014, she could steal Matt's phone and save the videos before Justin entered the dream. She tried for several weeks to get back into the dream but was unsuccessful. But one night, out of the blue, she started having a romantic dream about Larry.

# 46

I woke up to go to the bathroom and tried to recap everything I saw in the previous dream. I wondered if Harold and Matt's plan to prevent the conception of Lila worked. Without the chip in my head, Dina wouldn't be able to see the altered timeline. I went onto the computer to see what I could dig up on social media, but much to my surprise, all of Melanie's accounts were deleted. I wondered if she was still alive. I fell back asleep and suddenly found myself in a clinic with Melanie. She was passionately kissing me.

"Melanie, is this your dream?"

"Yeah, I think."

"Where are we?"

"We are in a gay-conversion therapy clinic," she responded.

"Wait, what?"

"It's a long story, Larry."

"Let me guess, Matt had you committed here, right?"

"Yes. How did you know?"

"Well, a couple of hours ago, I had a dream Harold, Matt, and Bryce were plotting to prevent the birth of Lila. They sent Justin into a scene from your dream archives. I saw the scene on the monitors."

"So you know? You know that their plan worked then, right? Lila was never born in the altered timeline. They erased my little girl, Larry." Melanie began crying.

"I didn't know if it worked. I'm sorry Melanie."

"Did you see what was on Matt's phone?"

"No, I couldn't make it out. I don't think Harold or Bryce could see it either."

"Well, apparently, he, Justin, and some woman named Heather have been having some kind of three-way affair. That's why Matt insisted on sending Justin into the dream. He needed him to hide the evidence on the phone. Justin was on the phone watching us in the act. It was a perverted fantasy the two of them had. If Harold and Bryce had seen these images, they'd have told Beaumont, and this would have precluded Matt from being on the space colony."

"Wow. That's probably the craziest thing I have ever heard, and that's coming from me. So how did you end up here?"

"I threatened to expose the videos of Matt. In exchange for my silence, Matt agreed to sneak me into the lab and have my chip removed. He needed that chip out too because I was liable to conjure up the images of what was on the phone in a dream and thus Harold would be able to see what I saw. He took the chip out, but then injected me with something to knock me out. He then altered the videos to make it look like it was you, me, and Justin in the dream. So they committed me to the sex addiction wing in one of Beaumont's gay conversion therapy clinics."

"What about Justin?"

"It looks like Matt double crossed him as well. He's down the hall. His chip is gone as well. But my little girl, Larry. They took her from me."

"Maybe we can go back into the dream and get her back."

"I've been trying, but I can't get back into the dream without assistance from the OC17 chip. Besides, I'm so disgusted by Matt right now, I'm not sure I can go back and conceive a child with him again knowing what I know now."

Melanie was inconsolable, so I walked up to her and put my arms around her. Then, my mind must have went into full desire mode because we were suddenly having sex. I couldn't tell if it was me controlling the dream, Melanie controlling it, or both of us. So, I just went with it. I was bummed when I woke up back at the ski lodge by myself.

# 47

Melanie woke up from the dream back in the clinic in 2018. Although she was quite taken with the sex dream with Larry, she was still determined to get back to the penthouse dream from 2014 to prevent Lila from being erased. For the next month, she tried relentlessly, but couldn't get back into the dream. One day, she woke up and felt queasy. She thought it was a virus, but since she didn't really interact with people, she was perplexed as to how she could have caught it. After about a week, she told one of the doctors at the clinic, who agreed to run some tests. The doctor came into the room with a curious look on his face.

"Ms. Merriman, I have some very surprising news for you. It seems you're pregnant."

"What? That's not possible"

"Well, we ran the test three times to ensure it wasn't a false positive. Now I'm assuming the father is your husband, Matt?"

Melanie thought for a minute. She had not had sex with Matt since 2014 when Lila was conceived. However, the doctor didn't know that, after all, Matt did come and check on her every couple of weeks. For all the doctor knew, they were having conjugal visits.

"Oh, yes, right. It is. I mean Matt is the father," Melanie responded.

"Would you like us to let him know?"

"No, that won't be necessary. I'll tell him when he visits later in the week."

"Very well. Now this clinic is not equipped to deliver babies, so we will have to temporarily transfer you to another hospital when that time comes."

"Of course," Melanie responded.

As the doctor left the room, Melanie remembered the dream with Larry. Was that even possible? Could she get pregnant from having sex in a dream? No way, she thought. She must be hallucinating. She thought the clinic might have been drugging her and she wasn't thinking straight or maybe someone raped her in her sleep. But that was ridiculous, she would have known. She slapped herself in the face to make sure she wasn't dreaming and threw some water on her face from the sink. She was awake. The dream with Larry was the only plausible explanation.

But what was she going to tell Matt, she thought? Perhaps it would be best not telling him and denying his visits for the next eight months, but she realized that wouldn't be possible. The clinic belonged to Beaumont, and Matt could come and go as he pleased. Then she thought she might have to seduce Matt and have sex with him the next time he showed up, then conceal the pregnancy for another month and then tell Matt the baby was his. There were also few other male patients at the clinic; maybe she could seduce one of them, or better yet, just convince one of them to lie about an affair. Since being intimate with Matt repulsed her after she found out about his sexual escapades and that sleeping with a stranger also grossed her out, she decided going back into the dream and changing the timeline was the best option. Then again, her pregnancy might also be her ticket out of the facility where she most likely would be imprisoned indefinitely or at least until the meteor collision.

For the next few days, Melanie tried to get back into the dream but was unsuccessful. Then, out of the blue, Matt showed up with Bryce Patrick.

"The doctor tells me you're pregnant. How is that possible?" Matt yelled.

Melanie had to think fast. "I dreamt we were back in the penthouse, but it wasn't from 2014, it was a dream in present time. We had sex in the dream, Matt. I think that's how I got pregnant!"

"Wait, what? That is bullshit and not scientifically possible. You slept with another patient or one of the doctors, didn't you?" Matt yelled back.

"No, of course not. You know me, Matt. You know I could never do that. Besides, there are cameras and security everywhere here. They know everyone who comes in and out of the rooms at all times."

"Well, they could have altered the footage."

"Well, have one of the techs at the lab analyze the footage."

"I will," Matt yelled back.

Matt stormed out of the room and grabbed one of the doctors.

"What the hell is going on here, doctor?"

"What do you mean, Mr. Brennan?"

"You know what I mean. Who had sex with my wife?"

226

"You mean your ex-wife. But I'm not sure what you mean, Mr. Brennan," the doctor said.

"But I can assure you, she has not had any sexual relations with any of the staff or patients here. Does this have something to do with her pregnancy?"

Matt didn't answer. "Where is the server room? I'm going to need all the security footage from the past two months."

"Well certainly, Mr. Brennan. Actually, Harold Mitchell should be able to access it remotely since he has top security clearance in all digital databases."

As Matt and Bryce stormed out of the clinic, Matt dialed up Harold Mitchell to have him access the security footage.

"I'll get some of our techs working on it right away, but it will take some time. What is going on?"

"Melanie is pregnant," Matt responded.

"And I'm assuming it's not yours?"

"No. She claims it was from sex we had in a dream."

"Hmmm, well, since you took her chip out without my permission, I must remind you that we are not able to verify that," Harold answered somewhat sarcastically.

"I know. I realize that. But is that even possible? Could she get pregnant from a dream?"

"Unlikely. Possibly if she was dream-sharing with someone. And so far, she has only shared dreams with—"

"With Martin. Larry Martin," Matt interrupted.

"What should we do about this, Mr. Brennan? You know, a child from two parents with dream altering ability may have exceptional abilities."

"Yeah, and?" Matt asked.

"Well, we could put the child in the dream maker program. With Justin locked up in the clinic, and Claire's days numbered, we'll need to keep the program going when we are on the colony. We already have started Will and this new child would be a fine addition, that is given the child doesn't have any abnormalities," Harold explained.

"So, we just let her have it?"

"Indeed."

227

"And what do we do with Melanie?"

"Well that's up to you, Mr. Brennan. Do you think she still may jeopardize the space colony?"

"I do."

"Then we may have to eliminate her after she has the child. With Will and the new child in the dream maker program, we really don't need her anymore."

"We'll have to see what Beaumont thinks." Matt hung up the phone.

Matt thought about it during the car ride back to his penthouse. He now had Heather to pose as his wife to fit the part on the space colony, but he was unsure if he could kill Melanie. After all, he did really love her at one point. He also needed a way to get Justin out of the clinic. He was going to have Heather pose as Justin's partner, but since he was now hot and heavy with Heather, maybe he could work a deal with Melanie to pose as Justin's love interest. He could blackmail Melanie by using Will and the other child as bait.

# 48

Melanie continued to try and alter the dream, but still couldn't find her way back in. If only she could conjure Larry the two of them could certainly figure it out together. But then Matt showed up again.

"Okay, so this is how it's going to work, Mel. You're going to convince everyone that you and Justin had an affair here in the clinic and that the baby is Justin's."

"And why the hell would I do that?"

"It's the only way to keep you alive, Mel. Beaumont, Bryce, and Harold want to eliminate you. With Will in the dream maker program and the new child, you are now expendable. They still think you may jeopardize the colony. I actually think you will, too, which is why I'm making this deal."

"Ahh, so I see. I pose as Justin's woman which makes him look straight. This will allow him back on the colony and allow you to continue your affair with him. You tell everyone I cheated on you, which makes your relationship with Heather seem legit. What's in it for me? I'd rather die!"

"Well, it's not just your life, Mel. What about Will? Harold already has him in the program; he and Beaumont will certainly want the new child as well. If they leave you here to die, you will never see them again. Do you want that?"

"What makes you think I just won't go back and alter the dream again?" Melanie asked.

"Because. This child is your only way out of this clinic. It's the only way to ensure you will be on the colony, and the only way you will ever see your kids again."

"And what about Lila, Matt? She was defective in your eyes and you erased her from existence. What if the new child has some sort of one of your so-called defects? Then we're back to square one."

"Well, let's hope he or she doesn't," Matt responded. "So do we have a deal?"

"Did you ever really love me, Matt, or was it all for show?"

"I will always love you, Mel, just not in that way."

"So what's with Justin and Heather?"

"I met Justin shortly after we met. I didn't realize I could ever love a man until I met him. I started dating Heather shortly after I had you committed to make things look straight, but eventually developed feelings for her as well. I guess sometimes I feel like Burger King and sometimes I feel like McDonalds. I'm sorry all this happened, Mel, but these are the very consequences Harold warned us about when we alter history."

"The bottom line is you threw me under the bus to protect your own ass. Do you really think you, Justin, and Heather will ever be able to continue your three-way relationship on the colony? Beaumont will have all three of you ejected into space."

"That's a chance I'm going to have to take. But we can make this work and it can be a win-win for both of us."

Melanie thought about it. She really had no other choice.

"Fine, I'll do it."

# 49

Matt walked into his weekly meeting with Ned Beaumont, Bryce Patrick, Harold Mitchell, the vice president, and various other department heads regarding the exodus of the people from the ten sites into the space colony, which was now less than two years away.

"Mr. Brennan. Mr. Patrick tells me there is a situation with your ex-wife. Is she going to be a problem?"

"No sir. I'm glad you brought that up. I confronted Melanie last week. It seems she and Justin had an affair at the gay conversion clinic and she's now pregnant with Justin's baby."

Harold Mitchell chimed in. "Oh really? So the baby is not from the dream with Larry Martin?"

"No."

"Well, we will need to confirm that once the baby is born," the president remarked. "Because if she is lying and she did conceive with Martin, we'll want to get that child in our custody for monitoring, otherwise the three of them together could jeopardize the entire mission."

"Indeed. Whether the offspring is Justin's or Larry's, he or she will have exceptional dreaming abilities. We'll definitely want to test the child as soon as we can," Harold replied.

"Yes, she's willing to allow us to test the child and enter him or her into the dream maker program," Matt answered.

"That is if there are no problems with the child. We had to make a correction on the girl," Bryce remarked.

"I don't want to know about it. Just do what you have to do. So does this mean Justin has been rehabilitated?" The president asked.

"It seems so, sir," Matt answered.

"Excellent! I knew they could do great things at that clinic." The vice president chimed in.

"Great. So, you and Heather, Justin and Melanie, your son William, and Melanie and Justin's new child will all be on the colony. See how things work out, Mr. Brennan?" The president said.

"Yes sir."

"Is there any other pressing news from the dream makers, Mr. Mitchell?"

"Well, with Justin and Melanie in the clinic, we were down to just Claire and Bryan. Claire's abilities seem to be fading. Bryan, however, did dream of the location of Saxxon's lab that we were able to destroy."

"Yes, he should be commended on that. Did we confiscate all their equipment?" The president asked.

"Yes. It seems they were working on drone lasers that could be launched to counter some of the meteors."

"Could have those really worked, though? I mean, come on! A tiny little drone?" Bryce interjected.

"Well, in theory, one of the drones has enough power to destroy several large meteors, but this would only protect maybe a sixty-square mile area. We confiscated six of them during the raid," Harold explained.

"Are we sure the team hasn't regrouped?" The president asked.

"If they did, they do not have enough people or time to develop any more drones," Harold answered.

"And how are our evacuation sites looking? Has there been any attrition?"

"Not much. Our initial screenings were concise. We only had to weed out a handful of misfits. Most of the other residents have remained and are ready to go on their *space vacation*," Bryce explained.

Everyone in the room chuckled.

"Right, their ten-year vacation," The vice president added.

"And the nuclear warheads? Do we know which meteors will be enhanced?"

The head of NASA's Near Earth Object center, Robert Smyth, stood up and piped in.

"We are getting closer, sir. We have three, large two hundred-mile meteors that we're currently watching. One is going to hit near the Texas-Mexico border, one is going to hit in the Atlantic, and the third will hit somewhere near northern Africa."

"Oh Christ, it looks like we built that damn border wall for nothing," the president joked. "And good, Africa is a shithole. I'm glad that one is on target. I went there once and have never been so disgusted."

"But we'll certainly need more than three to ensure the human race is completely annihilated, right?" Asked Harold.

"Indeed. The good news is the largest meteor is about the size of our moon. This one will break up into thousands of pieces ranging from the size of a baseball to the size of Texas. We should be able to get better projections as we get closer to the impact date."

"And do we know the exact date?"

"We have it narrowed down to a three-day window. And get this: July 3rd, 4th, or 5th 2020. It couldn't be more fitting, right?" The scientist giggled in a nerdy manner.

The president didn't laugh, nor did anyone else in the room. "Do you think this is funny, Mr. Smyth?"

"No, of course not, sir."

"Good. Because one screw up and this whole plan will go to shit!" The president stood up. "Until next time, gentleman."

# 50

After about six months in the ski lodge, Scott Saxxon and Dina Lawrence still were working with a skeleton team. In addition to Scott, Dina, and myself, the team only consisted of Sherman, Lorie, James, Todd, Sam, Rachel, Margaret, and twelve students that weren't captured in the raid of the lab. Sherman, Lorie, and James were working remotely at a small camp near Lake Champlain, but nobody seemed to know exactly what they were working on, which made me somewhat suspicious. I told Saxxon about Lorie and James visiting me to get a set of my plans for the underwater colony I designed as an undergraduate student in his class.

"Yes, James is actually still pursuing his PhD in structural engineering. He needed a project for his dissertation. He's actually building a small-scale version of your colony in the lake for his project."

"Really?"

"He has Sherman helping him with the funding. The site will be a good cover for us to complete the construction of the drone-laser. We can just tell people all the work is for James's dissertation. There is a large garage on the site and an area that we may be able to launch the drone without it being detected."

Scott went on. "The site also has enough abandoned cabins for the rest of the team to reside, that is, once we get them out of that prison camp near the border."

"And how are we going to get them out?"

"Since Beaumont has detained so many people, the detainment prisons are hiring more security guards. Beaumont and his team have never seen Sam, so we have him applying for a job on the inside as we speak. Because the prison is on the lake near the U.S.-Canadian border, we will evacuate people via water."

Later that week, Scott, Dina, and I loaded all the gear into a van and Scott's car and drove to the lake site. The site was an old campground that had been deserted since Beaumont cut all funding to state and federal parks. There were about twenty rustic cabins overlooking the lake. The site was heavily wooded and there was a small island about one hundred yards off the shore. Seeing a site as pretty as this made me sad knowing it would most likely be destroyed in the meteor collision.

I fell asleep out on one of the screened porches of one of the cabins and soon began to dream of Melanie. We were once again out swimming in the lake together.

"Larry, where are we?" Melanie asked.

"Oh, this is a small camp on Lake Champlain. Do you like it?"

"It's beautiful, but you have to listen to me. I've been trying to dream of you again for the past six months."

"I know. Me, too. I wish I could just relive that night we had together."

"Well, yes, about that night. I'm pregnant"

"What? With Matt again?"

"No, silly. With you."

"What? How is that even possible?"

"Well, it seems I can get pregnant in dreams."

"That is completely, scientifically impossible," I yelled.

"As impossible as altering history by going into a dream? Larry, we don't know what is possible with this gift, or this curse, whatever you want to call it."

"When are you due?"

"In a few months."

"Does Matt know?"

"Yes."

"Does he know it's mine?"

"Yes. But here's the thing. I worked a deal with him to keep the baby safe. I have to pretend that the baby is Justin's. This way, he looks straight and can inhabit the space colony."

"And what do you get out of the deal?"

"I'll get to see my kids. Otherwise, Matt, Bryce, and Beaumont would probably just have me eliminated seeing I was still sharing dreams with you."

"Can you trust Matt?"

"I don't have a choice."

# 51

Bryce, Harold, and Matt entered the meeting room in the White House where Robert Smyth from NASA and Derick Englesby, the chief engineer overseeing the space colony construction, had the real-time cameras of the construction of the space colony up on one of the monitors. One of Beaumont's news networks was up on the other monitor covering the construction. The headlines across the bottom of the screen read, "Beaumont's outer space resort ahead of schedule." Beaumont entered the room and everyone at the table stood up. In addition to Smyth and Englesby, the vice president, the Joint Chiefs of Staff, and department heads from the rest of the cabinet were also present.

"Mr. Englesby, when can we go to space?" The president asked right away.

"About three more months, Mr. President. We are still testing the energy and air systems."

"Excellent. And where are my quarters again?" The president asked while looking at the monitors.

Englesby positioned the camera around the colony and zoomed into the presidential suite. "Ahh, right there, sir."

"Is there a hot tub?" The president joked.

"Of course, sir," Englesby answered.

"Really? I was just joking when I requested that, but now I'm even more excited."

The president went on. "Do we know which of our resorts will be evacuated first? I've been getting a lot of emails."

Matt Brennan chimed in.

"Yes, sir. We'll start with the eastern most resorts first and move south and clockwise around the country. Each ship holds five-hundred passengers, so there will be two launches per each site. We will start in about three months when testing is complete. There will be one launch a day, so it will take just about a month to get all the people on board."

"And what about the astronauts working on the colony? Do we have to eliminate any of them?"

"That's already been taken care of. There were about a dozen or so who were suspicious that the colony was more than a resort. A couple even transmitted pictures of the project to people on Earth. I'm happy to report all these people had unfortunate space accidents."

"Excellent. When do I get to board?"

Englesby chimed back in. "We were thinking toward the middle of the launch just to ensure there are no unforeseen problems. You know, test things out a bit with the inhabitants."

"No, Mr. Englesby. I want to be there first thing. My family and my team, first thing," The president said as he looked at Bryce, Harold, and Robert.

"Certainly, sir. We can accommodate that."

"Is there anything else we need to discuss? I'm late for a golf game."

Just then, Justin from the dream maker program came storming in the room.

"Justin, what the hell are you doing here?" Harold yelled.

Two armed guards came running behind him. One of the guards apologized.

"We're are sorry. Justin broke out of the clinic!"

The president motioned with his hands for everyone to be quiet.

"It's okay. It's fine. Let the man speak. Obviously, he has something important to say."

Justin ran over to the computer with a thumb drive. "I have something to show you all."

Matt stood up. "Someone grab him and don't let him touch that goddamn computer."

The two security guards grabbed Justin.

"No, wait! I just had this dream. It affects the colony!"

"Is this true, Mr. Mitchell?" The president asked.

Harold pulled out his phone and connected to Justin's OC17 chip to examine his dream bank.

"I don't see anything, Mr. President. Justin, what the hell is this all about?"

"I'm curious. Let the man bring the files up," the president remarked.

Matt grabbed the president by the arm. "Mr. President, I would strongly advise against that. He may be trying to sabotage the entire network or steal footage of the space colony."

"Mr. Brennan, let go of my arm. Go ahead, Justin, show us what you have."

The security guards let go of Justin. He put the flash drive in and brought up a series of videos of him and Matt having sex. He then started to shout.

"That's right. That's me and Matt Brennan and we are in love! I'm not hiding it anymore! And Matt, to try and cover this up by telling everyone that Melanie and I had an affair?"

"This is obviously fabricated! Those videos are doctored. That is not me," Matt yelled.

Justin went on. "We can't be on the space colony because we are gay. So what. I'd rather die here on Earth than live a lie in that space colony."

"Mr. Mitchell, can you examine the footage to see if it has been altered?"

"Of course, sir. I'll get on it right away."

"And Mr. Brennan, if this turns out to be true, I will be very disappointed in you. Until then, please escort Mr. Brennan and Justin to the holding area. I can't have either of you fleeing."

After the meeting, Harold took the footage back to the lab to analyze. He then phoned the president.

"Mr. President, the footage of Justin and Matt is real."

The president hung up the phone and chuckled. Bryce Patrick was standing at his side.

"Huh. So it's true. It seems Matt and Justin are a thing."

"So now what? Should we put them in the gay-conversion clinic?"

"No. I don't think that place works. After all, Justin has been in there for a couple of years now. That clinic was the vice president's idea."

"What should we do? Eliminate them?"

"No, Mr. Patrick. I'm not a monster. Have them detained at one of our prisons. I hear there is room at the one near the Canadian-U.S. border."

"That's essentially the same as killing them, right?"

238

"Absolutely not, Mr. Patrick. Who knows, they might survive. We still don't know the extent of the damage the meteors and nuclear arsenal will cause. So no, I don't equate this with murder."

"And what do we do with Ms. Merriman? Justin is not the father of her baby, I'm assuming."

"Ahh, right. We'll need to find out who is. If that baby has dreaming ability, I want it on the colony."

"Right, Mr. President. I'll get Harold working on it."

\*\*\*

With Justin's escape, all hell broke out at the gay-conversion clinic. Melanie was able to get out of her room and eventually out of the building, but being nine months pregnant, she couldn't get very far. She ran down the street to the train station. She could now see where she was—somewhere north of New York in the Catskills. She bought a ticket to Vermont. After boarding the train, Melanie quickly fell asleep. She started dreaming and saw Matt and Justin imprisoned in one of Beaumont's containment centers. She then dreamed she was in a shopping mall and had a strange ability to jump inside people's minds and hear their thoughts.

# 52

I worked with James, Sherman, Todd, and Sam for the next couple of weeks on James's dissertation project, where he engineered the structure and the energy systems of the underwater colony I designed as an undergraduate. He had a small model that he started with, then he progressed to a larger scale model, and much to our surprise, he started one at full scale. The first challenge James had to solve was how to simulate the pressure in the scaled models. James initially thought that a one-quarter inch model at a ten feet depth would be equivalent to a full-scale construction at an eighty foot depth, which is about the minimum depth the colony would have to be to provide adequate barrier to the radiation from both the meteors and any nuclear missiles. However, Sherman was still working on getting some type of submarine or deep underwater vessel to construct the full-scale portion. Deeper colonies around the sixty-foot depth are either constructed open to ambient pressure, which means that the interior atmosphere pressure is equal to the surrounding water pressure, or are constructed closed to the water with air-locked hatches, whereby interior pressure is less than the surrounding water pressure. Open systems are frequently employed in lab settings where divers are submerged for long periods and entering and exiting the lab into the water on a frequent basis. Since the pressure inside the lab is equal to the water pressure, there is no need for decompression each time the diver swims back into the lab. However, since people would not be entering and exiting the colony on a frequent basis, my original design called for a closed system.

The original design had an interconnected series of pressurized domes ranging from one to ten thousand square feet. James scaled this down to five-hundred square feet domes for his project. The colony was constructed of high strength titanium for the structure and six inch acrylic glass for the windows to maintain the interior air pressure at one ATM and called for a pressure shaft that extended from the colony to the water surface. James was able to build a pressure shaft for the one-quarter inch model at the ten-foot depth but would simply not have the resources to build one at the hundred-foot depth if it ever came to fruition. Once again, a submarine would be needed for construction and for the transport of people into the colony. The oxygen supply was generated from the electrolysis of water. A small distillation plant was installed to filter the lake water to make it potable, and power was generated through solar panels at the surface. The panels at the surface would have to be encased to withstand any impacts from the meteor collision. A back-up nuclear generator was also included in my original design, but this was something beyond James's expertise.

Sunlight was to be "siphoned" from the surface using solar tubes that use advanced optics and these, along with high pressure sodium grow lamps would be installed in the greenhouse where food would be grown.

Working on the dissertation gave me a new sense of purpose. I always needed a project to sustain myself, and seeing this was my design, I started to develop a new interest in the design-build process. We joked that we all might have to cram into the five domes if our laser didn't stop the meteors.

Seeing I was working about sixteen hours a day on the project, I was sleeping fairly sound and having many vivid dreams. One particular dream was really interesting. I was walking through a shopping mall that was abandoned in 2010. The mall was two floors with an open center and a glass atrium on the ceiling; the second floor had a row of shops and a balcony overlooking the courtyard below. This mall had a canal down the middle where you could rent kayaks or take gondola rides. There were bridges over the canal and extensive interior vegetation. A monorail ran through the building and connected the mall to rest of the city. The upper level was retrofitted with housing units, while the lower level was a mix of retail, entertainment, movie theatres, restaurants, and gymnasiums. I gathered from the dream that this had to be the future. I was familiar with the mall and as far as I know, it was still abandoned. But if it was the future, I wondered if that meant we somehow survived the meteor collision that was set to occur in less than a year?

Anyway, in this dream, I was able to jump into a person's mind. All I had to do is walk up to someone, touch their arm, and I was inside their conscience. I could hear their thoughts, see through their eyes, and communicate with them. I thought about the mental health applications.

Most of the people walking around in the mall were people I knew, or more particularly, people I dreamt of in the past. I saw Cindy, Gina, Raja, Ng, Sam, Todd, Phil, Donna, Maryanne, Kristi, and Michelle. Michelle was the first one I locked onto. Since I never went back and changed the timeline, Michelle ended up marrying Jason, the same guy who date raped Cindy in the original dream I altered. I could see Michelle was not happy. I could feel her anxiety and hear her thoughts about Jason. She said to herself as she looked into a clothing store window, "I bet I'd look good in that dress; I wonder if Jason would think it was too slutty?"

I blurted out, "Who cares what Jason thinks!"

Michelle stopped in her tracks and frantically looked around the mall.

"Who said that?" She asked.

"Wait, you can hear me?"

"Yes, Larry, is that you?"

"Yes!"

"What the hell is this? Where are you? Is there a chip in my head?"

"No, I'm somehow able to jump inside people's minds."

"Why don't you buy the dress?"

"I think I will, Larry."

I couldn't quite control who I was latching onto or "mind jumping" in the dream. I kept getting stuck onto each person that walked by. I was amazed at the variety of different thinking patterns and thoughts that people had. I saw depression, anxiety worse than mine, excitement, love, hate, good, and evil, and I could manipulate all of them. In the wrong hands, this power could be extremely dangerous if it actually changed the timeline like the other dreams did. But I was unsure if it would alter the timeline. After all, it was the future, and there was really no way to know until that time arrived. In my other future premonition dreams, I was only able to see what happened and unlike the dreams going into the past, I was unable to alter the timeline in future dreams. I could only react to something in the present that I saw in the dream in the future. However, maybe this new mind jumping would change that?

As I was perusing the mall, I suddenly saw Melanie. She was walking toward me with determination. She touched my arm and suddenly I could hear her in my head.

"Larry, if you stay inside of someone's head too long, your physical body takes on the form of where you left it," she yelled.

"What?"

"Go back into Michelle's head and look at yourself from her eyes."

As I did this, I saw what she meant. I was standing next to a bench and I saw my body slowing fusing with the floor and the bench. I jumped out of Michelle's head by grabbing a structural column in the mall. I slowly fused with my body by the bench. Melanie then jumped back into my head.

"See," she said.

"And if anyone else has this ability, they can steal our bodies permanently while we are in someone else's head."

"Holy shit! How long have you had this ability?" I asked.

"I just discovered it while I was pregnant. I thought it was just the hormones, but this is real."

Just then, someone walked by and sneezed. I turned my head and covered my face with my hands. I felt some of the mist hit my hands and I started to freak out.

"Jesus, Larry. Is this how you feel all the time? This is awful. How do you live like this?"

"It's a day to day fight, Mel."

As I looked around, my OCD kept spiraling. Melanie whispered to me softly, "Larry, there is nothing to worry about. I'm seeing what you see and there is nothing dangerous here."

The panic started to subside. What great treatment, I thought. Melanie grabbed onto a bench and pulled herself out of my head and fused with her body. "Do you want to see something else that we can do?"

She walked over to a bookstore in the mall and grabbed a book off the shelf. It was a music history book. She opened to a picture of Jim Morrison singing with *The Doors* at the Whiskey A-Go-Go in the sixties.

"Here, look at the page and touch it," she told me.

Soon, the two of us were at the concert. Then he was, Mr. Mojo Rising right in the flesh.

"But we only have a couple of minutes, I think. We have to get back to our bodies before they disintegrate or get hijacked."

We pulled ourselves out of the book and were back in the mall.

"So how does this work? Does the timeline alter?" I asked.

"I don't think so since it is in the future. It also seems we have to be in this dream at this mall for the body-jumping to work. We can't jump into a person or image when we're awake or in any other past, present, or future dream."

"That's probably a good thing because this is much too scary. If this got into the wrong hands …."

"I know," Melanie said.

Melanie started to feel contractions and woke up. She looked out the window and saw she was near Saratoga Springs. She fell back asleep at ended up back at the shopping mall.

As soon as I saw Melanie reappear, I jumped into her head. She didn't have to say anything. I knew where she was. When she would wake up on the train, I was able to see out of her eyes. In addition to being in her head in the dream in the shopping mall, I could also see where she was sleeping in the "real" world, given she opened her eyes occasionally. Luckily, since the train was so bumpy and noisy with people, Melanie kept going in and out of sleep. Then I saw a station.

"Saratoga?"

"Yes, I'm on a train and I'm headed to you, Larry. I escaped out of the clinic!"

"The train ends in Rutland. I'm on my way!"

Melanie fell back asleep and saw Matt and Justin being taken to a prison near the Canadian border. She saw them being tortured, woke up screaming, and realized she was in labor. Luckily, she was at the station.

I ran to Melanie as she exited the train, but then heard a swarm of helicopters above.

"Larry, they must have tracked me!"

We quickly loaded into the Jeep and I started driving north toward our camp on the lake.

"Mel, I have to get you to a hospital."

"No, I think I'm okay now. Let's try to lose the helicopters."

Luckily, I knew some wooded backroads to lose the choppers. As we got closer to the camp, Melanie's contractions started again.

"Oh shit, Larry, I think the labor is for real this time!"

"We're going to the hospital," I yelled.

"No, there's no time. We'll have to do this here!"

I pulled the Jeep into the camp and started yelling for Dina and Saxxon. We recently converted one of the cabins into a medical unit and luckily, before becoming a paranormal psychologist, Dina worked as a nurse in Florida.

"Quick, bring her into the infirmary," Dina yelled.

After about six hours of labor with no anesthesia, a baby girl was born.

"What do you want to name her?"

"Lila, of course," Melanie responded.

# 53

By our calculations, the meteor collision would start in about three months. Even though the end was inevitable, I was probably as happy as I ever was in my entire life. I was with Melanie and Lila, we were living on the lake, and albeit at a smaller scale for James's dissertation, my underwater city design was coming to fruition.

Saxxon, Sherman, and I geared up the boat to go and rescue the rest of our team at the concentration camp near the border. As we were loading, Melanie came outside with Lila.

"Larry, I have to ask a favor."

"Sure, anything."

"Matt and Justin are in that camp as well. They are being tortured. Now I know they haven't always done the right thing, but I do still care for them. Matt is still Will's father, and Will does still love him. And I must get my son back. Matt may be able to help."

"Do you still love him, Mel?"

"No. Not in the way you're thinking. But I do still care for him and segregating and torturing him for his sexual orientation is just wrong."

"But isn't he the one who made that a policy on the space colony?"

"He is, but I think he's seen the flaws in in his thinking. I've seen it in my dreams."

"Yes, I know. I actually read that thought in the shopping mall dream."

"Will you get him out of there?"

"Do you think we can trust him?"

"I think so. Like I said, I think he knows he was wrong."

"Well, we're going to free the whole prison, so he'll get free as well."

"Thank you, Larry. I really do love you."

# 54

Sam had been working at the concentration camp for about six months. It was enough time for him to learn where the blind spots and weak spots in the security were located. Seeing these prisons were just temporary, the infrastructure was really not that sophisticated. The main reason Beaumont constructed the camps was to ensure they would get a direct hit from one of the missiles, ensuring all the "abnormal" people inside were killed.

We now had six functioning drones, but only one laser to attach to combat the meteors. With the rest of the research team locked in the prison, we would be unable to complete more lasers in time for the meteor collision. In addition to the real-time aerial footage, Saxxon and Sherman retrofitted one of the drones to be able to carry and drop twenty golf ball sized capsules containing a lachrymatory agent. The trick was to get the capsules deployed before the drone was detected. Sam was able to steal the gas masks from the security's riot gear closet to hand out to the escapees.

The camp was laid out as a series of temporary metal buildings in an orthogonal grid, so there were clear strategic points to drop the capsules. From the aerial footage and Sam's description, there were only twelve guards at the facility at any given point. Sam was going to tranquilize the guards in the main building and the capsules should take care of the guards on the perimeter.

Saxxon launched the drone. He was like a kid with a video game at Christmas. The capsules dropped and all mayhem broke loose. The guards started firing their rifles blindly. Sam ran and unlocked as many buildings as he could but unfortunately, he only could do three before some of the guards broke through the cloud of gas. Sam guided the members of our research team into a bus and headed for the lake to our boat. Several others in the prison also boarded the bus, while others ran for the gates.

The security team was able to regroup and contain about half of the captives. They then sent armored trucks after the bus and those who ran out of the facility. Sam drove the bus right out onto the dock, causing the dock to collapse into the lake. The security team opened fire. There were several causalities—two from our group and four others I didn't recognize. Sherman pulled the boat out full throttle. Several shots hit the boat, but it didn't seem to sustain much damage.

We made it about five miles down the lake toward our camp when we heard several boats and helicopters approaching. Sherman drove into a secluded harbor, and we exited people from the boat.

"Plan B. Scott. Call Dina." Sherman shouted.

Sherman then put the boat back in drive and aimed it toward the western shore of the lake. We watched from the woods as the police boats and helicopters surrounded it.

We ran the group to the road where a flatbed truck driven by Dina awaited us. As we loaded the truck, I was getting a better look at the people we rescued. A majority were researchers from our old lab at the university, but there was a handful of unknowns.

Scott interjected, "I'm afraid this is where the journey stops for some of you. No offense, but we don't know you and can't trust you. I'm sorry it has to be this way."

One of the people from the group spoke up.

"That's no problem. We're just grateful you got us out of there."

As the group broke up and went separate ways, Sam shined his flashlight over by a tree.

"What are you two planning on doing?" Sam asked.

The two slowly walked out. It was Matt and Justin.

"We also want to thank you. Especially you, Larry. I know we've had our differences and you probably want to kill me but thank you."

"It was Melanie's idea. You're right, I probably would have left you there," I said.

Scott gave me a strange look. I don't think he ever saw me get tough before.

"But then again, no one should be imprisoned for the way they look, their religious beliefs, or their sexual preference. Do you see that now, Matt?"

"Look, I know I've made some mistakes, but I was under pressure from Beaumont. He's the bigot; he's the bad guy. The rest of us are just following orders."

"Well, there is something called free will, Matt."

"You're right. Look, we want to help take Beaumont down now. With my knowledge of the plan and Justin's dreaming abilities, we could be valuable assets."

Scott, Sherman, and I glanced at each other. Scott said, "That's a generous offer, Mr. Brennan, but we have no plans in attacking Beaumont. We never have."

"Come on, Saxxon. Aren't you the one who leaked the meteor collision to the press?"

"No. Not me. Not any of us."

"So what is your game?"

"Survival, Mr. Brennan. We're just trying to survive. Unless you can provide us a defense system in the next three months capable of blowing up the meteors, there's not really much you can do."

"We can do that. I still have the access codes to our missile defense system that's orbiting Earth. I also know which meteors Beaumont is going to enhance with nuclear warheads," Matt responded.

"Don't you think they would have changed the codes after they rid you from their colony?" Saxxon asked.

"Not necessarily. They didn't know I even had the codes."

"We'll need proof," Dina yelled from the cab of the truck. "But we need to get out of here now. The helicopters are headed this way."

"Fine. Get in the truck. But you'll need to show us this now. Sherman, grab a laptop." Scott ordered.

The truck peeled out and Sherman gave Matt the computer.

"Okay, Mr. Brennan. Show us the system." Scott commanded.

Matt typed in a few codes and handed the laptop back to Sherman.

"That's the entire space defense system at your fingertips."

"Is it legit?" I asked Sherman.

"It appears so," Sherman responded.

"This could be a game changer," Scott responded.

"I still don't trust them. Either knock them out or put a blindfold on them so they can't see where we are going!" Dina yelled from the driver's seat.

"Come on, Ms. Lawrence. I just gave you the solution. Is that really necessary? There are no windows back here anyway"

"Did you frisk them? And here, scan their heads with this and make sure neither of them have any tracking chips injected." Dina handed Scott a device shaped like a television remote.

"They took my chip out at the conversion clinic," Justin responded.

"They're telling the truth, Dina. The scan is negative." Saxxon responded.

The camp was about sixty miles south from the prison, but Beaumont's team would probably cover that search radius within a week. However, with all our equipment and the underwater pods at the camp, it would be difficult to leave.

Three days after the prison break, we started hearing helicopters and drones over the camp. We hunkered down in the underground tunnels which were now quite extensive seeing as engineers expanded them over the past year and were using them as an entry mechanism to the underwater pods. The tunnel went down about thirty feet, and then a horizontal tube with a watertight hatch connected to an entry tube which descended another seventy feet or so to the bottom of the lake. There were several nooks carved out at the landings of the staircase where groups of people gathered, which were around forty now. To play it safe, James decided not to tell or show anyone the connection to the underwater pods.

On the fifth day after the prison break, an entire team scoured the surface. We could hear the search dogs sniffing around the cabins, but luckily, we had emptied all the contents into the tunnels. When the search team moved out, several people slowly moved back to the cabins. After about two weeks, Melanie, Lila, and I decided it was safe to go back to the surface. As we were walking toward the lake, Matt approached us.

"So, you still ended up having a baby girl. It must have been fate. What is her name?" Matt said to Melanie.

Melanie picked up Lila and held her tight.

"Her name is Lila Mae," Melanie answered.

"Lila? Really? You reused the name we picked out?"

"No. I used the name I picked out. And yes, I reused it because that is what her name was destined to be. Besides, this is Lila Mae, our first child, the one you erased, was Lila Ann."

"Oooh, big difference, Mel," Matt said sarcastically.

250

I had to admit, it was kind of odd that she kept the name relatively the same, middle name changed or not.

"But I'm not here to fight. I'm happy that this situation was rectified. You know I had no choice, right? It was to ensure our survival."

"No. You had a choice, but like you said, I don't want to fight. I'm too tired."

"Well, good. Because from the bottom of my heart, I want to thank you for breaking Justin and I out of that prison. You know I'm going to help take down Beaumont and help with the missile defense."

"Really? I don't believe it," Melanie said emphatically.

"I already hacked into the space missile defense system. Ask Larry, he saw it."

I looked at Melanie and nodded.

"No offense, Matt, but I no longer trust you," Melanie said.

"I understand that. And you have good reason. But I will help mitigate this situation. Beaumont was pressuring me. I have seen the error of my ways."

"Well, that remains to be seen. But more importantly, what about Will? I want to get my son back, Matt."

"Our son, Mel. Our son. And yes, I agree. But you know there is only one way to get him back, right?"

Melanie looked at me with sad eyes. I read her thoughts, as I was often able to do.

"No. Out of the question. You are not turning yourselves in," I yelled.

"It may be the only way, Larry. And it may be the only way to ensure the survival of Will and Lila."

"We can keep them safe here in the—" I stopped myself. I didn't want Matt to know about the underwater pods.

"Where, Larry? How will you keep them safe?" Matt asked.

"Well, I thought you were going to hack the missile defense system?"

"I will, but that's no guarantee. That will only prevent Beaumont from exasperating the meteor impacts with the nuclear warheads. There's no guarantee it will prevent destruction from the meteors. Face it, Larry, Melanie and I turning ourselves in is the only hope we have."

"What makes you think Beaumont won't kill you on sight?" I asked.

"He needs Melanie and Lila for their dreaming ability. His entire success was built on that dreaming program. He is totally dependent on it, and the last I heard, he only has one dream maker left."

"He still has Claire and Bryan, so he has two," Melanie answered.

"No. Claire is out. Apparently, Beaumont made a sexual advance towards her. She rejected him, and she's been missing. Bryan is the only one left and he's not very good. Definitely the weakest of the five dream makers."

I grabbed Melanie by the arms. "We'll find another way. I can't lose you again. We just broke over three-hundred people out of a prison. We should be able to devise a plan to break into the Pentagon and get Will back."

"There's no way, Larry. That prison was child's play. Beaumont has a quarter of the military guarding the Pentagon right now."

"I'm going to talk it over with Sherman. He still has some contacts in Washington," I said.

"Well, you do what you have to do, but I'm telling you, turning ourselves in is the only way inside that facility," Matt answered.

Matt walked away and went over to Justin who was eerily lurking in the woods. The two kissed. Melanie gave me a strange look. She was as liberal and open-minded as anybody, but seeing her ex-husband kiss another man was still a bit unsettling for her.

Matt then whispered in Justin's ear. "Were you able to find a cell phone?"

"Yup," Justin answered.

"Good. I'll make the call," Matt answered.

# 55

The following week, Saxxon called a meeting with me, Melanie, Dina, Sherman, James, Todd, Sam, Rachel, Lorie, and Margaret and the other researchers we rescued from the prison. He started the meeting off in a lab coat like how he used to start his lectures. It was difficult to tell if he was in character or not.

"We have less than three months to go before the first meteor impact. There's a good chance we'll not be able to defend against the meteors and/or the nuclear arsenal Beaumont plans to use. We need to start thinking of a contingency plan. We may have to utilize the underwater pods. James, Sherman, do you want to start this off?"

James started talking but nobody could understand him, partly due to his dialect, partly due to his technical wording. Sherman interrupted him.

"We have twelve pods constructed, ten of them are one thousand square feet, one is for utilities and one has to be used as a greenhouse to grow food."

"Yes. And we scaled down Larry's design. Each pod is designed to house about five people. So right now, we can just barely sustain everyone who is here, and it will be tight." Saxxon added.

The energy in the room seemed grim.

"Honestly, no offense, but I'm not sure I can live down there with all of you for ten years. I may take my chances up here," Todd said.

"Well, maybe it won't come to that. What about the access to the missile defense system Matt Brennan provided us?" Margaret asked.

"So far, it checks out. I am seeing if there are ways to reprogram the missiles," Sherman responded. "But even if we can launch them all and actually hit the targets, it may only save a small percentage of people from direct impact. There's no guarantee that they will be safe from the radius of the radiation from other meteors that actually do strike."

"And there is really no guarantee that one-hundred feet of water will keep us safe, either, is there?" Todd asked.

"No, but the research I did back in NASA in the seventies did test some of this, but it was on a much smaller scale. The other issue is we only tested it in salt water. It's unclear if the fresh water will provide the same protection."

"Oh man, this gets grimmer by the minute," Todd said.

"Indeed. We need to inform the rest of the team. Let them know if there are any last items of business that they need to take care of."

"Can we tell our loved ones?" Rachel asked.

"You may want to say goodbye, but I wouldn't tell anyone the specifics. It could cause more panic and more heartbreak," Saxxon replied.

# 56

Sherman, Sam, several of the student researchers, and I loaded up one of the drones into one of the vans and were headed to Washington to see if we could break into the Pentagon to get Will back. Sherman arranged a meeting with a crew that he formerly worked with in his days at the CIA.

As we were loading up, Matt approached us. "I still think this is a suicide mission, but I want to help. I know the layout of that facility better than anyone. I know where Harold Mitchell's lab is located. That's where Will is being held."

"Sure, why not," Sherman answered.

I kissed Melanie and Lila goodbye. Matt did the same with Justin. Saxxon and Dina wished us good luck.

As we approached New York City, we came to a halt in the traffic on the Tappan Zee Bridge. Suddenly, Matt jumped out of the van and a large tractor-trailer rammed our van over the side rail of the bridge. The van smashed into the Hudson River and everything went black.

When I came to, the van was half submerged in the frigid water and was quickly sinking. Sam and Sherman were still buckled into the front seats and were both unconscious. I unbuckled them and pushed them out of the windows. I opened the side door of the van and swam to the surface with Sam in one arm and Sherman in the other. As I reached the surface, two helicopters came from above. At first, I thought they were there to rescue us, but then they started shooting. I was able to make it the shore and drag both Sherman and Sam into the woods. They were both gone. The helicopters hovered above and continued shooting. I ran about ten miles and ended up somewhere around SUNY New Paltz. I climbed up into the back of a semi and realized one of the bullets hit me in the upper chest. I managed to get the bullet out but passed out from the pain. I woke up in Rochester, New York, my hometown. The truck driver grabbed and threw me out of the truck and threatened to call the cops. The only place I could think to go was back to my old house where I grew up.

Most of my neighborhood was completely abandoned. I wondered if people here somehow found out about the meteor collision. My house was completely empty. The people who lived in the house after us must have gutted all the newer materials we added, leaving the house with its old sixties' décor exposed. I fell asleep in my old bedroom. My mom started talking to me in a dream. Then I felt a huge jolt and the entire house tilted up on one end.

And then I said to her, "That's it, Mom, this is the end of the world."

# 57

I woke up and my mom disappeared as my eyes refocused from the dream. The house sustained significant damage, but was for the most part, still intact. The superior mafia construction certainly was a factor. I ran down the street and could see fire and smoke in the distance. My guess was a meteor struck to the north somewhere in Lake Ontario. One of my neighbors, who had lived in his house since it was built in the sixties, collected cars. He had added onto his garage and had six vintage cars. Most of them were white Cadillacs, but he had one 1978 Camaro complete with flames of fire painted on the hood and the side. Since he was nowhere to be found, I decided to borrow the Camaro. I left a note for him in the event he was still alive or if he was going to return. I fired up the Camaro and headed back to the camp in Vermont. Most of the communities were abandoned. When I drove to higher points through the Adirondacks, I could see more meteors falling to Earth's surface in the distance.

When I arrived back at the camp in the Vermont, it seemed I was too late. Most of the cabins were in flames. Beaumont's crew had the camp surrounded. And then I saw two armed guards escorting Melanie and Lila onto one of the helicopters. I ran out of the woods. I didn't care at this point if I got shot again. I was still in pain from the bullet I took on the Hudson.

"Melanie!"

I ran towards her and kissed her. Lila ran to me and hugged my leg. In the distance, I could hear Scott Saxxon's voice.

"Larry, get down!"

I don't know what happened first. The bullet hitting me, Saxxon and Dina firing rounds at the guards and helicopters, or the meteors hitting.

I woke up in a glass dome on the bottom of the lake. Scott, Dina, Rachel, James, Todd, Lorie, and Margaret were all standing over me. In the background, I could also see several of the others I had helped in past dreams: Cindy, Kristi, Maggie and her mom from Niagara Falls, Raja, Ryan, and Heidi, to name a few. Dina was holding Lila. She put Lila into my arms.

"Where's Melanie?" I asked.

Scott and Dina hung their heads in despair. I started crying and suddenly fell back asleep with Lila in my arms. I was back in the house that I lived in my undergraduate years. I tried to get back to the underwater colony, but I couldn't seem to wake up. Suddenly, the visual distortions of my surroundings that were commonplace in my dream state seemed to come into focus and everything seemed eerily real. I looked at the old RCA tube television and saw a live broadcast from *Saturday Night Live* with a skit featuring Chris Farley. Indeed, it was 1996. I laid down on the bed and closed my eyes to try and figure out what was going on. I then saw Melanie in a dream. She was drifting quickly away from me. She yelled and asked what was happening. All I could mutter was, "I think this is the end of the world, Melanie." And everything went black.

# About the Author

Michael A. Richards grew up in a town outside of Rochester, NY in the 1980s and 90s. As a child, he spent countless hours exploring the medium to old growth forest that surrounded the neighborhood. The woods provided a peaceful and tranquil environment where he was able to escape from reality and hone his creativity. In the mid-1980s, the town decided it was going to expand the road network to accommodate the increase in people, cars, and related infrastructure. Several of the road expansions destroyed much of this surrounding forest and unfortunately much of his utopia. This childhood heartbreak is what ultimately led Michael to choose environmental studies as major in college. He further went on to study architecture in graduate school with the hope of integrating his environmental sensibility into the built environment. After graduate school, Richards went on to publish several papers and a book entitled Regreening the Built Environment: Nature, Green Space, and Sustainability, that further expanded the notion of transforming architecture from a building-centric discipline into one more concerned with conserving natural resources. Although the book has been well received, Richards felt it only tapped a small fraction of his vision and creativity. This, essentially, is what led him to write Dream Makers. The fiction medium allowed him to explore without limit some of the stories and fantasies he imagined in the woods as a youth and some of the dreams and surreal moments he experienced as a graduate student. When he is not writing, Michael enjoys skiing, hiking, kayaking, swimming, and playing the piano. Michael has also played keyboards with several bands in Buffalo, Rochester, and Vermont and still plays with 7Lbs of Pork and The Shady Trees.

www.ingramcontent.com/pod-product-compliance
Lightning Source LLC
Chambersburg PA
CBHW021218260626
47172CB00002B/497